AGENT G: ASSASSIN

A SCI-FI SPY NOVEL

BY C. T. PHIPPS

I picked up the Sidewinder-7 from its case in the back seat and hastily loaded it as the back window shattered from a stray chain-gun round. I gave a swift look over to Claire and saw that it had passed between us and gone through the front windshield, which would have shocked even the most seasoned combat pilots. Somehow, Claire managed to maintain control over the vehicle.

"So much for bulletproof windows," I muttered. "We need to get up level with it!"

"I'd ask if you're insane, but that goes without question. You better get this right, or we're both dead."

"I couldn't ask for finer company."

"That's not reassuring!"

The Zero-7 aircar lifted into the air right as it was about to dip down and get us, and the factories we were passing disappeared, replaced with a mile-long graveyard and park. Claire brought the car level with the helicopter. I didn't bother with the sunroof and mounted the Sidewinder-7 sniper rifle on the broken glass of our rear window.

"Bye," I said, aiming not with the scope but my enhanced cybernetic vision and shooting both helicopter pilots before putting a round through the dashboard computer. Deprived of all navigation, the helicopter spun out of control and landed in an artificial lake approximately two hundred feet below.

I looked over at Claire. "I think they're dead."

FOREWORD

Welcome to the third installment of the Agent G series. I'm very pleased we've made it this far, and for those who are of the opinion this is going to be the final installment of the series, it is not. Indeed, there's so much room in the story for expansion, we're going to be continuing indefinitely—or at least for two more books.

Fans who think this will mean less of a focus on the characters and more on the events shouldn't be worried. I think the protagonist and his supporting cast have a great deal more development awaiting them. As much as I love writing the intricate spy adventures with their double and triple crosses, I think of getting into their heads as the real focus of the series. Well, that and being able to set up the new world we'll be getting into in *Agent G: Assassin.*

When I first started the series, I said it was my goal to start the story in the then-present of 2017 and move to a dystopian cyberpunk future. That event finally occurred with the release of all the hidden Black Technology plans on the internet. It's promptly followed by a disaster I predict will probably happen in the not-too-distant future. We'll be making a time skip of about fifteen years in this book, and it's been an enormous amount of fun figuring out what the world will be like after such a world-changing pair of events.

My biggest worry with this transformation wasn't that I'd change the nature of the stories, which was always the plan anyway, but that I'd lose focus on the characters across the fifteen-year time skip. I thought long and hard whether it would be better to take my books through the resulting time or whether to trust that I could pull off keeping them recognizable, but older. These fifteen years turned out to be the perfect place to put surprise changes as well as flashbacks. In other words, I'm not going to spend years unraveling the "Meereenese Knot" like another author.

I think fans will appreciate the new world we'll be visiting. G, or "Case" as he's known now, has significantly expanded his social circle and gotten a chance to show his softer side to a small number of individuals. However, the previous books have hardened an already hard man into something even tougher. No one ever said being a cyberpunk protagonist was easy.

As always, kudos to my fans who have been contributing their fan art, trailers, and reviews to this work. The Agent G series wouldn't be nearly as successful without all your inspiration. As usual, I encourage perceptive fans to notice all the homages and references I've scattered through the story, from *Blade Runner* to *Resident Evil*.

Enjoy!

PROLOGUE

I soaked up the sun's rays while laying back on my chaise lounge. I was on an Indonesian beach I hadn't bothered to learn the name of. I'd changed my features, voice, and identity with the practiced ease of a Letter. I had no doubt there were parties in the U.S. government and various megacorps who wanted to track me down, but my guess was they'd have a hell of a time doing it. The only people on Earth who knew my location were the AI known as Delphi, Lucita Biondi, Marissa Sanchez, and S.

I wasn't worried about any of them. Delphi was enjoying manipulating the stock market, S was off the grid, Marissa was in Washington trying to deal with the collapse of the global economy, and Lucita was three feet away in a chair like my own. I questioned the necessity of tanning when she was a Shell, but she said the synth-skin that made up her body was photo-receptive. A year ago, I'd been a Letter, a man with no identity other than the letter G, who worked as an assassin for a private mercenary company called the International Refugee Society under then-President Douglas. Both had used me with no care for my humanity, which turned out to be nonexistent since I'd been created in a lab with false memories.

Crazy huh?

I'd managed to turn the tables on them and pull a Snowden, uploading millions of terabytes of "Black Technology" information, along with secret files, onto the web. It had brought down the Douglas administration and destroyed my ex-employers, but had changed the world as well as technology. I'd been smart enough not to attach my name to the data and was planning to spend the rest of my life enjoying the local hospitality. Lucita, a fellow cyborg assassin but not a Letter, had decided to join me.

I sipped my margarita. "You know, you should probably wear a swimsuit when tanning."

"Eh," Lucita said, wearing only a pair of sunglasses. "Not my problem. It's our beach, after all."

"Technically, it's *my* beach," I corrected her. I wore a pair of mirror shades and red swim trunks. I was tempted to remove them and enjoy the environment like Lucita. We weren't a couple, but we enjoyed each other's company. Assassins with benefits, if you will. It was probably the most serious relationship I was going to have since I'd never be able to share who I was with anyone else. Those people I'd trusted most had turned out to be the people most likely to betray me. In the end, it was just me, an AI named Delphi and cyborg hiding with me from the governments we'd pissed off.

"Then what am I?" Lucita asked, lowering her sunglasses to the bridge of her nose as she gazed at me.

"You're a guest who doesn't pay rent."

"I'm fun," Lucita said, shrugging. "Besides, you'd grow bored with just the local women to keep you entertained. What's the latest one's name?"

"You know her name," I said, frowning. "Besides, it's interesting having a lover who isn't either paid or trying to kill me."

My need for human companionship transcended my need for honesty and I'd made dozens of friends under my fake ID. As far as the locals were concerned, I was Mr. Case and I'd made my fortune in the tech industry. I'd made up friends, family, and a tragic backstory which was all verifiable on the internet save for the fact I had no decent pictures on Facebook. Sometimes, I even believed my fake backstory myself. Was it an adequate substitute for genuine human intimacy? How would I know? I wasn't human.

"If you say so," Lucita said. "Do you think it's serious?"

"No," I said, sighing. "In addition to bartending and spearfishing, Toni likes to tell fortunes. Per Indonesian astrology, I'm going to eventually get married again. Two more times, in fact."

I'd been married once before to a fellow Letter named S. S

had never loved me, was sometimes not even my friend, but we'd shared years together as man and wife in a cover identity. I'd never been as good at compartmentalizing as other Letters. It was possibly why I was the first one to rebel and the only one who'd actively turned against his employers. Personally, I put as much stock in tea leaves and divination as I did in the honesty of politicians. Still, it was a nice thought even if I suspected it was also a way of Toni telling me we weren't going to get serious no matter how often I paid her rent.

"Marriage is just a tool to enslave the economically dependent partner," Lucita said, stretching. It was distracting. "Is your future wife a cyborg? Do you see it happening soon? If so, I want a heads up so I can kill someone for their mansion before you force me to move out."

"The zodiac did not say," I said, putting down my margarita and looking down at my Karmapad handheld computer. I was currently reading last week's news since I didn't keep an internet connection near my home. Instead, I downloaded my books from the public library's server and bought local papers in town to enjoy.

"Anything good?" Lucita asked, clearly bored with paradise. She needed to take up a hobby, hopefully not involving murder. Unlike her, I was perfectly content to read and soak up rays until my cyber-brain shut down in however long its warranty remained working. Given it was originally only supposed to last ten years before I'd jury-rigged it, that was something I didn't count on being long.

I read her the news. "President Karl Trust has done a bunch of embarrassing and unconstitutional things. The economy is up. The Democrats are fighting. He's not going to press charges against President Douglas, though. She's decided to stick with public speaking and writing a book about her experiences being the first woman President."

"A small punishment for being an autocratic technocrat," Lucita said. "How many people did she have you kill?"

Too many. "Eh, it's probably the worst thing that could have befallen her. Besides, the Invisible Hand really was every bit as dangerous as she foretold. I may have misjudged her."

The Invisible Hand were the Military Industrial Complex, which wasn't a conspiracy so much as a sociological phenomenon. A dozen of the world's biggest military suppliers and technology companies had gotten together to make the International Refugee Society. I'd been their puppet for years before switching sides to President Douglas. In the end, I'd fought for my own side as I wanted to work for the one person who didn't want me to continue being a hired killer. I'd ended up exposing their secrets, Snowden style, and sharing all the top-secret Black Technology that had allowed both to thrive. It had helped thrust Trust into power—but I considered that a small price to pay for wrecking the gameboard—even if I didn't like the guy or his policies.

"Any news on the Hand?" Lucita asked.

"I don't think there's a spot to download information about the Illuminati," I joked. "A credible one, at least."

"I meant the companies we know they're involved with," Lucita said. "I owe them some payback too, you know."

Lucita was referring to her deceased father and friends, whom I'd played no small role in killing. Honestly, her feelings were more than a bit complicated on that matter, since the late Papa Biondi had been what we in the assassin business liked to call "a rapist child-abusing shithead." I was glad he was dead, and so was Lucita. Still, she was Italian and they had very specific ideas of what to do when someone killed your relatives. Thankfully, she blamed the Hand for it rather than me. You know, the guy who pulled the trigger.

"Ah. The lawsuits against Karma Corp and the other Big Twenty will drag on for years," I said, shrugging. "There's been a lot of suicides, resignations, and firings, but I suspect the real power players will escape with a slap on the wrist. They always do. Black Technology is claimed to have been stuff they were just heavily testing, and its release was a breach of national security. Six Fortune 500 companies have gone bankrupt, though, while thousands more startups making their own variants have risen to power. It's no longer a Big 20, but a Big 100. Their power is diluted if nothing else."

"Sounds like you're just trying to convince yourself that you didn't change the world."

"A little girl is running with new legs in Hong Kong, North Korea has surrendered to South Korea after their failed attack, and after Delphi revealed herself, the United Nations began drafting a universal human rights bill that will cover AI rights. I'm okay with how things have turned out."

"All you had to do was lose yourself billions of dollars in Black Technology secrets by giving them away."

I shrugged. "Giving away billions is easier if you already have billions. Just ask Bill Gates."

Truth be told, change was happening at a more rapid pace than I could have imagined. Venezuela's economy had returned to stable levels within two months of the release. They had created the world's largest solar farm and were in negotiations to build a space elevator. Knock-off cybernetics were everywhere, and plastic surgeons proclaimed they'd be able to supply new bodies within two years. Plenty of people weren't willing to wait that long, and a few grisly stories of homemade Shells had already emerged. Slicers—the Black Technology equivalent of Hackers—had also successfully crashed the Ukrainian stock market on behalf of Russian backers. Then, two days later, Russia suffered a reprisal that had almost triggered World War III. It was a new world. Or maybe just the old one revealed.

"Any word from Marissa?" Lucita said. "I know you still want to bang her. That's why you're stalking her."

"No," I said, rolling my eyes. "I'm not stalking her."

Marissa had been the only woman I'd ever loved. Truly loved. She was also a woman who had turned me over my insane brother (clone base? father via genetic donation?) Daniel Gordon. It had been to save her sister's family, but you didn't come back from something like that. Still, the wound in my soul from her betrayal was as fresh that day on the beach as it was a year prior. Some things you never got over.

"Come on."

I sighed. "She's working with a cybernetic commando named Stephen Wilcox. He's a member of Task Force-22."

"Ah," Lucita said, her voice dripping with condescension. "Replaced so soon. Any word on the others?"

"I wish Marissa the best," I said, half suspecting we'd end

up back in each other's lives again. It was just how the system worked. "As for the others—no idea."

That wasn't entirely true. James Madison had gone public with his story of being held prisoner by an American-based paramilitary organization. No one had believed him, but his story got a large amount of publicity, enough for him to launch his own technology firm. As one of the world's leading experts on Black Technology, James had already attracted something like ten billion dollars in investment capital. Last I heard, he was already chilling in a Silicon Valley mansion with a paid harem. Good for him.

"No word from E or S?" Lucita asked.

I'd distributed a nanotechnology-based cure for the ten-year lifespan built into each Letter. It was something I'd nicknamed "The *Blade Runner* Curse." It wasn't much of a gift since only a few of us were left. We'd ended up killing most of each other off. Still, it meant freedom, and if we were a race doomed to extinction, then it was better we have a chance to live our lives to the fullest. It wasn't like a bunch of incredibly strong, super-intelligent machines were going to starve in a world hungry for killers.

"Nope," I said, shaking my head. "Whatever they've decided to do with their share of the Society's money, they haven't seen fit to include me in on it."

"That's insulting."

"I'm okay with sitting here and reading *Cthulhu Armageddon*," I said, tapping the paperback novel beside me. "I am done with killing people."

Lucita snorted.

"I'm serious," I said.

"Old soldiers don't retire. They just get blown away."

"That's literally the opposite of how that saying is supposed to go."

"Then the old saying is wrong."

That was when I heard a helicopter approaching. Flipping over the side of my chair, I grabbed the REM-7 pistol hidden underneath and aimed it at them. Lucita flipped over herself and grabbed a composite assault rifle hidden in the sand. Hovering above us was an AR-27 Whisper helicopter whose sides opened before rappelling ropes shot out. It could have wiped us out if its members had planned to do so. Apparently, someone just wanted to make an entrance.

Six individuals wearing tactical body armor with familiar faces descended to the beach. I recognized E, S, W, I, J, and K. They were all the fellow Letters I'd recruited into Task Force-22 and very possibly the last of us since no one had heard from the others in over a year. They also had white berets on, which were just adorable. They looked like the Cub Scouts of the apocalypse.

"Are they here to kill us?" Lucita asked.

"No," I said, standing up. "We'd already be dead."

That was when the sunlight started to disappear. I looked up. Something dark raced across the sky, and it didn't look like clouds. Instead, it was a pure blackness spreading from beyond to devour the light.

"What's up?" I said, lowering my pistol.

"I take it you haven't seen the news," S said.

"No," I said, looking around. "Although just about everyone was absent from the estate today. I thought it was a holiday."

S shook her head. "Wyoming is gone."

I blinked. "What?"

"The Yellowstone volcano Delphi predicted has gone off. The President declared a state of martial law, as have half the other countries on Earth. Civil wars and riots have broken out over the implications. It's going to be a very long winter for the next few years, and society is going to be defined by who has the most wealth as well as technology."

I stared at her, cursing God and my luck in equal measure. "What do you want me to do?"

"We want your help in fixing the world. To make amends for the hundreds of people we've murdered."

"And make a lot of money in the process," E added, as if the two weren't mutually exclusive.

"I'm in," Lucita said.

S glared. "You weren't invited."

"I'm in," Lucita said, laughing as if we hadn't just heard twenty million people had died.

"Fine. I was getting bored of retirement anyway," I said, lying.

It was a flippant response to the beginning of the Dark Age of Technology. We had all the machines we could want, but no machine could keep the barbarism and ruthlessness at the heart of the human spirit from rising up.

God help us all.

CHAPTER ONE

I woke up with a blinding headache, tangled in a silk-sheeted bed in my Los Angeles penthouse. I still dreamed, usually—which answered the question of whether androids did. I dreamed of the past, and my mind was constantly forced to cycle through the various memories I had from living twice my allotted lifespan. I was twenty years old now, two lifetimes for a Letter, and had successfully managed to survive well over a thousand combat engagements. Most of them had been in the first ten years after the Big Smokey Event when my opponents had been starving, desperate, and dying refugees. The last five years had been better. Those were criminals, professionals, politicians, and corporate executives. Killers like myself, paid security guards, mercenaries. People in the Great Game.

"Mmm," a voice spoke beside me, and I looked down at Heather Rollins. She was a pretty, but not beautiful, young woman with fire-colored hair who was studying at the University of California to be a dentist. She was also my paid mistress.

Prostitution was just one of the things that had been legalized by the State of Emergency Government as part of the efforts to rebuild the United States economy once the Long Winter had ended. Because of the extreme wealth disparity, pretty men and women happily traded themselves for survival as the one percent of one percent doled out a trickle of their money.

I should have been ashamed to be part of the super-rich, who had somehow managed to become even richer after the near end of the world, but I'd suffered enough to know it was better to be the boot than the ant. I'd met Heather online and took her on as an employee before she'd not so subtly suggested she could do more—I'd found out most of her money went to keeping the rest of her family out of the refugee zones that had become America's version of Brazil's *favelas*. I remember what she'd said when I'd pointed out I could just give her a raise: "I'm not a parasite, sir!"

But who was I kidding? I wasn't straining against the system either.

"Hey, Heather."

"Bad dreams?" Heather asked, reaching over to get her glasses off the sideboard. She put them on and stared at me, blinking a few times for emphasis.

Heather could get her eyes fixed for 250 credits at the mall but apparently thought the glasses added a bit of distinction to her features. Plastic surgery and body modification were ubiquitous in the new world to the point that even the poor were beautiful. Which meant, ironically, the little flaws were now marks of attraction. I admitted, they were cute on her.

"Are there any other kind?" I asked, shrugging.

"I suppose that's part of the life of a samurai," Heather said, giggling.

Heather was referring to a bit of co-opted cyberpunk lingo in corporate samurai culture. It had begun as a joke that the megacorporations—now the Big 200 instead of the Big 100—had enough soldiers to qualify as armed nations. That included troubleshooters who didn't just do private detective work but also covered assassinations and special operations.

It was a joke that had lost its punch line, since I was an executive at Atlas Security providing troops across the globe to both public as well as private organizations. I also did all the highly illegal wetwork and black ops that I used to do for the International Refugee Society, which was now standard operating procedure for the world's companies.

Heather seemed to find it dashing.

"Yeah," I said, joking. "Television on."

The International News Network showed an image of a visibly aged and corpse-like Karl Trust delivering a half-hearted speech in Washington, DC for the new Smithsonian dedication.

Trust had been a puppet for the State of Emergency Government (SOEG) for years now, after a massive stroke a good eight or nine years ago left him all but brain dead. His son and associates had kept him going with cybernetics, allowing the country to slip firmly out of democracy into dictatorship. As far as I knew, no one cared but a handful of radicals who had no answers about how to fix the continuing disasters that afflicted the country. I'd been one of those idiots with hope, the big bad resistance to the corporations, but had pulled away when they'd become more about crushing the corporations than saving the planet.

"Nothing ever interesting happens in the news," Heather said, sliding out of bed. "I don't know why you bother."

I shrugged. "I like to know what is being fed to the masses."

Atlas Industries was the smallest of the Big 200 Corporations, but was in preparation for a merger with Madison Electronics and Global Construction. It was part of my efforts here in Los Angeles to do some aggressive negotiation to make it and Chicago part of the "revitalized" cities that would help restore the United States to its former first-world status.

It was all very beyond me as I was more a professional killer than a negotiator, but apparently, that was my role to play in the discussions. So far, the Ishikawa-Kazagumo Combine had agreed to our every demand since I'd sat down in the meetings.

"How dramatic," Heather said.

"Not really," I said. "Same shit, different toilet."

Heather and I took a shower together before I changed into a black suit identical to virtually every piece of clothing I wore. I hadn't been to the beach in years, and what was the point, really? Almost all were owned by the government now. It had been snowing last time I took a drive there in July, anyway. Heather slipped on a pair of panties and a University of California sweatshirt, doing her best to be attractive while casual. I could sense her fear, from the way she moved to the smell of pheromones in the air. The fear of losing her patron and being totally at the mercy of a society that would consider her washed up at 30. Her hope of finishing a degree and finding employment also depended on my patronage. As part of my paranoia, I'd read her letters to her mom, and she was desperately hoping to get a job at Atlas before I got bored.

This was the world she lived in.

We lived in.

Heather took my arm as we entered the lounge of my penthouse, which occupied the entire upper floor of the building. It was full of lush shag carpet, metal furniture, and portraits on the wall designed to maximize my sensory intake. Andrew was in the kitchen, a blandly pretty man in his twenties who served as my butler and housekeeper. Heather was sleeping with him, and he was also sleeping with the paid boy toy of the man who owned the apartment beneath me.

It wasn't so much that the number of heterosexuals, bisexuals, and homosexuals had changed, but that people were far more flexible as to what qualified as such nowadays. It was fascinating, watching the changing nature of human culture while being out of its reach. None of that was my business, as far as I was concerned.

"Good evening, sir," Andrew said, his expression empty but pleasant. It was a sign he was taking Lethe and using his overly generous payment to stay high as a kite. The drug dramatically reduced the lifespan of its users, but with the general hopelessness of the New World, I didn't blame its users. I considered confronting him about it, but the advantage of Lethe was it never interfered in your work—indeed, you could work yourself to death using the stuff without ever feeling a moment of boredom.

Did I have the right to try and clean him up? Did I care? I wasn't a white knight, and it wasn't any of my business. I could pay for his rehab, but he wasn't my friend; he was my employee, and I'd long since passed the point of redemption. I was part of the system that made everyone in this country desperate and willing to beg for scraps from the uber-rich.

"Is it evening?" I asked, looking out the windows. It was hard to tell with the change in climate thanks to the Big Smokey.

"Seven p.m., sir," Andrew said. "Shall I prepare you something?"

"Just order out," I said simply. "Ask for Daphne."

Daphne was Heather's best friend and from the Los Angeles

refugee zone. Daphne was a crude, angry, and hateful woman who despised the rich with the passion of someone who saw them living like kings while the rest of the world starved. I liked her a lot. She'd also robbed me several times, and I'd ignored it.

"Sure," Andrew said. "Hey, sir, random question, but are you bulletproof?"

I paused and looked at him. "Excuse me?"

Heather blinked.

I wondered if Andrew had been replaced by a Shell. After a second's pause, when I realized he could have gunned me down if he'd been armed, I realized that it was just him coming off the Lethe and asking stupid questions.

"Bullet-resistant. Depends on the caliber, really."

"Know how many people you've killed?" Andrew asked.

"Andy!" Heather asked.

"Is that a bad thing to ask?" Andrew asked, blinking rapidly.

I walked over to my liquor cabinet and pulled out a bottle of scotch and a glass. "I don't keep score."

"Ah," Andrew said, going over to the household terminal and starting to type. "Your usual?"

"Yeah," I said, pouring myself a drink. "Chinese food. Get something for yourselves."

"Cloned swan?" Heather asked, perking up.

"Yeah, if you like." I looked up from my drink. "Want one?"

"No thank you," Heather said, nervous.

Heather been taking alcohol from my cabinet and watering it down for her friends when I wasn't inside the penthouse. It was cute the way they kept thinking themselves criminal masterminds. Then again, I supposed they had every reason to since I didn't bother to punish them for what they did. Honestly, what did I care about a few trinkets and watered-down liquor? People were dying outside.

"Harriett, any messages from Atlas?" I asked the interior computer.

"Yes, sir," a female synthesized voice spoke. Harriett was a dummy AI for my apartment building. Delphi and others like her had global citizenship and massive financial resources of their own but the majority of gruntwork was still done by glorified Siris and Cortanas.

"Great. How many?" I asked.

"You have a priority one e-mail from the Atlas Corporation's CEO, sir," Harriett said. "It was sent twenty minutes ago."

I mentally cursed. "Why didn't you wake me up?"

"I don't know, sir," Harriett said.

I shook my head. "I'll take the call in my private room. You guys, do whatever it is you want to do. I'll probably be gone for a while. Also, everyone should just call me Case. No more of this sir stuff."

"Yes, sir," Andrew said.

"Of course, sir," Harriett said.

"Wow," I said, shaking my head. "Everyone is a comedian."

"Mmm hmm." Heather nodded, eating a piece of insta-toast from the fridge. It was warm straight out of the package. I walked past the lounge to a side room, which contained a biometric lock built into the wall that scanned me and my voice. The door slid open to reveal a personal chamber filled with guns, swords, and books—my private collection. There was an electric sheep toy sitting in the oversized comfy chair facing the vid wall. It was a gift from Lucita, and one I recognized the symbolism of.

My weapons were kept from the rest of my live-in servants even when I was away, since the devices were capable of tearing through a small army. I disliked the fact that I could name every single element of every single weapon inside this room as well as their combat capabilities. After I'd released Black Technology into the world, I'd thought I could live without being a professional murderer and spy, but I'd ended up falling back on my old habits. I'd never learned to be anything else than what I'd been created to be.

The world hadn't wanted me to be anything else.

I picked up a carbon-fiber katana designed for the purpose of slicing through cybernetically enhanced synthmuscle and fiberbones. It wasn't a practical weapon, but I'd seen it used by the Yakuza (who'd given it to me), who had sacrificed their bodies for the chance to experience life as nearly unkillable machines.

"Contact S," I told Harriett. "I want to see what she thinks is so damned important."

"Yes...Case," Harriett replied.

"I'm genuinely confused by the fact you added an annoyed pause."

"I'm sorry, sir."

The west side of the wall turned black as an Atlas logo appeared on it along with S's chosen name, Samantha Sanders. I gave my sword a few practice swings before sheathing it. My body seized up and my head twitched before I clasped the sides of my face. I was having a flashback, another sign the quantum computer inside my brain was suffering glitches.

"Dammit," I said, sitting down. "Just ride it out, Case."

I was chasing a cybernetically enhanced police officer across a rooftop. It was another memory that told me my IRD implant, the quantum computer that made me as ensouled as a human, was starting to break down. Rain poured down on us, and I had orders to kill him.

The man, Thompson Wilkins, had collected damning evidence against Atlas and had also killed two of our operatives. He thought he was the big hero and was exposing corporate corruption that would save lives in the long run. The irony was he'd been funded by Karma Corp, who wanted to steal Atlas' security contract with Los Angeles. Karma Corp wanted to be the one to have Rent-A-Cops and soldiers on the ground rather than us. The sad fact was that if Thompson succeeded in exposing our bribes and eliminations then nothing would change.

A few hundred more people would die due to gang violence while the city settled out which firm to hire, but in the end, it would be business as usual. The only thing different would be the color of the mercenaries' armor. The lost of the world may have increased in number but they were still the same people the rich sacrificed to their gods of wealth and apathy. He was chasing windmills in pursuit of a justice that just didn't exist.

Thompson fired at me as the rain poured down on us both. The bullets from his gun buried themselves in my suit's reinforced plate interior. It hurt like hell, but I pushed forward, raising my gun.

"You don't have to die, Thompson! We can end this peacefully!" I shouted, not even breathing hard. Outdated as my technology may be, it was still superior to any natural human being's speed and stamina. I could chase him all night and was doing my best just to wear him down. I wanted to take Thompson alive. You needed those little moments of mercy to keep yourself sane in the frozen hell the world had become.

"Fuck you, assassin!" Thompson said, reaching the edge of the building. We were forty stories up. "I remember what the United States used to be like! We used to have rights! You can't replace real cops with thugs!"

"The city replaced the cops," I said coldly. "The Emergency Government approved it."

"You've killed people!" Thompson said, raising up an infodisc, which had replaced flash drives. I knew it was a distraction because he had a memory CRD implant. "The file they gave me told me just what kind of monster you are! You're not even a person!"

"I'm jamming the frequency of your implant," I said softly. I wasn't going to dispute what he said. "I've been doing it all night. You can't distribute the information to who you want. It's over."

"Nothing is over," Thompson said, staring at me and realizing that his gun was probably useless.

Also, that I wasn't firing.

"Life will go on," I said, meeting his gaze. "But this isn't the past. This is the future. You have to live here now."

Thompson raised his gun, then aimed it at me. I wasn't going to fire at him because I didn't want to kill him.

Instead, he walked off the side of the building.

"G?" S spoke, shaking me from my repose.

My involuntary flashback had ended and I was back in the real world, so to speak. I looked up to see my ex-wife, a woman with long black hair and cheekbones you could cut glass with. S was a woman who was capable of masquerading as nearly anyone, but had chosen a look that was attractive but not beautiful.

She was wearing a faux military uniform with brass buttons and a somewhat antiquated look—the "dress" uniform of Atlas. Personally, I found the whole thing ridiculous.

"Hi," I said, blinking. "Sorry, zoned out there for a second."

"That's a common problem with us all lately," S said. She paused. "Doctor Madison claims our memory systems weren't designed to handle the excess of life experiences even if we've overcome the physical time limit of our bodies. He says the maximum we probably have is fifty years, and that's pushing it."

I shrugged. "Thirty years is a long time to work a medical miracle. Especially since I'm probably going to be long dead by gunfire before then."

S smiled. "You've survived this long, old man."

I paused. "What's the emergency?"

S blinked. "There's been an incident at our regional head-quarters in Chicago."

"And?" I asked. "I may be the CSO, but we're a frigging security company. It's not like I have to personally manage everything."

S narrowed her eyes. "It happened just thirty minutes ago. We've found a body in the upper floors. It seems to be Marissa's."

I stared at her. "I'll be there in two hours."

CHAPTER TWO

My next flashback was voluntary, a chance to go back over the days gone by and experience them once more. A useful trick which came from having a computer-brain that stored every sight, smell, and touch with perfect accuracy. I occasionally used it as free porn but, let's be honest, who wouldn't? Right now, I wanted to remember Marissa and not under those circumstances. I wanted to remember the day I walked back into her life during the worst of the disaster years.

It was five years into the disaster and the final months of the refugee crisis. Well, at least as the government defined it. Afterward, it would cease to be a crisis and become the new reality for the people driven from their homes. From this point on, they would live in the outer walls of America's largest cities. It was a bad time, but not as bad as it had been before.

The snow poured down on the refugee camp in the former city of Detroit. The United National Alliance (UNA) had taken over the duties of FEMA, and that had been a blessing even if it was stretched far beyond the limits of its resources. So many people had been forced from their homes in hopes of relief, and they were still located in camps like these, especially given the distribution of food was erratic outside of them. Erratic here some days, too.

The camp was composed of thousands of pre-made shelters and trailers, most of them bearing the Atlas Security logo. It was disgusting to profit off the suffering of others, but no one was else doing the job, and these camps were places we recruited others to help themselves. Their families ate because they helped with the process of acquiring, scavenging, or distributing food.

Holding a crumpled picture of Marissa and myself in my hand, I walked through the section of the facility that was currently being taken over by the United States Army. They were carting out laborers to the government camps that had been set up to handle rebuilding. The Great Reconstruction Project had already killed more people than the Panama Canal but was widely held as a triumph for the Emergency Government.

It was also a time to meet old friends—and enemies. Walking past huge concrete garages full of food and guarded by armed men, I passed a wall where a dozen men had been executed for looting. I finally arrived at the former fire station, which was presently serving as the dual communications center for Atlas and the army to care for the refugees. The government was much harsher than Atlas, though, mostly because it had the authority to be.

I wore a thick winter coat, and I could see my breath in front of me. The cold didn't bother me because I was more machine than man (to quote Obi-Wan Kenobi and Elsa both), but I wasn't about to go advertising my status as a cyborg. The United States military had taken to upgrading their troopers with enhancements, but it was still rare enough that I half expected people to tear me apart with chains and tractor trailers if they knew what I was.

"Man, I can't remember when I was last warm," I muttered, heading into the fire station and walking up the staircase to the side while watching dozens of soldiers communicating with the refugee stations across the nation. The walls were covered with posters straight from World War II, advocating obedience to the government and suggesting citizens sign up for the Citizens Reserve. In a future all too much like one out of science fiction, it felt a bit like we'd regressed.

A part of me wondered why I'd even bothered staying out here in the thick of things. The fighting was over, and there were far better administrators. Atlas had eliminated hundreds of gangs, petty warlords, and even a few traitorous military units when the government was still getting its shit together, but there was nothing requiring a cyborg assassin anymore. I wanted to selfishly get back to one of the civilized cities of the world. A place where they still took credit cards. Yet for reasons I couldn't understand, I was still here.

Reaching the top of the stairs, I saw the woman who had both ruined and saved my life. Marissa Sanchez was a Hispanic woman with black hair tied in a ponytail, wearing a light brown colonel's uniform that was two ranks up since our last meeting. The fact that she was working with the Army despite being an agent of the NSA wasn't new. Task Force-23 had authority over virtually every department of the government as it was the President's personal hit squad. Here, she was talking to a major before spotting me. She dismissed him, leaving us alone by a window.

Marissa gave a somewhat bitter smile. "You know, when I last saw you, you said you were going to go live on a beach somewhere."

"I did," I said, shrugging. "It turns out it's hard to sunbathe in a volcanic winter."

"I understand you and the others are Atlas."

"So, they tell me," I said. "Multi-billion-dollar government contracts await to reform the prison system, corporate-run zones, and security because apparently, the government can't do any of that."

"It's cheaper this way," Marissa said. "Which is somehow a concern with mass starvation."

"How's that anyway?" I asked.

"Better than it has been," Marissa said. "The genetic information in the Black Technology files let us create crops that could be grown year-round with minimal sunlight. It just required us seizing massive amounts of land and forcing people to work it."

"The Soviet Union is laughing from its grave," I replied.

"So is Russia," Marissa said, looking out the window. "Things are stabilizing, at least. Unfortunately, I don't think we're going to be getting our country back anytime soon."

"*Our* country?" I asked, wondering where she got off talking about my patriotism. The United States had used and abused me along with every other Letter. We had been disposable tools to them.

"Oh, that's right, you don't think you count as a citizen,"

Marissa said, with surprising judgment for a woman who knew Karma Corp had made me out of test tubes and wires to be a disposable super soldier.

"I'm a citizen of the world," I said, putting my left hand over my artificial heart. "The only problem is just about everywhere is suffering from one set of problems or another. I can assure you, I'm solely trying to save as many lives as possible, so I can get back to a life of sleazy self-indulgence."

Marissa smirked. "I've missed you, G."

"Case," I said, correcting her. "You were the one who gave me that name, after all."

"By Egyptian beliefs, that means I could control you," Marissa joked.

"Yes, well, we're not in Egypt," I said. "I haven't forgotten all the lies and betrayals."

Because of Marissa, I'd managed to bring down the Carnivale, the International Refugee Society, the Reapers, and President Douglas. I should have felt good about all that, but the simple fact was all those accomplishments had come from her using me as a tool against the people she'd been ordered to take down. Her loyalties had been mutable, and she'd gone from double to triple to quadruple agent before everything was said and done. I could have forgiven her all that, but the worst of the betrayals had been turning on me.

Love died hard.

Marissa smiled. "I was born on the streets of Los Angeles, Case. I learned the only way to survive was to learn to make sure you could play the people around you like a fiddle. The National Security Agency refined those qualities before the Task Forces perfected them. Even if I wanted to, I don't know if I could ever stop manipulating everyone around me. I incorporate every bit of data I learn into profiles, then become the person people need me to be. You needed someone to love you and cherish you. A cute goth girl hacker who was half Lisbeth Salander and half Angelina Jolie's character from *Hackers*. If it's any consolation, I liked that Marissa better than most."

"Is there a real Marissa, or are you just a borderline personality sociopath blank slate?" I asked, not having intended to come there to insult her but clearly failing miserably.

"I'm here to help other people," Marissa said. "We owe you, Case, for all you've done. If Black Technology hadn't been distributed to the world, then casualties would have been far worse. Billions might have died."

"Instead it's just hundreds of millions," I said bitterly.

The death toll was impossible to calculate for the Big Smokey eruption, but a rough estimate was five hundred million people had died worldwide from the initial eruption itself, freezing to death, starvation, civil wars, and other conflicts. It was the worst disaster to hit humanity, arguably ever, but certainly since the near extinction of the Toba Explosion circa 70,000 years ago.

"How's your life?" Marissa asked. "Are you still with Lucita and S?"

"I'm not with anyone," I said, shrugging. "They're their own women."

Lucita occasionally did work for Atlas but had decided to make sure she waited out the apocalypse in style. As such, she'd moved from employer to employer while keeping away from the worst of the disaster. I didn't blame her. Not everyone was cut out to be a hero and I wondered who I was fooling trying to do some good out here. S and I had a cold but formal relationship. Whatever had been between us before didn't exist anymore now that there was no cover identity for us to maintain.

Marissa paused as if dissecting that. "If it's any consolation, I'm not with anyone else."

"It's not," I said, honestly. "I'm not going to be your puppet again."

"Good," Marissa said.

I paused. "You're lying."

Marissa smirked. "You're right. You're one of the best soldiers I've ever worked with. I'd very much like to use you in the future."

"Fat chance," I said. "I'm never working for the government again."

Marissa smiled, almost amused. "I'm not going to be working for the government after we finish transferring the last of the refugees from the camps."

"Oh?" I asked, curious.

"Yes, I'm hitting the private sector after this," Marissa said. "I can't stand the corruption anymore."

I snorted. "You're making a lateral career move then."

"Am I?" Marissa asked, her voice calm and collected but carrying more bitterness than nearly anyone else I'd talked to this year—and this was a refugee camp. "I think the Invisible Hand is back in power."

I blinked. "Err, duh?"

"Duh?" Marissa asked. "Are you a thirteen-year-old girl?"

"I use the internet a lot," I said, shrugging. "It's amazing that it's stood the test of time."

"It was made to survive a nuclear war, and Delphi made sure plenty of satellites were there to keep going through the worst of it," Marissa replied. "What do you mean 'duh,' though?"

"I know Karma Corp and most of the other companies were fronts for it," I replied, staring at her. "I also know the Trust Administration bent over backwards to make sure they were immune to prosecution as well as able to field their own armies to keep them producing for the United States through the worst of this."

"I don't think the Trust Administration had much choice," Marissa said. "The State of Emergency Government is the real power in the country. Still, I'm not going to stand by and see the world fall into the hands of private business."

"Well, good luck with that," I said, raising my hands. "You can continue chasing windmills for as long as you want."

Marissa raised an eyebrow. "Why did you come here, Case?"

I shook my head. "I don't know. Wondering how you were doing? As much as you did to me, I also owed you for awakening me to my past. Maybe I wanted to see how you were doing or if you'd managed to find anyone yourself."

Marissa shrugged. "I have four boyfriends and two married men I'm sleeping with. All of them mean precisely nothing to me. They're all a little in love with me, though. Three of them have killed for me. The other three provide information."

"Do they know about each other?"

"Of course not."

I closed my eyes. "Shameful."

"Says the assassin to the spy," Marissa said, her expression empty. "Despite everything, we went through a lot together. Would you say you owed me for revealing the truth to you about Project: Letter?"

"No," I said, frowning. "Because I paid you back by saving you from my brother."

"Yes, but I saved you from him at the end." Marissa lifted an imaginary rifle and made a boom gesture.

"Still doesn't count," I said, realizing I should probably get out of there before she persuaded me to do something I didn't want to do.

"What if I could do you a favor now?" Marissa said after a pause.

I blinked. "What do you mean?"

"I'm the Deputy Director of Refugee Relocation in the Department of Homeland Security," Marissa said, showing once more she was able to move to whatever department she wanted. "You've been here for over a year, making sure the people here survived as best they could. I even noticed you set up the Christmas celebration."

"Kids deserve a Christmas even in a frozen hell," I replied. "I don't like where this is going."

"I'm just saying there's probably someone you care about that's in need of a little bit of government assistance."

I opened my mouth, slack-jawed. "What is this? Are you actually blackmailing me with the fate of refugees for a future favor?"

Marissa paused. "I'd prefer to say bribing. The simple fact is it's a dangerous world out there, and I don't think it's a bad idea to have the world's best assassin as a friend."

Third-best assassin, technically. S and A were both better than me back at the International Refugee Society. Of course, S was now primarily an administrator, and no one had seen A for years. For all I knew, he'd been in Wyoming when the place had become an enormous crater they were considering turning into collective farms.

"You disgust me," I said, turning around. "I should have known this was a mistake."

"I promise it'll be someone bad and I won't be there."

I laughed, then stopped mid-step. Goddammit.

I took a few pointless breaths. "I know I'm going to regret this, but could you look up Barbara and Kathy Gordon?"

Marissa paused for less than a second. "Done."

"What?" I asked, turning around.

"I had my brain put in an IRD case," Marissa said. "Most of my body is a Shell now."

"I thought your breasts were bigger."

Marissa narrowed her eyes. "Smooth, James Bond. Real classy."

"Hey, you're the one who did it."

Marissa rolled her eyes. "They're stuck in Canada on half-pay. They're both alive but pretty heavy in bills."

I paused. "Can you get them a spot back in America with easy work?"

"How much of a favor will you owe me?" Marissa asked.

"One," I said coldly. "I regret even entertaining the thought, but unless you manage to suddenly put me up with the most charming person on Earth, one is going to be all you get. Lord knows I want to get out of murder and espionage for hire."

Marissa shrugged. "Done. I'll keep it for a rainy day."

"You're never going to change, are you?" I asked, disgusted with myself and her.

"You've got to have hope," Marissa said.

Little did I know how I was going to eventually hate that word.

CHAPTER THREE

Ten years later, I regretted making that deal with Marissa. Two hours after receiving S's message to come to Chicago, I was sitting in the First-Class section of a Vertical Lift Off (or VLO) transport. They were one of the creations of the modern era's technology and had replaced the jet. I had no idea how they worked, something about magnetism, but they moved across the globe at ridiculous speeds.

I had a private jet, but it was faster just to take one of the Atlas Security transports headed to our newest building. The VLO's interior was comfortable, with leather seats to cradle the latest employees of our company as they were transported to take up their new jobs in one of the few thriving businesses in the new world: war. My only problem with them was the company—specifically that they considered themselves in a position to make friends with our companions.

"So where were you when Big Smokey erupted?" asked a blonde woman sitting beside me. She was middle-aged, with several plastic surgeries and a right hand that my cybernetic eyes detected as artificial, along with her kidneys.

"On a beach," I said, thinking about how my life of leisure had become one of cold-blooded, ruthless service. Voluntary this time. Mostly.

"I was with my brother," the blonde woman said, sighing. "We were vacationing in Florida when the world changed. It was like the apocalypse, wasn't it? I wasn't planning to vote for President Trust. He seemed so… goofy."

"Yes," I said, taking a deep breath. "He's certainly changed the world."

"I'm glad they're letting him run again," the blonde-haired woman said. "We don't need a change in government right now, and term limits don't make sense to me, anyway. Why shouldn't I be able to vote for whoever I want?"

"Obviously," I said, trying to hide my disdain. Not for her caring about the show elections where the results were predetermined by the Emergency Government (my company was providing security for the ballot boxes being fixed) or the belief that the President was still in charge, but that I cared to discuss politics on a plane.

"Oh, look at me," the woman said, chuckling. "I've been prattling on this entire time. I've not even asked your name. What do you do, Mister—"

The VLO started rocking, and I knew we were about to set down on the top of the Atlas Security Corps Building. Thank God. The building looked rather obnoxious with its glass spiral design that seemed designed to show off the artist's deranged sensibilities. It was a Tower of Babel in the middle of a city that was still half leveled. Still, it was soon going to be number 166 of the Big 200 and was replacing the police forces of not only Chicago but also all the other super-cities.

The State of Emergency Government had devoted massive amounts of resources to the creation of arcologies, basically self-sufficient super-structures. They were meant to rescue the United States from its pit of destruction. Ten cities, curiously beginning with Las Vegas, had been designed to handle the massive population overflow while also having an industrial base to rebuild the rest of the country. There were mile-tall buildings now, and cities that had layers in the sky. The research done for building the International Space Elevator (which was probably not going to be built—at least in this century) provided the future metals strong enough to do it. It made for some breathtaking vistas, but the shining ziggurats of electricity and transparent steel cast long shadows over the poverty below. So at least some things hadn't changed in the country.

"Case Gordon," I said, simply. I didn't expect her to recognize that I was Atlas' Chief Security Officer even though she was apparently another refugee being allowed to work in our

Chicago offices. "My friends call me G."

"Oh." The blonde woman blinked. "That's an interesting nickname."

"It's from my childhood," I said, glad the ride was almost over. "So, what made you decide to work for Atlas?"

"Oh, I don't want to work for Atlas," the woman admitted, not having bothered to give her name, or maybe I'd just forgotten it. "They're a bunch of thugs and rent-a-cops playing soldier. However, you go where the work is."

I smiled. My respect for her had gone up, at least a bit. "I totally agree."

The VLO's side opened, and the passengers began to disembark. I unbuckled my seatbelt and claimed my luggage, which included a katana hilt attached to a carry-on bag that also carried several other pieces of equipment used in assassination. The blonde woman's eyes widened before I chuckled and headed to the door, stepping out onto the rooftop where the new employees were being sorted.

The Atlas Security logo of a hand wrapped around the world in a circle was sprayed on the ground instead of the traditional H. Soldiers in black and white plastisteel armor stood watch next to the uniformed officers scanning everyone's identity cards. Standing off to one side was Colonel Lucita Biondi.

Lucita was a beautiful golden-tressed woman who had a single braid hairstyle and a black beret to go with her urban camouflage pants and gray shirt. She had a swimmer's body even though her actual form was almost entirely cybernetic. She wasn't dressed for combat and looked more like a model than a soldier, but she could throw a car, so who was I to tell her what was appropriate?

As I walked over to her, one of the soldiers saluted me, and I rolled my eyes. "Hello, Lucita."

"Case," Lucita said, walking up and giving me a passionate kiss on the lips. Her hands moved inappropriately down to my leg.

"Please, we're in public," I said, uncomfortable.

"Oh, no one cares," Lucita said. "One of the few benefits of the end of the world is people are starting to mind their own business for once. Besides, it's not like you've ever been shy. My harem misses you."

"Do you really call them that?" I asked, shaking my head.

"They prefer it to slaves," Lucita said, smirking. "Why, what do you call yours?"

I sighed and wondered for the millionth time if I knew anyone who wasn't a sociopath. Perhaps I shouldn't have been too judgmental, though, as she was one of my few friends to stand the test of time. I'd never love Lucita, and I doubt she was capable of the emotion herself, but I could count on her to come to my aid when the chips were down and vice versa, despite the times we'd almost killed each other. The fact that our relationship was sexual was almost an afterthought—like a handshake between two people that life had chewed up and spit out.

"Funny," I said.

"I'm not joking," Lucita said. "In any case, I assume you're here to confirm the Wicked Old Bitch, at last, is dead."

Lucita wasn't fond of Marissa.

"Assuming it's her. A corpse isn't quite what it used to be."

Lucita, who had left the flesh and blood body she'd been born with behind long ago, nodded. "S has ordered the area cordoned off and garrisoned, but no one has gone in since the initial identification."

I nodded. "Thank you. This is personal."

"You don't still love her, do you?" Lucita asked, looking ready to gag.

"No," I said softly. "I stopped loving her the moment she tried to kill me."

Lucita snorted. "I tried to do that. Stop loving her for all the other stuff."

She had a point there.

"Let's get going," I said, looking over at the other people offloading the VLO before shaking my head. "We can discuss places you've been and people you've killed once we've got confirmation."

Then I could figure out who was responsible—or if this was another one of Marissa's tricks. It said something about our relationship that the discovery of her corpse meant I was leaning toward the latter instead of the former.

Lucita gave a short grumble of assent, looking down over the rooftop's edge to the neon-illuminated buildings below. Chinese translations accompanied English and Spanish advertisements for everything from legalized drugs to sexual performance enhancers. Huge holograms were projected into the air, and the night sky provided an insane tableau of sensory input. We'd recovered from the near-end of humanity to double down on commercialism.

Maybe I was being too hard, though, and maybe it was because we had survived so much that mankind wanted to forget the horror it had left behind. If so, they were willing to do it every which way technology allowed while catering to the lowest common denominator. I'd seen plenty of advertisements for lifetime service contracts in the same sort of job Heather worked, plus virtual reality experiences to replace your existing life. I didn't judge desperation, but I also knew the predators were always lying in wait for those willing to throw away everything for the promise of anything to give their life meaning.

"Come this way," Lucita said, gesturing to a nearby private elevator.

"How's business?" I asked, stepping into the stark white elevator beside her. As we turned around, the elevator doors closed in our faces, and we descended into the depths of the building.

"Booming," Lucita said. "The United States military is too bogged down in the Antarctica Wars to handle the ninth arcology construction security. It doesn't help that the Pentagon isn't even trying to hide the fact it's for sale."

"Oh joy," I said, smiling.

"You asked," Lucita said.

"Sorry, just trying to take my mind off things," I said.

"Try porn, it's less depressing," Lucita said, smiling. "You can do simulations in your mind with the latest uploads, and no one would be the wiser."

I stared at her, surprised. "Do you?"

Lucita snorted. "Please. You actually believe I can't do better than the hacks out there? They should sell my memories.

Hmmm, there's a thought."

"Did you ever see her again after the Big Smokey eruption?" Lucita asked, showing even she wasn't sure how she was supposed to react.

"Who?" I pretended I didn't know who she was talking about.

"You know," Lucita said, frowning. "We don't have to talk about it."

"A couple of times," I said, lying. "Mostly she wanted my help for a few minor things. I refused, of course."

"Jesus," Lucita said, shaking her head. "The nerve of that woman."

"I'm not in any position to throw stones," I said.

I'd killed something like a thousand people in my life. Most had it coming, but there were others who'd simply been in the wrong place at the wrong time. Small comfort as that might be to my conscience.

"You never betrayed anyone you loved," Lucita said, her voice low. "That's the difference between you and her."

"So they say," I said, knowing there wasn't much difference in the end. Not after all I'd done for HOPE.

The doors opened seconds later, revealing a still-incomplete area of the office full of computers, cubicles, and a stark white decor that was vaguely unsettling. Plastic covered a lot of the machinery and devices, and I could smell the blood hanging in the air. About a dozen Atlas security officers were hanging around the location along with forensic scientists. They were all avoiding the actual crime scene, which meant they were following S's instructions to the letter.

There was a strange body sitting in a chair, which told me this hadn't just been an incident involving Marissa. Still, we should have had security footage of the area and Delphi monitoring the situation.

"We still haven't gotten this building completely working, have we?" I asked, walking out.

"No," Lucita said, shaking her head. "The price of trying to get this fucking smart building working. Delphi wants everything perfect, and I'm getting sick of listening to her demands."

"We can't do this without her."

Lucita rolled her eyes. "That's just because she mothers you."

I shrugged. "Maybe. I don't think she's anyone's mother. Though per the tabloids, someone should really tell her to dial down on the drugs and parties."

Delphi was the heart of Atlas Security's success and also one of the reasons why humanity had survived the Big Smokey eruption. She'd been preparing for months before it happened as a possible end-of-the-world scenario, and while it hadn't been long enough to get much done, she'd done enough to save many lives. She was also based on my mother—or Daniel Gordon's mother, to be precise—which made our relationship unique. That didn't stop her from using drone bodies, male or female, to indulge all of humanity's pleasures. Apparently, she considered her job finished and thought it was time to enjoy herself.

"*You* tell Delphi she needs to tone it down," Lucita said, missing that I was contemplating deeper things than the fact that our AI was a party animal. "Dee doesn't listen to me. She's giving us a bad name, though. You might think there's no such thing as bad publicity, but people don't want their army's general showing up at raves."

"I wouldn't know where to begin. It'd also be massively hypocritical," I said, walking over to where the bodies were kept. "Have the Chicago police visited?"

"No," Lucita said, taking a deep breath. "It happened on Atlas property, so it's a corporate sovereignty matter. Besides, they'll be out of a job in a few months, and most of them want to work for us rather than transfer."

I wasn't sure about that. "Did Delphi see anything? Anything at all?"

"No," a soft female voice spoke via my cyberlink. "Marissa got inside the building using a series of blind spots and chose this floor because it's off my grid. Still, I spotted her twice and informed security the moment I noticed her. It's also perhaps why she was killed."

It was Delphi, all right. No one else could get past my

defenses. Mostly because she'd created them all. "*If* she was killed. Let's not forget how many times she's escaped death before."

"The Grim Reaper gets everyone eventually," Lucita said, walking beside me. "We've just made him wait more than most people."

The first body on the ground was an Atlas security officer with a white beard, metal arms without synthskin, and a chest that looked like it had been blown apart by grenade bullets. The interior was completely artificial, which made me think he was a Shell or a drone. Drones were the cheap knock-offs of Letters that had appeared on the market lately. Mostly, no one used them because they were too expensive and the legal rights they possessed were murky. It was one of the reasons why the other Letters and I hadn't come forward with our inhuman nature.

I couldn't bring myself to look at Marissa's corpse yet.

"Who is this guy?" I asked. "I don't recognize him, and one of the advantages of a computer brain is I know everybody in our army. All two million."

"Charles Porter," Delphi said. "That's what his identity card reads, at least. However, it's a forgery and was entered into my system by a slicer. He has no identity in any existing database, which means his body is almost certainly newly acquired or he has no identity."

"Shell or drone?" I asked.

"I'm inclined to say drone," Lucita said. "There's organic material in his brain, but it looks harvested. My guess is some assholes grew a brain in a vat, slapped it in there, and attached electrodes to keep it alive while the real business took place in his RealBrain implant."

I frowned. "Well, that eliminates the usual suspects. Most rival corporations know regular humans are cheaper and more expendable."

"Government?" Lucita suggested.

"Even more inclined to use cheap and expendable labor," I said. "Is he the one who killed her?"

"No," Delphi said. "Examination of the crime scene

indicates it was done by a second subject." Taking a deep breath, I turned to look at Marissa's body. It slumped in a chair where both had repeatedly been struck by armor-piercing bullets. The damage done was considerable, but not quite as bad as it could have been if she'd been completely human. Instead, it looked almost like a Hollywood reproduction of a crime scene with her glassy, artificial eyes staring back at me while the holes leaked rather than bled.

Marissa was a beautiful Mexican-American woman with long dark hair and perpetually youthful features. Her skin was light brown, tanner than usual, with eyes the deepest shade of blue. She was thinner than I remembered and wore a beige business dress rather than her usual Goth attire. In her right hand was an infodisc.

"I'm sorry, Case," Lucita said.

I put on a pair of black plastic gloves, designed to cover up DNA and fingerprints, before reaching over to touch Marissa's cheek. The feel of it was undiminished by the gloves and moved with a greater buoyancy than regular human flesh. It was synthflesh, professional grade quality but also upgraded for military use. Not entirely unlike the kind Letters had.

"It's not her," I said.

Lucita did a double take. "Are you sure?"

"There's no seams," I said, using the slang term for synthskin graft edges. "This is a full body transplant, and that takes six months to recover from. I've talked to Marissa more recently, and she was working with an older model body."

Lucita frowned put her hands on her hips. "A couple of times, huh?"

I shrugged. "I was visiting my other partner."

Lucita blinked.

That was when one of the security team shouted, checking the janitor's closet only to have a short redheaded woman in jeans and a red jacket run out. Apparently, somehow, they'd missed someone hiding for the entire three hours. Goddammit! I thought we were employing people who weren't Keystone Cops!

The security guard raised his gun to shoot her.

"No!" I shouted, chasing after her.

I recognized her as the partner I'd mentioned.

Claire.

She was the bait Marissa had lured me in with to become her slave. One of the few people I'd ever cared for.

Goddammit.

CHAPTER FOUR

There were some advantages to being an inhumanly fast cyborg. Those seconds had passed, and I'd managed to cross the entirety of the office to wrap my arms around Claire Morris. Thankfully, that was before the security staff gunned her down in a fit of trigger-happy idiocy. Hopefully, they wouldn't shoot after I was in their line of fire and fulfill the American dream of killing their boss.

Panicked, Claire struggled in my arms and kicked the air before elbowing me in the face. The blow was far stronger than any woman (or man) punching the equivalent of a skin-wearing metal statue should be. For a second, I believed she might be another imposter like the "Marissa" I'd found shot up nearby. However, as my hands accidentally moved underneath her shirt across her stomach, I found a scar that told me no, this was her.

As she spun around and made a move to knee me in the groin, I caught it and stepped back. "It's me, dammit!"

Claire, who had been reaching into my jacket for my hidden Red Desert-20, stopped in mid-motion. "Case?"

"Yes," I said, staring at her. "It's my building. Sort of."

Claire stopped and stood still. "Oh, right."

Eight Atlas Security guards surrounded us and aimed their laser-sight-equipped M25s at us.

Lucita glared at them as she caught up after a less-than-impressive jog. "Okay, Case, who the hell is she and what's she doing at our crime scene?"

Claire wasn't wearing her usual style of a hoodie and jeans. Instead, she wore the sort of business dress common enough that someone who didn't know her might mistake her for a secretary. Also, a pair of glasses that were purely an aesthetic choice these days. The fact that Atlas Regional Headquarters had facial recognition software and a frigging AI monitoring everyone who entered meant such disguises were pointless, though. Had she managed to hack the system to get a false identity too?

"No," Delphi said in my mind. "I identified her immediately. I just thought she was coming to your place of business for money, a sexual encounter, emotional support, or some combination thereof. She has, after all, done so before."

"I thought I told you never to record what goes on in my office," I thought back to her.

"I have exceptional microphones. Believe me, you're not the only one using your office that way."

"Ugh. Thanks, Mom."

"I don't know what she was doing up here, though," Delphi admitted.

I stared at Claire's hands and noticed powder burns. I looked back at the closet she'd fled from and noticed an automatic ARC-57, the King of Uzis, sticking out.

"I think she's our killer," I said, holding her by the shoulder. "Which, as the Chief of Security, means she's in my custody, and I'll be taking over from here. Everyone get their guns off us, or I'm going to get very upset."

The security personnel looked to Lucita then at each other. It made me think I'd have to do more to associate with our staff. I might know all of them by name, but they didn't know me and clearly didn't have any reason to be loyal to me. That was the problem when you were a millionaire recluse who hated dealing with people.

"Go," Lucita said.

The security personnel broke up and put their guns away, leaving us and heading back to the bodies.

"Thanks," Claire said, taking a deep breath. "I have a good reason for everything I've done."

"I'm sure you do," I said, not really caring whether she did or not. She could have shot up the Oscars, and I would have done my best to protect her.

"You didn't answer my question," Lucita said, looking between us. "Who is she?"

"This is Claire Morris. She's an associate of mine and Marissa's."

"Helps-you-kill-people associate or naked-and-screaming-in-ecstasy associate?" Lucita asked.

"Both," I replied.

"Case!" Claire said.

"Oh, like you're alone in that," Lucita muttered. "I do my best to sleep with my associates. It makes them less inclined to turn on you. Well, sometimes more, but only if you're stupid about it."

Oh, Lucita, what would I do without you? Oh right, not be embarrassed and have to clean up as many bodies. "In any case, I think she'll be able to provide us with information about the situation."

"You think?" Lucita said. "Either way, I am willing to let this go if she killed Marissa."

"I did not kill Marissa," Claire said, her voice cold and harsh. "She's my friend."

"Okay, now I'm against her again," Lucita said, shaking her head. "I suggest you throw her off the building."

"Lucita!" I snapped. "Not funny."

"Not joking," Lucita said, growling. "I'm your best friend, and it astounds me you're still involved with that woman. Jesus, Marissa is like a virus."

"Sure," I said, trying to wrap my head around why Claire would want to meet with Marissa in the middle of a half-constructed Atlas building. As known associates of HOPE, they would have been stopped by security, and the only people who would have let them in were Delphi and me. Hacktivists and cyber-terrorists were not the normal sorts of people security companies liked to associate with. Hell, my association with both would have gotten me "retired," or at least forced me to fake my death if my non-Letter partners found out about it. "Do we have any idea who our fake Marissa was?"

Claire looked down. "I don't know. She and the others were apparently sent to kill me and retrieve the data I was bringing here."

The plot thickened. "Perhaps you should explain from the beginning."

Honestly, I wasn't too surprised about the discovery that the body wasn't Marissa. Death could catch any of us at any time or any place, but I somehow knew she was too clever to be caught in such an obvious way. Cybernetic enhancements didn't make it impossible for you to be killed, but it did make sure it was much harder to kill you. Body doubles, face-sculpting, Shells, and even artificially accelerated clone growths were all possible with today's technology. Ryan Gosling had been reported killed like three times thanks to the fact that he'd licensed out his visage to the public. It had become a popular conspiracy theory, but the second time had been real, and a Shell had replaced him in his subsequent movies.

"All right," Claire said, taking a deep breath. "I was born in Seattle to a mixed Odawa and Irish family that lived on the border of Canada. My brother joined the army first—"

Lucita narrowed her eyes. "I meant with Marissa."

I gritted my teeth. "She's a member of HOPE."

Lucita's eyes widened, then she covered her face. "Delphi, did you know about this?"

"Yes," Delphi said simply, speaking over the building speakers.

"Why didn't you tell anyone?" Lucita asked.

"I am fully prepared to destroy this entire company to protect Case," Delphi said. "Everyone else is expendable."

Lucita looked up at the ceiling. "Well, at least we know where you stand."

"On a mountain of corpses, overlooking an infinite vista of information," Delphi said. "Reality is made of information, you know."

"How long have you been a member of HOPE, Case?" Lucita asked. "You know, the organization that routinely bankrupts billion-dollar corporations?"

Lucita was exaggerating, but not by much. HOPE had been formed in the wake of the refugee crisis and ended up about halfway between Anonymous and the Weatherman Underground. They engaged in actual sabotage and political activity that sometimes-included violence. They also engaged in blackmail, espionage, and the occasional bit of wetwork for hire. The organization, unbeknownst to the public, donated billions of credits in vital humanitarian aid to the most desperate parts of the country as well. None of which would keep the Emergency Government from executing them all if they could track them down.

"I'm not a member," I said simply. "Just an affiliate. I—"

"How long?" Lucita asked.

"Eight years," I answered.

"Jesus," Lucita said. She then paused. "Marissa is the head of the organization, isn't she?"

"Founder. At least as far as I know."

Lucita looked about ready to explode. "Why? Just why?"

I blinked, thinking back to the mission where Claire had recruited me. It had been after Thompson had thrown himself off the rooftop. "I was tired of being the bad guy."

"There are no good guys!" Lucita said, shaking her hands in the air. "There never have been. There are only bad people and worse people!"

I didn't want to believe that and working for HOPE made me feel different. "If you want me to resign, I will."

Lucita blinked. "Case, I drowned a man in my toilet once. I'm not that hypocritical. I just don't know how you can serve both God and Mammon."

I was surprised by her show of support. As much time as S and I had spent together, I was sure she'd have me thrown into a hole and forgotten about me for endangering her company. "God *is* Mammon when it comes to the megacorporations. It's why I'm trying to tweak their nose enough."

Lucita took a deep breath. "White guilt has ruined you, Case."

"My mother was black," I said. Well, the mother of the extremely light-skinned biracial man I was cloned from.

Lucita raised an eyebrow. "Really? You don't look—"

"Can we get back to the fact that people just tried to kill me and Marissa?" Claire spoke up.

"That's Tuesday for us, dear," Lucita replied condescendingly.

"Also, I hate Marissa and don't know you from Eve."

"Is Marissa all right?" I asked, realizing for the first time since finding out her corpse had been a fake that my ex could actually be in danger.

"I don't know," Claire said, frowning. "The information I mentioned earlier is all stored in my mnemonic drive. Terabytes of data about all of Karma Corp's dirty deeds, and hopefully, enough to finally bury them if it's all released at once."

"Karma Corp?" Lucita interjected again. "Your target is Karma Corp? The head of the Corporate Council? *Numero uno* of the Big 200? The first company-state to be on the United National Alliance Security Council? Ugh, English doesn't have enough swear words for what I'm feeling right now. I'm going to have to switch to Italian."

Lucita let forth a series of choice profanities that somehow still sounded beautiful. It was her command of the Romance language's epicness that made even variations on *cazzo idiota* come out sounding lovely.

"Aim big, and you'll never miss your target," Claire said, reciting a line from her days in the Marines.

"Karma Corp has been a target of mine for a long time," I said softly. "I owe it many debts."

I wasn't a crazy person and didn't anthropomorphize Karma Corp. Companies weren't people, no matter what the law said, and couldn't be evil in and of themselves—only the people inside them. Most of the people involved in the Letter Project were long dead or had been replaced. Still, the company was the heart of the Invisible Hand and had never stopped its vilest experiments.

Indeed, with how cheap human life had become after Big Smokey's eruption, it had gotten even worse. If Marissa or Claire had discovered something that could cripple or even dismantle the megacorporation, then I was all for doing it. I'd probably be able to make a tidy profit for myself and a mega-profit for Atlas Security along the way.

"What's on the disc, anyway?" I asked.

"I don't know," Claire said. "Need-to-know operational security and all that. I probably shouldn't know it relates to bringing down Karma Corp, but Marissa occasionally lets details slip."

"In bed?" Lucita asked.

I stared at her.

"What?" Lucita asked. "Spy work should always be lurid. Otherwise, it's just wiretaps and hacking."

"Marissa contacted me to meet her here with the decryption drive. Except when I arrived, it was a fake and she was an assassin. I shot them both up and hid when the security corps arrived. They didn't do a very good job searching. They seemed more interested in Marissa's body than in looking for the assailant."

"Why were you having your clandestine meeting on Atlas soil anyway?" Lucita asked, as if the Atlas Regional Headquarters were a fucking embassy. Which, legally, it was kind of was, but she was still taking this corporate sovereignty thing way too seriously.

"We use Atlas Security property to hold most of our meetings," Claire said. "Case said it would be okay if we stayed off the grid."

Lucita turned to look at me. "Case, I withdraw my earlier statement. You need to resign immediately."

"I don't care. It'll give me more time to play video games and kill people." I was joking, sort of.

"I overrule that with my Chairman's veto," Delphi said via our cyberlink. "You're not allowed to resign, Case."

"Isn't that my choice?" I asked.

"No," Delphi said. "You owe me too much."

"Fine."

"Why don't you have an encryption key and why didn't Marissa have a copy of the data?" I asked the first questions that popped into my head. I couldn't think about the fact that someone had very likely intercepted and killed Marissa. I'd been thinking about that all the way over there, and it had left me numb. I couldn't afford to be numb now. I needed to be sharp.

Claire rolled her eyes at that before turning to me. "I kept the data in my cyberbrain to avoid the possibility of leaks. If Karma Corp knew HOPE had as much as we did, they'd send the Feds or their own mercenaries against us. They'd also spare no expense in crashing our system with Black Hat slicers. Marissa believed keeping the encryption would prevent me from deciding to use the data early."

"I see," Lucita said. "A nice way to make sure your subordinates stay under your thumb as well."

"Says the woman who calls hers slaves," I replied.

Lucita shrugged. "That's a fair cop. You don't know if you can trust a relationship if they have other places to go, though."

"That's horrifying," I said.

"Says the man who lets his employees steal from him as long as they fuck him," Lucita said.

"They don't have to fuck me," I corrected her.

"Marissa didn't trust herself with the data either," Claire said, looking as disgusted with this conversation as Lucita had been earlier. "Honestly, I think it would have been better to keep it with a third party."

"The 'why now' actually matters," I said, trying to put pieces together. "We've been trying to take down Karma Corp since Mississippi."

Claire slumped her shoulders, defeated. "We've run out of time. Zheng Wei is going to be making an announcement in two days. Our inside sources indicate he's managed to get nanotherapy working."

Zheng Wei was the Chief Technology Officer of Karma Corp and the pioneer "visionary" of nanotechnology as a new force in human medicine. Theoretically. Truth be told, he'd done amazing work in micronizing surgery and advanced medical treatments, but nanotherapy had proven beyond his capabilities despite extensive human experimentation. The miracles at Lourdes had a better track record than nanotherapy healing. If he actually had gotten it working, it was the opposite of information that could destroy Karma Corp. It could be enough to make them bigger than the next ten in the Big 200 as well as give them a monopoly on modern medicine.

Lucita blinked, credit signs passing across her irises. "Seriously, I thought that was a myth. We need to buy Karma Corp stock heavily and get ahead of this."

"They're the worst of the Big 200," I said.

"And if we're to be even half as effective, we need to be more like them," Lucita said, unashamed. "Nanotherapy has the possibility of ending disease on Earth. Fuck, it could reverse aging, or at least retard it. The number of in-born medical conditions it could fix—"

"Which is why Karma Corp needs to be taken down now," I said, nodding my head. "The moment that announcement goes out, it won't matter how many thousands of people they've murdered in their experiments to get these results. The ends will have justified the means."

"Won't they have?" Lucita asked. "The only people who care about the means are those who haven't succeeded."

She had a point.

"Oh, come on," Lucita said, shaking her head. "Surely, Case, you're not going to argue good and evil with me."

"I leave God to judge," I said, shrugging. "Everything I do is based on my own little pseudo-Nietzschean world. Karma Corp is a sick twisted giant who has hurt the people I love. It also made me its slave, so I don't give a shit about how many aspirins or clone hearts it makes. I intend to take it down, and they can distribute nanotherapy knockoffs across the world after the other companies have looted its corpse."

"Says the guy who has a love slave," Claire said.

"Heather's not a slave," I said.

"What's wrong with slavery?" Lucita asked. "I mean if it's not racial and applied equally."

I felt my face. "Stop helping, Lucita."

"Sure."

Claire smirked. "Still, a badass speech, Case. You know, despite misusing both God and Nietzsche."

"You're going to end up distributing the technology to everyone, aren't you?" Lucita asked, sighing. "Again?"

I laughed. "I gotta be me."

Lucita shook her head. "At least give us a copy of the information. We'll get a head start on it."

I looked at Claire, who nodded. "Sure."

"Have you tried to contact Marissa? The real one?"

Claire's expression was unreadable. "I sent calls her way immediately. Nothing. I tried calling you, but you had your cyberlink off."

I grimaced. "I had it restricted to Atlas frequencies. Sorry, I thought I was coming here to identify Marissa's body."

"You still might be," Lucita said, more harshly than usual. "You realize the most likely scenario is those are a pair of Karma Corp's samurai out to scuttle HOPE's ill-conceived plan to screw them over."

Claire looked ready to go for Lucita's eyes. Instead, she responded with an icy "I'm aware."

I thought about the bodies nearby and proceeded over to the fake Marissa. The guards and forensics teams had taken Lucita's order to leave literally, and thankfully, I didn't have to explain why I was stealing evidence. Then again, I was Chief of Security, so I could just order them away. I really needed to start doing my job one of these days.

"What's that?" Lucita said.

"The fake Marissa was trying to give me that when I shot her," Claire said. "It can't be the encryption key."

"Are these computers operational?" I asked, looking at the various machines covered in plastic all around us.

"Yes, Case," Delphi said. "Do you want me to isolate them from the rest of the network?"

"Yes," I said, sitting down. "I have a feeling they weren't here to kill Claire, though they may have been here to steal your information."

Claire looked confused. "Then they didn't know me very well."

"Obviously," Lucita said.

Sitting down at one of the cubicles, I booted up the system and uploaded the infodisc.

"It's attempting to reach an outside cyberlink," Delphi said.

"Allow it as long as it doesn't reach any other systems," I said. "I don't want this turning into a bad spy movie where a single virus takes out the entire agency."

"That would be stupid," Delphi said. "Also, I liked *Skyfall*. Just not that scene."

Seconds later, a video link began on the screen, and I saw the image of a handsome black man in his mid-thirties with a short, businesslike haircut. He was smiling broadly with no emotion behind it, just an artificial pleasantness taught by Karma Corp's trainers in the early days of the Letter program.

A flood of images filled my mind from the man, too jumbled to form a coherent narrative. I remembered him beating me every time we fought during training. I remembered him sharing his phone's photo section of artfully arranged corpses he'd created. I remembered how he'd told me every Letter should be forced to kill a baby to eliminate weakness from our ranks. I also recalled how he enjoyed Snickers bars and pizza. He was the best and worst of us. The living embodiment of an indestructible, unstoppable killer with no humanity—made by fools with too little idea of what they were unleashing. Fools like my father and mother.

Shit.

"Hello, A," I said softly. "Long time no see."

"I prefer Arthur now," A said, chuckling. "Though I never bothered to give myself a last name. Maybe Arthur X would be a good choice. My fellow Letters might confuse me for X, though, who was kind of a shit agent."

I took a deep breath. "Where is Marissa?"

"She's fine," A said. "But indisposed. I'm afraid she's going to remain that way until I get what I want."

Lucita kept her cool, but Claire looked ready to rip the computer monitor out from its console and throw it against the wall.

"Where is she, *Arthur*?" I asked, staring at him through the screen. He was identical to the way he'd looked Pre-Crisis. I'd thought he'd have changed his body by now or died of cybernecrosis, but it seemed he'd found a cure for the condition the same way Atlas' Letters had.

Arthur sighed. "G, you really are a bother. It's always about you and your assistant. You're like E in that. What's he up to?"

"He's currently in Russia investigating a cybernetics harvesting ring," I said, willing to play along with his chit-chat tone for now.

"Ah, how cute. Mister E is a detective," Arthur said. "You

never did invite me to join your little corporate adventure."

"You were too busy snorting mountains of cocaine and banging three hookers at a time," I said.

Arthur frowned. "Yes, I suppose that would be an impediment. I still would have helped through, though. Delphi knew that."

"I did," Delphi said. "I wanted no part of you near any of my objectives. I predicted you'd eventually try to kill the others to seize control of the company yourself."

"I'd fix you first," Arthur said. "Machines should do what they're told. Thinking or not."

The irony was either lost on Arthur, or he didn't care. Did he not think of himself as a machine? I wished I had that luxury. Every day I wondered if I had a soul or not. With no answer to that question forthcoming, I repeated my earlier question. "Where is she, Arthur?"

The camera switched to an image of Marissa sitting on the side of a bed in the middle of a lavishly appointed room. The place had Old World decor with antique wooden furniture, bookshelves, and a fireplace. It had no windows, though, and a steel door. She was wearing a pair of sweatpants and a *Lucifer's Star* t-shirt which made me think they'd grabbed her out of bed. She had a gag in her mouth, and her hands were zip-tied behind her back.

Marissa hadn't changed much since our meeting in Detroit. Her hair was tied in a ponytail with the back-dyed blue and a tattoo of an ouroboros on the side of her neck. I didn't know why she'd gone back to the cybergoth look, especially since she'd aged out of the present demographic, but didn't care right now.

"She must be going insane without a computer," I said. "Assuming you're jamming her implants."

"Of course," Arthur said, as if the alternative were ridiculous. "It was the least I could do after I lost two men trying to take her."

"She's very easy to underestimate," I said.

"What do you want?" Claire asked.

Arthur finally acknowledged her. "I want the same thing

you want, Mrs. Morris. I want the devastation of Karma Corp."

"Why?" I asked.

"Because they created me? Because I'm a terrorist? Because I stand to make money from it somehow? Because of some bizarre ideological reason?" Arthur said, shrugging. "My reasons don't really matter. I do, however, want the entirety of that information in your mnemonic drive."

"You want to blackmail Karma Corp with it," I said. "This is about money."

Arthur smiled. "Perhaps. Either way, my demands are the same."

"If I give you this information, it'll never be exposed," Claire said, growling. "They'll get away with mass murder."

"I promise it will," Arthur said, sounding entirely insincere. "However, that is not my only demand."

"Which is?" I asked, unsure whether Arthur would kill Marissa anyway. This wasn't his usual style.

"I need you to kill Zheng Wei at his announcement for nanotherapy and have HOPE claim credit. If you don't, I'll kill Marissa, then go after your children. My operatives will be in touch with a drop location for the information. Don't try and copy it. I'll be able to tell."

Arthur logged off.

"Shit," Lucita said. "This isn't good."

"I know," I said.

Lucita shook her head. "I was really hoping Marissa was gone for good."

I gave her a sideways glance. "Really, Lucita?"

"What's the worst he could do? Kill her?" Lucita asked, shrugging. "I'd pay money to have him do it."

"There's more to it than that," I said.

"What?" Lucita asked.

I felt my face. "Marissa has a massive amount of blackmail material on us as well."

Lucita reached for a pistol at her side. "Delphi, permission to shoot your son."

"*Denied!*" Delphi said, sounding almost as angry. "*For now.*"

"Explain," Lucita said.

CHAPTER FIVE

I rubbed the bridge of my nose. "HOPE continues to exist entirely because the organization has created a Black Dossier."

Black Dossiers were something all the megacorporations have. They were a necessary part of business these days.

"That sounds made up," Lucita said, her hand still on her pistol. I hoped she was just holding it there to make a point.

"How I wish it were so," I said, sighing. "It's a massive file that exists in Marissa's mind and probably contains not only whatever they were going to exchange here but also a massive amount of actionable material on every other Big 200 corporation. Illegal experiments, bribes, sexual deviancy, ties to foreign powers, and more."

"Blackmail material," Lucita said, removing her hand from the pistol grip. "The goodie-goodie Antifa wannabes have a price like anyone else."

"You shouldn't be sharing this, Case," Claire said, looking uncomfortable.

"Tough shit. It's our building, and you brought us in here," Lucita said. "Also, we're apparently in this dossier. Did you provide HOPE with this information? What is it?"

"Nothing to concern yourself with," I said, a little too sharply. "I also didn't provide them with that information. Marissa and her cronies managed to acquire it on their own. As part of my efforts for HOPE, she removed part of it from her database every time I did a favor. She also provided me with plenty of information from it on other companies. Research material and plans built on Black Technology that kept us competitive when everyone else was falling behind."

Claire looked aside. "It's a reason why he's not a member of HOPE Real members don't need to be bribed or blackmailed."

Lucita visibly calmed down, as if the fact that I wasn't working for idealism made this all better. "How the hell did she get so much information on the power brokers?"

"A lot of NSA and Army intelligence officers were...unhappy when they realized the Emergency Government wasn't leaving power," Claire said, her voice letting us know she was one of them. "In the chaos following the Big Smokey, a lot of them were willing to share techniques for monitoring groups like the Big 200 through their cellphones as well as laptops. Things the government has safeguards against—safeguards we know how to turn off."

"I'm already intrigued," Lucita said. "Do you think we could—"

"No," Delphi said. "They have the support of Right Brain and Left Brain, the former NSA AI They're not fully sentient, but I'd rather not get entangled with them."

"So, what does this have to do with A?" Lucita asked. "I think we should call S and tell her about him."

"We have to get Marissa back," I said softly. "Because if he decrypts that information in her implants, then we're fucked."

"Is this true?" Lucita asked, looking at Claire. "Aren't you the encryption key?"

"I am," Claire said. "But Marissa claiming I was the only person she could use to decrypt her data strikes me as another one of her lies. One just designed to make sure the other members of HOPE feel comfortable with having that sort of power."

"This sounds like an excuse," Lucita said, pausing. "What's your real game, G?"

She wasn't calling me Case.

"I want to take down Karma Corp," I said, pausing. "But I'm also concerned about how this will backfire."

Lucita looked at Claire. "And her?"

"She's a friend," I said, taking a deep breath. "I don't have enough of those to toss them away."

"I'm your friend too, but you *can't* kill the CEO of Karma Corp," Lucita said, appalled.

"Obviously not," I said, thinking about the consequences. "If I did that, then anything revealed about them would be overshadowed. The company would manage to survive, and it would suffer only a minor bump in the long run."

I'd thought about ways to destroy Karma Corp and its subsidiaries many times over the years. There was no single keystone to destroying the company, though. It was like the mythical hydra, and even if I did manage to eliminate all its heads, then the best-case scenario would be it would develop a dozen more for each one cut off. The only way to eliminate it truly was to somehow get corporations large enough to replace it to do so. Or as the old saying goes, the only way to destroy an empire is to build another one over it.

"Yes, because that's totally what I'm worried about," Lucita said. "What do you suggest?"

"In simple terms, decrypt the information Claire downloaded and find out what Marissa was planning," I said, making up a plan to satisfy her. "We appear to go along with A's plans and then track him down before rescuing Marissa."

"This sounds a lot like the plot to *Johnny Mnemonic*," Lucita muttered.

"No, then she'd be dying," I corrected. "Though Claire does kind of look like Dina Meyer in her heyday. Didn't she make a comeback recently?"

"The benefit of so many actors dying," Lucita said. "I'm with this plan right up until the part of rescuing Marissa."

"What did she do to you?" Claire asked, her voice holding more reproach than someone betrayed by Marissa almost as much as the rest of us should have.

"She framed me for trying to kill Case," Lucita said, crossing arms. "Also, Marissa blew up a building I was in with a missile strike. That's in addition to the fact that she's a pathological liar and sociopath. There's also the trying to kill Case part. How many times did she do that?"

"Three times," I said. "But she was coerced."

Lucita rolled her eyes.

Claire looked to one side. "Yeah, there is that. She's also saved his and my life many times too."

"Oh, that's different then," Lucita said, turning back at me. "You're not seriously considering this, are you?"

"Yes, I am," I said, standing up. "We can use the situation to force Marissa to share the Black Dossier's contents with us."

Lucita narrowed her eyes. "Are you sure this isn't because you're still in love with her?"

"Yes," I said. It was because I was partially in love with Claire and she was in love with Marissa, at least a little.

"You're going to bargain with Marissa now?" Claire asked. "When we're so close to getting Karma Corp?"

I smirked. "There's never a situation too idealistic you can't bend to your own advantage."

"I don't recommend this course of action, G," Delphi said. "A is profoundly dangerous."

"No shit," I responded to her. "What I don't understand is whether he knew I would become involved if he kidnapped Marissa."

"I suspect he probably did," Delphi said. "Otherwise, why would he have killing Karma Corp's CEO among his demands?"

"That's part of what's confusing me," I replied, our conversation taking microseconds of real time. "If A wanted to frame HOPE for murdering Zheng Wei, then he'd be able to do it without us complicating the job. He's framed wives, children, mistresses, the U.S. government, and terrorists for his jobs with a lot less hassle."

"That is peculiar," Delphi admitted. "Maybe he's playing a game."

"Next time, let's do Virtual Beach Volleyball."

Lucita looked over at the bodies nearby. "There's a serious reason you can't cooperate with A. If he's after Karma Corp, he's not going to leave any loose ends. If you kill him, he'll eliminate Marissa and then you. He'll probably come after Case as well. Hell, maybe all of us."

That was one of the areas where I'd differed with A. Much to my disgust, I'd kidnapped and extorted people as part of my job working for the Society. I'd always abided by the letter of my agreements, though. It was fundamentally indecent to hold someone's loved ones hostage and then snatch away the hope of seeing them again. I recognized that as hypocrisy now, but my journey to becoming a not-terrible person started with baby steps like those.

"Do you really think he's ready to go to war with an entire army?" Claire asked, obviously hoping Atlas Security would stand by me in this.

"A and I only worked together once. In the South China Sea, we were supposed to go after a former associate of the International Refugee Society who had set himself up with an army of cybernetically enhanced soldiers. He had a full-on Bond villain island lair with security that included an actual rocket-propelled panic room. The place was damned near impenetrable, and after trying for three days to get at him, I admitted defeat without ever getting close. A, however, knew what to do to get the man off the island."

"Which was?" Claire asked.

"He shot down a plane with the man's son on it along with three hundred other passengers," I said. "Then he blew up a city block where the man grew up. He planned to kill every single person the man knew until he left the island—which he did. That was his strategy."

"What did you do?" Lucita asked.

I stared. "I tried to kill him, and he left me in a coma until he was done. I think, even then, he knew we were machines and how to disable me."

A was better than me at all the disciplines the International Refugee Society taught the Letters. Assassination, close-quarters combat, counter-espionage, interrogation, psychological warfare, mind-hacking, and more. I wasn't afraid of him—no, scratch that—I *was* afraid of him, but I was even more aware he was in control of the game board. I also wasn't discounting the possibility he was in Marissa's employ, and this was another one of her attempts to manipulate me.

Claire too.

"There's more going on here than we're seeing," I said. "A's behavior isn't consistent with his usual *modus operandi*."

"It's possible time has changed him," Delphi said. "A... Arthur was a man with great wealth and influence within the

Society. While you and the other surviving Letters have gone on to great wealth, he's remained off the grid. It's possible he's motivated by a desire to get back at you and the others. He might have created the plan once he discovered you were involved with the members of HOPE."

I frowned. "I don't think so."

"Why is that?" Claire said.

"Just a gut feeling," I admitted before speaking to Delphi via our cyberlink. "A was always into being an assassin. More than any of the other Letters. It was his calling in life, if you will. If he was jealous of what we've established here in Atlas, he'd just take us all out or ask us for a job."

"Which you wouldn't give him," Claire said. "You'd kill his ass, right?"

"Of course," I said, not so sure. "No, I can't help but imagine this is something he's been ordered to do. Arthur was the quintessential corporate samurai and not the kind of guy who would ever go into business for himself."

"If he was working for the Big 200, then we would have seen him before today," Lucita said. "We know all their regular operatives. The governments of the world are even less discreet."

"There's another possibility," I said. "The Invisible Hand."

"The goddamn *Illuminati* are not employing him," Lucita said, her voice dripping with disdain.

"The Invisible Hand is not...never mind," I said, sighing. "But they are a possibility."

"I don't care who employs him as long as we kill this guy," Claire said, looking between us. "How do we find him?"

Lucita looked at her as if she were a toddler. "If he was easy to find, then he wouldn't be a very good assassin, would he?"

"I was unable to trace Arthur's signal," Delphi admitted. "The technology protecting it was extremely sophisticated, even by my standards. We might be able to get more clues to his location by examining the bodies, but I wouldn't be surprised if he's going to move Marissa now."

"I'm still not sure why we're devoting so much effort to that woman," Lucita said.

"Because A is a threat to this company," I said, cutting her off. "Also, because it's important to me."

Lucita cursed. "Fine. Case, you have my complete support. It wouldn't matter anyway. Delphi would support you jumping off a bridge."

"I'd survive falling from most," I said. "Either way, I have a plan."

"Oh, this I've got to hear," Claire said. "Case, I love you, but your plans tend to revolve around shooting until the problem goes away."

"Only because I'm a bloodthirsty homicidal maniac," I said, raising my right hand in objection. "We need to get the information in Claire's head decrypted and copied. Then we send it to A with a tagger program and follow it back to his location. We kill A, rescue Marissa, and only kill the CEO of Karma Corp if we really want to."

"He'll be ready for that," Lucita said.

"Do *you* have a plan?" Claire asked.

Lucita looked away.

Delphi gave us an option. "Decrypting the data won't be easy, nor will encoding a tracer program which A won't be able to detect or go against. Mnemonic drives are designed so data can't be copied or decrypted by anyone but the original uploader."

"I just thought it was because someone was obsessed with old Keanu Reeves movies," I muttered. "The fact that they're designed against that doesn't mean it's impossible, does it?"

"Usually, it does," Lucita said. "At least in my experience."

"There might be someone who can help with this," Delphi said. "The hacker known as BlackCat1."

"Seriously?" I asked. "We actually live in a world where people go by their handles?"

"I'm Cowgirl13," Claire said. "BlackCat1 is a legend."

"Yes," Delphi said. "She's a woman who claims to have found an exploit in mnemonic drives among other systems. The FBI hired her to get information from a Red Sword terrorist's cyberbrain after Madison Technologies refused to give them a universal key. A slicer working for the people she ostensibly opposes. She's very similar to you in some respects, Claire."

"I'm less than happy at the comparison," Claire said.

"Too accurate?" Lucita suggested.

Claire rolled her eyes. "We need this information either way."

"Have you even viewed it?" I asked.

"Not all of it," Claire explained. "I updated it every week with a special download code. Lots of information gathered by agents we've cultivated in Karma Corp. For all I know, my last download revealed that nanotherapy was powered by sacrificing children on the altar of Moloch."

"That is unlikely," Delphi said. "However, I'm one of the individuals who believe nanotherapy's potential is overstated, and the technology is not remotely near the level it needs to be to work on even half of its stated goals."

"Another reason the fact they've cracked it is such a big deal," I said. "Can you get us in touch with this BlackCat1?"

"Yes," Delphi said. "She'll be at my party tonight here in New Chicago. Black Cat is very skittish, though, and is unlikely to want to come directly to the Atlas Building. You should meet her there."

"So, what's your plan?" Lucita asked. "Or are we doing that thing where you juggle everything and pretend however it falls apart to be what you planned all along?"

"Cute," I said, not at all disagreeing that's how I usually operated. "Once we decrypt the data and send it to them to track him down, we eliminate him. If it doesn't work, though, we need to keep our options open. We shouldn't kill Zheng Wei, as that will just play into whatever plans A has. It'll also eliminate any need for A to keep Marissa alive. We need to look like we're prepping to kill him, though."

"Oh, joy," Lucita said. "How exactly do you expect us to do that?"

"Put me on the security detail and add Claire to it too."

Lucita smacked her face. "Sure, why the hell not."

"In the meantime, I'm going to go meet with BlackCat1."

"We both are," Claire said.

CHAPTER SIX

Claire and I walked through the Atlas regional headquarters' upper floors, not saying a word to one another until we arrived at the executive motor pool.

The top floor didn't have many employees but had row after row of the air car variants employed by the super-rich. Personally, I found combining planes and cars just made an inferior example of both, but the simple fact was they were useful for those who wanted to get across the country quickly. Most of the United States airports were still being rebuilt, and bullet trains, of all things, were now the primary means of transport after personal vehicles.

"So, are we taking the Aston-Martin or the Rolls Royce?" Claire said as we walked past expensive car after expensive car.

"Ha-ha," I said, frowning. "I don't actually own a car."

"Really?" Claire said. "I thought that's what you'd spend your fortune on."

"The part I don't invest?" I asked. "No, I use company cars. I like to mix them up too. Less chance of there being a bomb on them."

"That a common problem for you?"

"Yes and no," I said. "Just because you're paranoid doesn't mean they're not out to get you. I've had, like, a dozen attempts by people to kill me, but generally, it's just people trying to disrupt Atlas' business plans."

"Helping in the privatization of the U.S. military and police force was bound to piss some people off."

"That was happening anyway," I said. "We're just participating."

Eventually, we stopped at a sleek black air car with opaque windows and an armored frame. The Zero-7 by Madison Motors was a vehicle used primarily for the transport of VIPs. It was extremely maneuverable and had a sunroof that was unusual for its brand. I checked the back seat of the vehicle and pulled out a Sidewinder-10 sniper rifle, checked the magazine, then replaced it.

"You always keep sniper rifles in the back of your company cars?" Claire asked.

"Yes," I said. "But in this case, it's E's car. I'm sure he won't mind me borrowing it."

I still checked under the hood and carriage to make sure the vehicle hadn't been tampered with. After all, if the false Marissa and her partner could beat Delphi's security system, then A certainly could. I took a deep breath and did my best to control my fear. I would settle this, no matter what it cost me.

"Is it safe?" Claire asked.

"Yes," I said. "As near as I can tell."

"Do you mind if I drive?" Claire asked.

I raised an eyebrow. "Do you know how to pilot a flying car?"

"I can fly, drive, or crash anything that moves."

"All right," I said, tossing her the identification key. "I'll ride shotgun."

Most cars didn't require drivers anymore, and that was one of the reasons why the flying variant had become so popular. While all of Atlas' vehicles were equipped with a manual mode, most public vehicles weren't, and people were shuffled by computers to and from their destinations. Personally, I'd never trust my fate to a computer unless it was Delphi. I'd eliminated quite a few enemies by arranging all-too-convenient "accidents."

As Claire moved over to the driver's seat and I pulled open the passenger side door, she looked at me.

"So, what is your real reason to help me on this?"

"Excuse me?" I asked.

"I don't buy any of the excuses you gave Lucita," Claire said.

"Well, I'm not going to abandon any of the women I'm sleeping with," I said, shrugging. "It's ungentlemanly."

Claire rolled her eyes. "Classy, James Bond."

I looked at her strangely. "What did you think was the reason?"

"I dunno, loyalty to the cause?" Claire said. "HOPE needs you."

I slid on into the passenger seat. "HOPE means nothing to me. As much as I love tweaking the megacorporation's nose and hopefully finding a way to take down Karma Corp, I'm not interested in the quote-unquote cause."

"How can you say that?" Claire asked. "Don't you want the United States to return to what it was?"

"Was it ever what it was?" I asked, buckling my seatbelt. "The United States made me as a slave. A disposable artificial soldier. And it had plans for doing that to others if I worked out. The corporations may rule openly now, but it wasn't like they weren't in charge before."

"That's a cynical attitude to have."

"I prefer clear-sighted."

"We can do better," Claire said, sounding very much like Marissa at that moment. "HOPE is a tool for that."

"Through blackmail and petty terrorism?" I asked.

"Through any means necessary."

She started the air car, and it vibrated with the power of the massive engine. Thankfully, the interior was soundproof.

"This is the new reality, Claire. Maybe in a century, they'll look back to this time as the Dark Age of Technology. However, people aren't interested in democracy or corporate controls right now. They're interested in survival and entertainment."

"Bread and circuses are nothing new," Claire said. "They also don't make less of a tyrant who provides them."

"And neither does revolution wash away the stain of one's evil deeds," I said. "Marissa has been nothing but a murderer and liar since I've known her. A good cause doesn't change that for any of us. I'm your friend, and once I was her friend, but that doesn't mean I'm going to pretend any of HOPE's actions are making the world a better place."

I remember murdering a Halifax International banker, making it look as if he'd run off with his mistress in order to cover up the fact that we'd embezzled millions to fund a free hospital in the Los Angeles refugee zone. The greater good was a Band-Aid on a far greater horror, but it was something I'd willingly done before. It was just one of the missions I'd done for Marissa.

The two of us sat in the car's black interior. The silence from earlier had returned, and it was still oppressive. A part of me wanted to lash out at her. I was better than this and didn't need to be treated like a whipped dog for just trying to be good to the person I loved. If she didn't want me, then I was happy to find someone else who did.

I was about to speak when Claire spoke first. "I'm sorry."

"Excuse me?" I asked. "Did you say sorry? Must I get my pistol and aim it at you? Because you are clearly not Claire Morris, but her sinister doppelganger."

Claire glared. "Stop acting like a fourteen-year-old, Case."

"No promises."

The air car took off, and my stomach lurched at the brief floatation of our bodies as we bumped from free fall to magnetic field.

There was a lot about this entire business that smelled worse than the refugee zones right before the monthly disinfectant teams sprayed them down. It felt very much like someone had put out the bait of a tantalizing mystery and expected me to just fall right into whatever trap they'd set up behind it—which I had, for all intents and purposes. Two old girlfriends, an old enemy, and the prospect of revenge against my ex-employers were just the kind of things you could use to lure me to my doom. Really, the biggest argument against a trap was I just wasn't important enough for that kind of effort.

Once there was a time I might have been worth it, but that was before I'd released all of the Black Technology research into the world. I was obsolete technology, twenty years old, with my current cybernetics limited in their ability to be upgraded. It wasn't like they could replace my CPU any more than you could replace a human's brain and still call them the same person. I could upload my consciousness into a new body, but that wouldn't be me. Someone might want revenge on me, but I couldn't think of anyone. Most of the people I'd wronged were long dead or had suffered much greater tragedies in the Big Smokey eruption than anything I'd done to them as an assassin.

Then there was Claire.

"May I ask why you're so interested in this?" I asked.

"Excuse me?" Claire asked.

"The last we saw of one another, you'd just found out Marissa had been lying to about your ex-husband being killed by Karma Corp," I said, remembering the events in Las Vegas's arcology. "I'd have thought you would have dumped her by then."

"You'd think," Claire said. "But it's not like I haven't lied, cheated, and murdered in the service of HOPE When I started working for her ten years ago, I was full of anger and idealism. I joined the United States military to help people. I saw the massive work camps, the overcrowded refugee centers, and the casual corruption at every level. HOPE promised we could change things for the better. I was willing to do everything I could to force the corporations to do the right thing. It was the only thing I could do to honor the dead."

"So, you have to believe it's all worth it?" I asked. "That's called a sunken cost fallacy."

"I wouldn't be so dedicated if I hadn't seen the other side of the equation with you," Claire said, looking sick as we flew over Chicago's skyline. "Black Technology combined with the excesses of the super-super rich is sickening. Every party is an orgy, and the drugs flow like water. I've seen everything from gladiator fights to people genetically engineering unicorns for their daughter's fourth birthday party. Did you know a man actually successfully had a brain transplant in Sweden? They put a seventy-seven-year-old man in a twenty-two--year-old's body. Only afterward did they find out the latter wasn't willing but had been sold by his family."

I knew the story was an urban legend. Transplants like that had been possible for years, but they were being kept under wraps lest everyone start to believe immortality was possible. Overpopulation hadn't been solved by the Big Smokey eruption, and there had been a second baby boom afterward. Resources were stretched thin enough. Humanity couldn't survive if the rich refused to die while the poor kept expanding.

"Yeah," I heard about that. "I admit, it's not easy being on the wealthy side of the rich/poor divide if you have a conscience. It's better than being on the poor side, though."

"So that's why I'm with HOPE," Claire said. "It's why we need to decrypt this data and find Marissa, so we can keep holding the bad guys to account. It's the only law they know."

"Except you're lying about not having the data decrypted."

"What?"

"Please, I do this for a living. There's more to this than you're telling. What is in your mnemonic drive? Really?"

"You know I don't know—"

"Bullshit," I said, annoyed she thought she could play me like this. "I don't buy for a second you don't have every bit of data scrutinized. I also don't buy for a second your story about not releasing the data until you have a killing blow. You would have torn down Karma Corp at the first opportunity and nothing Marissa could have told you would keep you from doing that."

"You're wrong," Claire said, looking like someone had socked her in the gut. "There was one thing I knew, though. One thing Marissa had showed me before getting the entire data file assembled."

"What did she show you?" I closed my eyes as I tried to make sense of this story. This story was making no sense, but I didn't want to push too hard. Why would Marissa have the encryption and not Claire, even if it was some kind of practice to make sure no one could go to the presses with the data themselves? Wouldn't the reverse make more sense? I understood why no single HOPE member, even Marissa, could access the Black Dossier themselves. They could make themselves fantastically rich or expose all the secrets at once—rendering it useless to the company as a whole. Secrets only had as much value as the inverse of how many people knew them. Also, how the fuck had A found out about it? Who in HOPE had told him about the Black Dossier? Because it sure as hell wasn't me.

"Not so much what secret as what kind of secret," Claire said. "Did you know Bill Gates saved six million lives by giving away twenty-eight billion dollars before his death in the eruption? HOPE has saved roughly ten million *every year* since we acquired the data at the outpost. All because Karma Corp donates their surplus production to us in exchange for not releasing what we have."

I paused. "I know how the system works. What blackmail material was she holding over Karma Corp? Is it related to nanotherapy? You can...well, no, you can't trust me. You can depend on me, though."

Claire was silent.

"Claire..." I trailed off.

"Nanotherapy doesn't work," Claire said, biting her lip.

"What?" I asked. I hadn't expected that despite everything we'd been through. That was something stupid even for Karma Corp's corrupt business practices.

We flew past an enormous holographic billboard of a geisha popping a pill. The irony didn't escape me. "Exactly what I said. Karma Corp killed thousands of people for three years testing their variations on medicinal nanotechnology and got approximately jack and shit from it. This despite the fact it's been selling the dream of using it to prop up their medical division from bankruptcy for the past decade."

"There's been progress."

"Not at all," Claire said. "What progress they have made with nanotechnology has been eliminating what doesn't work, but creating what does is miniscule. It's like announcing the creation of a plane without figuring out how to get an object to stay in flight. Nanotechnology is pretty much where it was when your father invented the first micro-disassemblers in ninety-nine."

"Too bad I killed him," I said, grimacing. "But Zheng Wei is announcing they've managed to crack it."

"Which means all our blackmail material might well be worthless now," Claire said, admitting HOPE wasn't as omniscient as they liked to claim. "It also could mean that they're making this announcement with full knowledge it's a hoax."

"If they're insane," I said, thinking about what a scandal that would be. The people depended on Karma Corp, but the government no longer defended them against lawsuits over medicine. The Corporate Council had, ironically, weakened U.S. power enough to mean it was unable to do the jobs it could do back when it was powerful but corrupt.

"The files contain the actual data on nanotherapy and its progress," Claire said. "Enough to make or break them."

I thought about that. "Maybe A is working for Karma Corp's board and is trying to get your information so he can assassinate Zheng Wei, then torch their facilities. They could pretend the work has been set back for years."

"You came up with that just off the top of your head?" Claire asked.

I shrugged. "I admit I've done similar hoaxes."

Claire looked disgusted. "You don't need to tell me those details."

"With great power comes great responsibility," I said. "Unfortunately, almost no one believes that but me and Spider-Man."

"Really?" Claire asked. "Spider-Man is your go-to philosopher?"

"There are worse. Besides, I take it farther than Peter Parker. Because I know power corrupts and absolute power corrupts absolutely. But to change the world you require power and the acquisition of power makes you responsible for the lives of those you can affect. Just having power means you bear responsibility for those you could help but choose not to if you don't use it."

"I'm not following you, Chief."

I paused. "I think in life you can either be good or do good. To do good, you have to be strong and to be strong, you need to do bad. So, life is just a compromise between doing the bad necessary to do good and not becoming so bad you can't be good or cease to care. Otherwise, you're just one of the good people who live their entire lives being good but doing nothing because it requires you to be bad."

"Or are just bad and don't give a shit," Claire pointed out. "Which is most people."

"I think most people are a combination of the two," I said.

"And what are you?"

"I'm here doing bad things and hoping they'll somehow turn out good for a bit."

Claire shook her head. "Right. Well, I'm just going to focus on driving for a bit."

I nodded. "I'll go relive some memories to pass the time."

"You can do that?" Claire asked.

"Benefit of being a cyborg."

I decided to relive the day we first met. Sadly, it wasn't because I was having fun. It was because something was off, and I wanted to compare Claire to her past self and look for discrepancies.

CHAPTER SEVEN

I had a perfect memory, at least in terms of recapturing moments I wanted to recall. Since I discovered my brain was artificial, I'd learned to control that. I knew how to call up the best moments of my life and suppress the worst.

One moment I was in the car with Claire, and the next, I was wearing a white suit with a Panama hat, briefcase in hand, and looking over a distributary of the Mississippi River. It was about eight years ago, almost nine, and there was still snow on the ground in the middle of summer.

Across the river was a large Southern-style plantation that was falling apart amid a row of almost a dozen other buildings. Much of the area had been evacuated as people had moved to the cities in hopes of getting government aid to survive the disaster's aftereffects. That was a mistake because many ended up devastated by earthquakes.

The mansion I was looking at, though, was still inhabited. The new owners, squatters certainly, had surrounded the property with seven-foot-tall fencing and had it rigged up with its own generator system. It was early in the afternoon, and there were electric lights going on as an occasional guard in a heavy coat patrolled the grounds with a Doberman that acted unnaturally calm.

Thankfully, my vantage point did have an excuse for my presence, as one of the last functioning gas stations in this area was nearby. I suspected that was the reason they'd set up shop at that mansion, since it allowed them to purchase enough fuel to keep their facility going.

I proceeded to finish pumping my gas, checking the price

at ten dollars a gallon before shaking my head. I was driving a ten-year-old 2014 Lincoln town car, which still ran on the increasingly outdated fossil fuel. Flying cars were possible now, though they functioned essentially like helicopters with just as much skill required, but such a vehicle would look even more conspicuous than me down here.

Having completed my casing of the location, I stepped into the driver's seat and started the car, only to have a woman in a green hoodie and sweatpants step into the passenger side before shutting the door. Her hoodie had a U.S. Army logo on it. I was tempted to put a gun to her head, but I didn't know if she was an enemy agent or just a girl hoping to bum a ride when a tenth of the population was homeless.

It was also possible, even likely, she was my contact, but I couldn't be sure. The woman was in her mid-twenties and Marissa hadn't been that much older when she'd joined the NSA. Still, I didn't take her for a spook since there was softness in her expression that I didn't normally see in my associates—especially after the eruption.

I gave her a once-over to make my judgment call. The intruder had smooth angular features, auburn hair tied in a ponytail, pale white skin with a couple of freckles around her nose, thick faded jeans, and a pair of combat boots. Her looks were pleasant and had enough flaws to let me know she was almost certainly all-natural. I also noted she was hiding a gun in her hoodie pocket as well as a knife in her right boot. Even the weapons weren't a confirmation of her identity, as she might have been a guard for the plantation, a robber, or just one of the many hitchhikers who knew it was better to stay armed.

"Drive," the woman said.

"No," I said simply. "Who are you?"

"Claire Morris," the woman said, buckling her seatbelt. "I'm a friend of Marissa's."

"If you are, you should know that doesn't put me at ease," I said before driving off. "What did she tell you about me?"

"That I couldn't learn from the infonet?" Claire said, smiling. "You're a billionaire, Mister Gordon. That's not exactly discreet."

"Not a billionaire. Not even close. Millionaire? Yes, but that's not what it used to be. I'm just the Chief Security Officer of Atlas Security," I said.

"Which is still a megacorporation's hatchet man. That's still famous."

"The purpose of being a hatchet man is *not* to be famous. I fix problems by any means necessary. I don't even have a photo on the infonet. Hell, I have three assistants who answer to a guy who most people think is the CSO. They're the guys who handle the day to day business of Atlas Security's ... well, security."

Truth be told, I was more comfortable taking orders than giving them. I enjoyed working behind the scenes and did a lot more field work than my position required. The simple fact was I didn't know how to be anything other than a killer, and it was a daily struggle for all Letters. It was why Lucita taught at the Atlas Academy and insisted on visiting the various frontlines we operated on every few weeks.

Claire seemed undeterred. "Yeah, well, Marissa told me your whole story. You're a biological android, your name was G, she gave you the name Case, and you're an okay guy when you're not murdering people. There's a lot of other stuff involving your father and brother being evil plus uploading all the world's Black Technology. Oh, and you love cats."

I frowned, debating killing her to keep that secret. I mean, if people knew I loved cats, then there would be no stopping my enemies. If anyone took Snowball and Mittens hostage, I'd be at their mercy. "Either you're very close to her, or she has become awful at keeping secrets. What's your connection to my ex?"

It had been a couple of years since our last encounter in the Detroit refugee camp. Things had been going smoothly if you ignored the massive poverty and technology used as a placebo for the ongoing humanitarian crisis that still afflicted the world. She'd called me a couple of days ago and told me she was calling in her marker. I didn't know what Marissa wanted, but I was glad to know she wouldn't be involved in the mission on the ground. I'd had enough of her interference.

"She didn't tell you?" Claire asked.

"You didn't come up," I said.

"Huh, that's strange." Claire looked embarrassed, which told me it was an intimate connection of some kind. Best friends, lovers, or something else? Claire's eyes and reaction to me implied an attraction, so I didn't think she was exclusively attracted to women. I filed that information away for future reference.

"Not an answer," I said.

"Sorry," Claire said, moving her hand from where she'd been keeping it pressed against her pistol. "We're both founding members of HOPE. You know, Humans Offering Peace and Enterprise."

"Never heard of you." In fact, I had. They were a widespread grassroots organization that got a lot of airtime while getting very little done. Also, they'd struggled really hard to make their name fit the acronym HOPE. It would be a few more years before they'd change into militant radicals.

"We're a non-profit organization devoted to trying to get the United National Alliance, Congress, and the megacorporations to make laws protecting people against the misuse of Black Technology."

I snorted. "Good luck with that."

"You don't think it's a worthy cause?" Claire asked, surprising me with her naiveté.

"I think every single government in the world is looking for an edge, and that goes double for the megacorporations."

"You'd know, I suppose." There was more than a little venom in her voice, more than pretending I'd never heard of them warranted.

I raised an eyebrow. "You don't much like the megacorporations, do you?"

"Does anybody?" Claire asked, brushing a strand of hair out of her face.

I shrugged. "Far be it for me to talk about class warfare, but wealth is generated by the corporations. As bad as they can get, we're in need of a lot of wealth if we're going to throw it around."

I just wished it was generated by anyone but the people it currently was.

"Or maybe you just don't care because you're rich as fuck."

"Maybe," I said. "Then again, I was made by a corporation to be a slave, so maybe I know the difference between the real evils and those just doing their job."

Baiting her was probably not the best option, but I wanted to know more about her, and people tended to let their guard down as much when they were angry as they did when they were comfortable.

Claire looked away. "Marissa said you'd be frustrating."

"So, who do you want killed?" I asked, deciding to cut straight to the point.

Claire did a double take. "What?"

"Unless Marissa wanted to set us up on a blind date, I assume the reason you contact the assassin is you want someone killed."

"You still identify as an assassin?" Claire asked.

I brought the car to a stop along the side of the road. "You're asking an awful lot of questions. I'm not exactly the kind of guy who likes sharing his secrets, and you know quite a few of mine already. All I know so far is you know someone whom I used to love but who betrayed me three. Also, that you're a tree-hugging hippie, except the trees are R2-D2 and C3PO. Neither of which are exactly on the market yet, so you'll forgive me if I question the need to fight for their rights."

Claire closed her eyes. "I'm twenty-eight, I'm a former Sergeant in the United States military, and I love motorcycles and gory horror movies. I'm more a dog woman than a cat, but I haven't had a new one since I adopted my daughter. Marissa and I were involved with the same man before he was killed by one of Karma Corp assassins."

"How did your career end with the U.S. military?" I asked, ignoring the last bit. We'd inevitably come back to that, I was sure.

"I was dishonorably discharged for conduct unbecoming," Claire said, frowning. "I refused to shoot some people who were looting food."

"Sounds like you made the right decision."

"They later murdered another family for their provisions." Claire sighed. "I was scouted by Colonel Gomez because I was full of anger and wanted to make a difference. That's when I met Captain Stephen Wilcox. Thinking back, I suspect Marissa used him to bring me in."

Yeah, that was Marissa all right. "Then he was killed?"

"How could you tell?" Claire asked.

"There's a certain wistfulness you use when speaking his name," I said. "It has a past-tense quality."

"You're good." Claire frowned. "He was found with a gunshot wound to the head and a printed-up suicide note. I knew Karma Corp did it and wanted to kill as many people as possible to get revenge. Marissa decided it'd be better to try to bring the corporation down completely. Hacktivism, whistle-blowing, protests, and so on."

"How did you know?" I asked.

"What?" Claire asked.

"How did you know Karma Corp did it?" I asked.

"Marissa helped me find the evidence," Claire said.

I nodded.

"So now you know my life story," Claire said.

"Assuming any of that was true," I said, staring at her. "I still don't know why you and Marissa wanted me to come out to the middle of bumfuck nowhere to look at a building with slightly better security than you'd think an otherwise abandoned one would have, especially if you don't want to kill anybody."

Claire pulled back the seat and turned her head to look at me. "I think it's a body shop."

"Nothing wrong with that," I said, shrugging. "Not everybody can afford proper cybernetics."

"I think they're experimenting on the homeless in there for Karma Corp."

I blinked. "That is a serious accusation."

"But not an unbelievable one," Claire said.

"No," I said.

Since the refugee crisis had "ended," a whole new slew of problems had emerged as new and deadlier diseases had raged through the cramped and dirty conditions of the world's cities. The arcologies also required cybernetically enhanced builders to work the newest equipment and interface with the self-guided machinery. The Big 200 had thus devoted a massive amount of research to make them practical for their workers. In the case of cybernetics, that required human trials being rushed through, and there were a lot of people no one would miss nowadays. Karma Corp, especially, was prone to accusations of this. After all, they were the ones who stood to benefit most from cheap, abundant enhancements. That was in addition to entertainment implants, gene-therapy treatments to treat the new diseases, and devices like 100%-effective birth control regulators designed to limit the poor's breeding. The horror stories from the unregulated market were things that surprised even me.

"I'll give you the short version of what we know." Claire looked behind the seat to the back window, facing the plantation's direction. "One of the researchers at this outpost got cold feet and tried to contact the authorities. His messages never got further than a couple of phone calls, but Marissa has the Federal Bureau of Entertainment, Technology, and Weapons—ETW—bugged. We sent someone down to meet with him, but they're missing. The researcher washed up on the shore forty miles away with a bullet in the head. I don't have much hope for our man."

"And you want to send me in there to find out the truth," I said. "Why not just call the cops?"

"I want this to be our win," Claire said. "I'll be honest, I'm less concerned about what's going on in there than about finding a connection to Karma Corp they can't just make disappear. I want to hurt them."

"I admire that kind of ruthlessness. Still, I wonder why Marissa thought I would help. Frankly, I came out here as much out of curiosity as anything else."

Claire shrugged. "Marissa thinks you might be willing to help HOPE if for no other reason than you hate Karma Corp. She thinks you do know the difference between the good and the bad among the corporations."

"Do you think I do?" I asked, raising an eyebrow.

"I'm reserving judgment."

I decided to let her know some more of my secrets. A dangerous move, but one I felt worthwhile to play. "I'm not actually a billionaire, and most of my money is tied up in Atlas stock. I give away roughly ninety percent of my cash every year because all I need is my home, suits, food, and whatever else is needed to serve my lifestyle. If you want me to write you guys a check, I'll happily do so as well, but I'm not sold on any of this."

"We don't need your money," Claire said, surprising me. If she was honest, they were the only NGO in the world who didn't. "We have plenty of that. What we need is someone to show our people how to—"

"Do illegal shit to take down the 200." Marissa wasn't building an activist group, she was building an army. The activist group was just a way to recruit the people necessary to get her paramilitary group running.

I was impressed.

"Yeah," Claire said. "Does that bother you?"

"No. I'll do it."

"All right." Claire blinked, clearly not expecting that answer. "I want to come with you."

"You didn't actually expect me to show up, did you?" I asked. "You were just going to wait until nightfall and go in yourself."

Claire didn't answer.

I was really starting to admire her ruthlessness. "Sorry to disappoint you."

"The contact we sent down here, Ronnie Simons, was my friend." Claire sighed. "I don't know how they do it from where you're from, but in my hometown, if someone takes out one of your buddies, you pay them back."

"I was born in a test tube, but I echo that sentiment," I said. "Do you want to go in hard or stealthy?"

Claire looked at me. "You're up for just shooting our way in?"

"What part of *professional assassin* did you not get on my resume?"

Claire smirked. "I'm starting to like you, Case."

"I've counted only six guards," I said, shrugging. "How bad could it be?"

Why, oh why, did I say that?

CHAPTER EIGHT

I regretted my decision to not be stealthier as soon as I ended up being smashed through a plaster wall by the military-grade cyborg whose dog I'd just killed.

To be fair, the animal wasn't a real dog—it was leaking oil and had sparking electric wires coming out of the hole I'd created on its side. It was also possible the man was more upset that three of his comrades had been sniped while they were watching TV. It had been a rather bloodthirsty plan, eliminating the artificial dogs kenneled behind the house first with my Red Desert-17 silenced pistol while Claire sniped his companions.

I was supposed to eliminate the sole remaining guard and his companion in the kitchen, but much to my consternation, his animal sensed my presence as I prepared to silence him, and his owner was now kicking my ass.

"Murderer!" the tall buzz-cut-sporting Caucasian man shouted. He looked like a parody of a human being with a body that Arnold would have envied in his heyday, barely covered up by military fatigues and a vest with a biohazard sign pin prominently displayed on its left side.

A quick scan of his enhancements told me he was sporting thirty-million-dollar equipment—which was less impressive than it sounded since the dollar was worth a quarter of what it used to be—but still, top of the line. He had an artificial skeleton, arms, limbs, and synth-muscle but wasn't a full shell. It was still stuff designed in the past year and better than my fifteen-year-old machinery in force if not quality.

"This doesn't have to—" I tried to grab his arm to throw him, only to have him grab me by the head and shove it into the kitchen sink. I managed to brace myself before I hit the counter, then elbowed him in the face before jabbing my thumbs into his eyes. They were real, and he screamed as they were crushed.

That was when I spun around him with the garrote hidden in my wristwatch and electrified him at maximum charge. It was enough to kill a normal human being but only caused a faint sizzling sound before I used the garrote to throw him over my shoulder. The cyborg howled as his head smashed through the cheap checkerboard tile on the ground. I grabbed the Red Desert-17 pistol I'd dropped on the ground and fired three silenced shots into his brain case.

The military-grade cyborg stopped moving.

Claire entered the back door, holding a Sidewinder-7 sniper rifle that had been assembled from the parts I kept in my trunk. The gun was almost as big as her but had a targeting computer, the ability to shoot through solid steel, and velocity controls. Few people could handle a weapon like that, and she'd used it to take down four targets.

"Thanks for the help," I said, taking a deep breath.

Claire stared at me. "Did you really want me using this thing while you were in close-quarters combat?"

She had a point.

Claire looked down at the sparking canine on the ground as well as his dead master. "Did you have to kill the dog?"

"That's a drone, not a dog," I said, wrinkling my nose at the thought of harming an animal. Like many people. "It's about as much a real dog as my car."

"It acted pretty dog-like," Claire said, sparing no comments for the dead humans. "So, did the others outside. Maybe artificial animality is catching up with artificial people."

"Animality is not a word outside of *Mortal Kombat*," I said, shaking my head. "Also, any stealth we might have had is ruined."

I gestured up to a security camera hidden behind the obsolete 2015 fridge with one door blasted open. The contents of the fridge were mostly beer, red beef, and plain yogurt, perpetually popular with cyborgs.

"Fuck," Claire said, covering her face. "Can they transmit that?"

"No," I said, lifting a small black box from my jacket. "I'm jamming anything being sent via infowave. They'll still be able to see it downstairs, though."

"Are we sure the lab's downstairs?" Claire said. "I mean, it could be in the attic or something."

"Not for the number of people you've said have gone missing. What was it, like thirty?" I asked, heading over to a nearby door between the entrance to the kitchen and the TV room. That was traditionally where the door to the basement was kept in houses like this. Through the doorway, I could see three headless bodies in front of a gore-splattered flat screen showing a football game between the Dallas Cowboys and the New Kansas Raiders.

Claire was a good shot.

"Yeah," Claire said. "Do you think they're just dumping them in the river?"

"No," I said, trying to open the door to the basement and finding it locked. "Then they'd be popping up everywhere. I suspect your researcher friend got dumped in the river because it was an unplanned execution. The people who killed him panicked and didn't use whatever method they're using to dispose of the bodies here. Assuming there are any bodies."

"There are," Claire said. "The report—"

"You have the word of a dead researcher who sounded like a crank to the government," I said. "It could just be they're experimenting on the homeless and letting them go. Tales grow in the telling."

"That's not what happened," Claire said, looking for a key to the basement.

I proceeded to kick the door down, and it revealed a long concrete staircase down to a reinforced metal door with a biometric lock. There was another security camera down there. There was also an eye scanner there. "I really regret gouging that guy's eyes out now."

Claire grimaced. "You don't think we can threaten them into opening the door, do you?"

"Nope," I said, heading down to the door. "However, we have one advantage over these security measures."

"Which is?"

"Brute force," I said, pulling out a pen and some chewing gum before applying both to the door's hinges. I then clicked the top of the pen three times before starting to run up the stairs. Claire, who'd been following me, did a double take before running up the stairs behind me. Both of us covered our ears before an explosion filled the stairwell with smoke.

Claire looked over at me. "Do you have the entire James Bond collection of gadgets in that coat of yours?"

I shrugged. "Blame Atlas' new quartermaster. Naoko Brown loves the classics."

"Stay the hell away from us!" a scared female voice shouted from the staircase below. "We've called in reinforcements, and this place will be surrounded any minute now."

"Do you have a landline?" I shouted down.

"What do you think this is, 1958? No!"

"Then you haven't called shit. Now we're coming down there, and you're going to cooperate, or this is going to get even bloodier."

"We're armed!" the woman shouted back.

"Lady, do you think that makes a difference now?" I called back. "Besides, this is corporate espionage."

"What!?" the woman called back.

Claire shot me a confused look.

I mouthed, "Just go with it."

Claire shrugged.

I shouted down. "We had to murder the Rent-A-Corps to get at what you have, but we're totally just here to steal information. None of you are on our list of targets. If you cooperate, then none of you will be harmed."

The woman paused. "All right."

"What's your name?"

"Myra!"

"Nice name," I said. "Just a warning. If any of you are armed and take a shot at us, I'll kill you all. Understood?"

There was a pause. "Understood."

"Throw out any weapons you have," I said, peering down the doorway to the basement. The smoke had cleared, showing that the metal door had fallen on the ground. Three Glock knock-offs were thrown through the door, not even enough to pierce my skin but enough to sting.

"Good," I said. "We're coming down now, and do not piss us off because if this goes south, I'm going to resolve this *Dirty Dozen* style. For those of you unfamiliar with the classic film, that means my friends are going to pour barrels of gasoline down there and then burn you alive."

"What the fuck is wrong with you?" Myra shouted back. "We're cooperating."

"See that it stays that way," I said, lifting my pistol and slowly descending the stairs.

"Nice job." Claire unloaded the Sidewinder of its ammo clip and popped the round in the chamber before pulling her own Red Desert-17 and following me below. The two of us walked, single file, over the ruined door and into the Karma Corp facility.

What we found was disappointing.

Given the expense of the hardware they had to protect the place, I'd been expecting something more elaborate, but the place looked less like a high-tech research lab and more like a small-town emergency room. The chamber was a large rectangular basement, obviously widened from the plantation's original cellar and filled with a dozen hermetically sealed chambers. Each of them contained a man or woman on life support. They all sported lesions, tumors, and other signs of having had something seriously fucked-up happen to them. All of them were unconscious and hooked up to morphine drips and IVs.

In the center of the chamber, huddled around a tiny administrator's desk, were four men in nurse's scrubs, two women wearing doctors' attire, and a plastic, bubble-topped, treadmilled PharmaBot drone—the kind that distributed whatever you needed. If this was the entire facility, it was a small operation.

One of the doctors, an African American woman in her mid-fifties, raised her hand. "We have all of our research here. Listen, despite what it looks like, we're helping—"

Claire took one look at one of the patients, an Indian man in his mid-twenties, then shot Myra in the head before shooting every single one of the staff in the chest and emptying her pistols' clip into their corpses.

I looked over at the man she'd looked at. "He your missing HOPE member?"

Claire went over to check the bodies and kicked one of them for good measure. "His name is Arav Vijun. Yeah, he's my friend."

I did a quick once-over of the place and found an incinerator in the back with large trash bags full of human ash stored in a dumpster. It was some Nazi-level shit going on, but nothing I hadn't seen before. Whatever Karma Corp was testing here, they were clearly not worried about it getting back to them, or it was valuable enough to take these kinds of risks.

After finishing my sweep of the place, I found Claire typing away at one of the dead staff's computers. She'd moved the bodies of the dead away from the administrator's cubicle and tossed a tarp over them.

"You've already got access?" I asked, impressed.

"They opened it all up for us," Claire said, taking a deep breath. "It seems they really did believe your bullshit about letting them live."

"It wasn't bullshit," I said, shrugging. "I would have happily let them all go if it meant we could use them against Karma Corp. Monsters go free every day. As long it takes a bite out of the institution. At least you got them, though. This is enough to bury anyone."

Claire didn't respond.

"Let me guess, I was being overly optimistic," I said. "There's nothing relating to Karma Corp, is there?"

"I'm not looking for that right now," Claire said. "I was trying to see what was wrong with the people here in hopes of seeing how we could get them cured. Artificial organs, Shell bodies, or just plain ordinary surgery."

"And?" I asked.

"They're brain dead, all of them, including Arav. They chemically destroyed their minds before they started their procedure. We can't take the bodies with us, either. The bodies are full of medical nano-machines. They've infected all them with dozens of diseases to see how long the people can be kept alive until they fall apart. The nano-machines are designed to break the bodies down unless they're given a daily recall code."

I stared at her. "Fuck."

Claire shook her head. "This batch has been kept alive for almost three months on diseases which should have killed them in minutes. Their nanotherapy doesn't work perfectly, as the bodies all break down with the machines degrading in their programming, but it's an actual medical advance."

I surveyed the people around me. "It's not worth this."

"No," Claire said, sounding on the verge of tears. "The numbering on this document makes me realize we're not going to be able to beat Karma Corp, though."

"Why?" I asked.

"The memos I'm reading say this is Facility Number 118. They have little outposts like this all over the country."

The implications sunk in. I tried to think of things to say. Instead, I walked over to her and gave her a hug. It was with that uncharacteristic gesture, I remembered, how all of this began.

CHAPTER NINE

I remembered lying next to Claire's naked body underneath the sheets of the Mississippi hotel we were holed up in. It had been five days since we'd gone on our assault against Karma Corp's body shop, and we were waiting out the consequences of our actions. I'd used my contacts to get the FBI sent in, the corporate sovereignty act not having been enacted yet, and there was national news about the event on television.

The sex between us had happened our first night together and hadn't been planned as being anything special. Just a release between two people who had just gone through a harrowing experience together. However, the next few days had been spent enjoying each other's company, and I felt it was in danger of becoming something more. I was strongly attracted to Claire and her to me, which made the fact that we were destined to part all the more painful. Not to mention she was working with my ex-lover.

"I can't sleep," Claire said, turning to look over at me. "How about you?"

"No," I said, looking up at the ceiling.

"*Do* you sleep?" Claire asked.

"I was programmed to imitate being a human man in virtually all respects. That included sleeping for up to eight hours a day. Truth be told, I don't need to. My brain compresses and files information during sleep, though. So, I try to get around four or five hours every night just, so I don't suffer glitches."

"Glitches?"

"Memory loss, flashbacks, and more," I said, wishing we could discuss something else. "I was meant to exist for a decade of continuous use, and I'm already past that. Lucita has the people in the lab working on patching our programming so we can function for a normal human being's lifespan, but it's a complicated process."

"Huh," Claire said. "Well, at least you imitate a human man in other ways without any issue."

I gave a half-smile. "I haven't had any complaints so far."

Claire smiled. "Do want to turn on the television and see if there's any more news on our little escapade?"

"It's three a.m., so I doubt it's on INN," I said, sitting up. "This isn't a story that has much national attention."

"Which is bullshit," Claire said, her expression frowning. "Those bastards should be all arrested and heading toward a firing squad right now."

"It's not so bad," I said, immediately regretting my word choice. "Even though the bodies have dissolved, they have left behind trace evidence. The fact that Karma Corp tried to blow the facility remotely also paints them in a bad light. I'm glad we disabled that before we left. And the fact that there's ten murders also means the FBI is going to keep this an open investigation far longer than I think the executives will want."

Truth be told, I already knew this wasn't going to go any further than it already had. Karma Corp shares had taken a serious hit, but they'd successfully covered up most of their connection to the facility. It was an "outside contractor" they'd been working with, and they had no idea about the horrible conditions there. We'd left a trail for the FBI to find the other facilities mentioned in the outpost's computer records, but there was no sign they'd followed up on them. HOPE would have to do the legwork themselves if they were going deeper into this. As I suspected, someone had been bribed or threatened into shelving this. It was almost like the world hadn't ended and human civilization had recovered. But it hadn't.

The United States was functioning again, but it was utterly dependent on the corporations, which owned everything the same way China had before the Big Smokey eruption. Most of the Corporate Council's executives had diplomatic immunity, and there was no way for their facilities to be raided by the government since they were sovereign territory. It was ludicrous, but with Black Technology "secrets" able to destroy the world the way the atomic bomb had, legislation had been passed by an exhausted legislature desperate for companies to promise imported food and medicine from countries less devastated. Now the companies were claiming sovereignty in the European Union, Russian Federation, Africa, and the former Democratic People's Republic of China.

"Fuck," Claire said, getting out of bed. I took a moment to admire her scar-covered backside, which I'd explored with my hands many times. "This should have been a game changer."

"It's the same game as ever," I said. "The only rule is the house always wins."

Claire chuckled as she slipped on her bra, panties, and jeans. "I'm going to go for a cigarette. Do you want anything?"

"I don't smoke," I said. "Watch yourself. You don't know who could be looking for you."

"You're a bit paranoid," Claire said. "We did a good job of getting rid of all trace evidence."

"We did," I said, taking a deep breath. "But I always like to be thorough. You have a daughter, after all."

Claire pulled on a t-shirt and put on her coat. "Yeah, my aunt is probably getting more than a little annoyed I've taken this long to get back to her. I love Fiona and wonder if I'm being selfish putting myself on the line like this. Do you have any kids? I mean, can—"

"No," I said, frowning. "Letters can't."

"Oh," Claire said, zipping up her coat. "Have you ever wanted them?"

"I'd like to have had the choice."

Truth be told, I'd considered adopting one or two in the wake of the Crisis. I've always had a hole in my life where family should have existed. Unfortunately, I couldn't imagine exposing a child to my life. I was a killer, hundreds of times over, and someone who had no experience with love or giving love. In the end, I'd decided to just donate what money I could to families who were struggling because of the disaster. It was all I could offer, and it felt hollow.

Claire looked at me for a long time. "Goddamnit, Marissa."

"Hmm?" I looked, up blinking.

Claire rubbed her temples. "Marissa all but told me I should sleep with you when I was here."

My gaze darkened. "I see."

"No, it's not like that," Claire said, taking a deep breath. "Not to manipulate you, though she might have been thinking along those lines. I'm not ignorant of what sort of person she is."

"I very much doubt that."

Claire's gaze sharpened before she shook her head. "It's just I have a type. I have a history of guys who are all about the deep brooding tragedy in their pasts yet have a hidden heart of gold. Blame my *Twilight* fangirl years."

"Mine is a heart of silicon rather than gold. Also, you're admitting you're a *Twilight* fan?"

Claire pointed at me. "Shut up, I moved on to slasher movies when I was fifteen. Listen, what I'm saying is I have a history with guys like you, and Marissa knew it. It's part of why I started dating girls exclusively after my discharge. At least until Stephen and Marissa. Man, I really need a cigarette."

"You were all together."

"Yeah," Claire said, looking guilty. "Don't judge."

"I wouldn't dream of it."

"I just can't help but wonder if the fact you're...you factored into her equations when she sent me rather than one of her other agents."

"You flatter me."

I could tell my short answers were frustrating her. Closing her eyes and sticking her hands in her coat, she took a deep breath. "What do you think?"

The truth was I was incredibly attracted to her. Drawn to her, even. Marissa had adopted the persona of someone vulnerable and innocent while she was seducing me. Someone good and pure who I could feel justified in protecting from the Society when she was anything but. Later, Marissa assumed the persona of a hardened professional who was still driven by idealism. Claire's commitment to stopping Karma Corp, her soldier background, and her own tragedy invoked all those feelings with me. Claire struck me as the kind of woman who wouldn't turn away from the horrible things I'd done but wouldn't encourage them either.

It made me suspicious. "I think you could be reading a little much into this."

Claire opened her mouth, then closed it. "Yeah, you're probably right. Are you sure there's nothing I can get you?"

"Do you mind getting me a bottled water from the gas station across the street?" I asked. "The tap water here tastes like it went through the fires of hell."

After she left, I reached over to my briefcase and pulled out my Madison Technology laptop. They were the most advanced portable computers on the planet and manufactured by one of my former associates. Possibly future associates, if the talk of Atlas and M-T merging had any truth to it. I pulled out its cyber-link cord and attached it to my neck interface before making a video conference call.

Seconds later, the image of Marissa came up. She was wearing a business suit with her hair up like Princess Leia in the Yavin Throne room. I could see the New York City skyline behind her and an Ahab's coffee mug beside her.

"Hello, Case," Marissa said, smiling. "Have you slept with Claire yet?"

"Always to the point, except when you're not," I said. "Aren't you going to ask how I got your number?"

"Case, you're a professional spy. I think you can get my number from Claire. Hell, you might have just asked."

I'd watched Claire enter her password into her cellphone and swiped it while she was asleep. Not exactly breaking into the new CIA headquarters in Miami (which I'd also done). "Fair enough. Yes, we've had sex numerous times. Claire has the suspicion you tried to set us up together."

"Oh yes," Marissa said. "I did. Both of you are incredibly tightly wound and needed this. Also, without Stephen, I had less of a hold on Claire. She's already killed for me, and I have need of that kind of commitment. Getting her involved with you was a 'kill two birds with one stone' deal, since everything I've compiled about you says you're still the same lonely man you were when I left you."

"I'm not lonely," I said, lying. "Also, I'd be ashamed of admitting I was serving as my lover's pimp."

"Sex is a tool," Marissa said, shrugging. "Just one more exploit in a sea of them which I am willing to use alongside cash, pride, and ideology. A lot of people believe hacking is about technological expertise, but it's not. The best hackers are social engineers who know the inner workings of the human mind. Once you can take a person apart mentally, their passwords become easy to guess—figuratively or otherwise."

"You haven't changed a bit. Did you set her up with your lover Stephen? Am I a substitute goldfish?"

"Claire doesn't need you to defend her. Sex is a need and providing it for my agents through my other operatives, depending on how and who they want it from, is a way of keeping them happy. Certainly, you never complained."

"How did Stephen feel about this?" I asked, wondering what he'd thought about his girlfriend setting him up with another woman to control him.

Marissa frowned and for a moment, I saw a flicker of guilt. "I pushed him too hard. He was a member of Task Force-23 and did a lot of things he wasn't proud of. I played on that and our love until he snapped. In the end, he didn't have your, or Claire's, moral certainty to go along with your flexibility. Introducing Claire and her daughter to balance the equation may have actually pushed him over the edge."

"So, Karma Corp didn't kill him?" I asked, wondering why she was telling me all this.

Marissa blinked slowly. "No. They didn't. Stephen's loss devastated Claire, and I needed to keep her on track. Revenge was a way of doing that."

"I'm not even surprised anymore. Why do you even want to point them at the megacorporations, anyway? What's your game?"

Marissa's expression didn't change. "I betrayed everyone and everything I believed in while working for Task Force-22 and President Douglas. Then I saw the American people elect and re-elect the walking corpse we've got as President during the greatest crisis in human history. I felt the need to make atonement as best I could by heading off the future we're going to. A future ruled by corporations keeping the people under control through a combination of advanced technology, debt, information control, and war."

"It sounds like you're describing the present rather than the past."

"I did start HOPE six years ago," Marissa said, frowning. "We've had successes: we blackmailed swing voters in Congress to extend the life cycle of the American refugee camps for two more years, forced a basic living standard in all corporate territories, and also stopped using mass data mining to determine which citizens should be allowed to live or die."

"Is that worth using those you care about?"

Marissa looked down. "I don't know. I've had to be a chameleon my entire life. When I was a little girl, I had to pretend to be stupid and easily impressed so the Barrio Maya wouldn't beat or rape me. When I was a hacker, I had to pretend to be an anarchist because it made it easier to move through the circles I needed to learn my skills from. With you—"

"You had to pretend that you loved me."

"It wasn't entirely lies," Marissa said. "Though I know you have no reason to believe that."

"Seeing how you treat Claire, you're right." I decided I would tell her everything and bring down this ridiculous group of Marissa's.

"I can't help it," Marissa said, taking her cup of coffee. "It's how I'm wired. Which is why I need you."

"Excuse me?"

"I hack people. Everyone is a bit of code to me, even the ones I care about most. I need someone to keep this organization on the straight and narrow. Well, no, that's not true. I need someone to help me keep this organization aimed at the people who are exploiting the crisis for their own aims. Who hide behind money and power. I need people like you and Claire."

I stared at her. "You can't be serious."

"You hate what you do," Marissa said. "Even though it's a much nicer business than what you did before, you don't think you're doing nearly enough to atone. You also want to look after someone. To have a family. Claire is a new mother and someone who needs support for her crusade."

"A crusade you put her on."

"Yes. I need someone who is willing to do what she can't but who can stop at the end."

I was silent, knowing she was manipulating me and ready to rebuff her. "Why shouldn't I tell her? Give her some peace."

"Do you really think it would? Or would it just devastate her? Remember how you felt when you discovered Marcus Gordon, your father, created you as a weapon to sell to the military? How you felt when you discovered Daniel Gordon, the man you were cloned from, was a psychotic rapist?"

"How I felt when I discovered your betrayals?"

Marissa looked like she'd been struck before closing her eyes. "Yes."

"Ignorance is bliss," I said, feeling unclean. "What do you want from me?"

"To become part of HOPE. To be our agent. To love Claire and be her partner. To do the missions which need to be done to bring down the megacorporations. You can even take the information we gain to help your corporation and friends. It'll be a two-way street since we'll also know plenty from your role as Atlas' CSO. Atlas is, after all, security for the best and brightest among the Big 200."

"You also want me to watch you and kill you if you go insane with power," I added, reminding her of that.

"I want you to be by my side too." Marissa's voice lowered. It became hungry, almost desperate. "I want you in my bed as well as Claire's, to be my lover and partner. To love me as much as I love you."

"I could never love you the way I once did."

"I know, but you can fake it."

CHAPTER TEN

I pulled out of the memory, not having any more answers than when I'd begun the event. We were still flying around in E's car with Claire doing the driving, the black and empty refugee zone of Chicago looking like a forgotten industrial center. Few lights were on, and I wondered how many millions were forced to live there, waiting for jobs and opportunities that would never come.

"What are you thinking about?" Claire asked, looking over at me.

I shook away my remembrances. "I was just thinking about how every time I get close to something beautiful, I sacrifice it for something immediately gratifying."

I accepted Marissa's offer and become her lover while I was also Claire's. Claire had known, and it had made her more comfortable with my presence—allowing her the illusion that what we'd had was simply an arrangement between friends.

I'd kept the secret of Stephen's suicide for years, even as Claire had dedicated herself to avenging her ex-lover. About the only reason Claire was still talking to me after it all came out was I'd eventually told her the truth—and she'd revealed her own secrets. It bothered me to think I was her Marissa, though I suppose Marissa was also her Marissa.

"Well, that's depressing."

"Is it? I take it as one of the signs I'm more human than machine."

Claire snorted. "Humans are machines. Biological ones designed for replication. The only difference between you and me is you're the result of humans taking control over their evolution."

"So, I'm like a dog to your wolf?" I asked. "Only electric?"

"Do you dream of electric sheep to guard?"

I chuckled. "I'd enjoy that reference more if I hadn't heard a few hundred variants over the years."

"I'll stick to *Terminator* references then. Has Skynet ordered you to kill me yet?"

"Delphi likes you, actually," I said, thinking of her as the closest thing I had to a mother. Certainly, I barely remembered Rebecca Gordon. I'd made no attempt to contact her in the past ten years either. "Delphi says you're a good influence."

"Clearly, your AI doesn't know me very well."

"Better a good influence on me than a bad influence on you."

"The two aren't exclusive."

Ouch. "Perhaps."

Claire paused. "So, you never told Lucita about us?"

"You're the one who is acting like it didn't count in the first place."

"Isn't she like your best friend and ex-wife? Which is weird, by the way. You're not supposed to remain friends with your exes."

"I'm friends with all my exes. Most regularly still show up for sex."

Claire made a sharp swerve with the flying car and almost caused me to bang my head against the window. "Sorry, wind shear."

I rolled my eyes. "If you want to be exclusive, just ask. If you want to never see me again, just ask. Don't keep me in limbo here, though."

"What do *you* want?" Claire asked.

I paused, surveying the city below. "I want someone who I can dedicate myself to. Someone I can call family and just find a piece of normality with. Everything else? The wealth, the power, the rush from completing a perfectly planned mission? None of that matters."

"I don't believe it," Claire said.

"You don't?" I asked.

"No," Claire said. "Not the part about you wanting all that, but that love is a magical cure-all for your problems. Normality is overrated."

"Says the woman who has a family."

Claire stared out into the skyline, which was overlooking the city's industrial district now. An endless horde of automated black factories shooting up fire and smoke as the United States struggled to produce enough advanced technology to replace its former infrastructure. Most of the owners were Chinese and Russian with a few Brazilian, but the rest were controlled by the megacorporations who had divided the former United States up like a cake.

It would have been worse if not for the dozens of lesser volcanoes and earthquakes that had ignited alongside Yellowstone's. People were still trying to figure out how the timing on that had worked out.

"My brother Shaun and I grew up pretty much on our own. My aunt Mary and I wouldn't reconnect until after the Crisis forced everyone to seek out their relations," Claire said. "Hell, I joined the army less out of a burning desire to serve our country than to get the hell out of the Texas trailer park I grew up in. Life wasn't too good for a pair of mixed Irish and Comanche kids."

"You're Irish?" I asked, faking shock.

Claire rolled her eyes. "Our mother was a drunk and died in a car wreck when we were both sixteen. Never knew our father. He liked to wander, I suppose, or maybe he saw what a mess our mother was. Either way, Sean had my back, and I had his. He believed in the kind of family you did. He also believed the world would be a better place if everyone did their part. Instead of the army, he joined the Dallas police. Ended up becoming a member of their S.W.A.T. unit."

"What happened to him?" I asked.

"Died breaking into a house with a tweaked-out asshole. I had been in the city to introduce him to Stephen. But you already knew this, didn't you?" Claire asked.

"You tend to repeat yourself," I said.

"Yeah, well, it said to me that family is great, but it's also not worth the pain."

"You don't believe that."

Claire paused. "I don't want to ruin my daughter's life the

way my mother did ours. I admire the fact you have made up your own family. You don't get the baggage that comes with being born to a big screwed-up collection of nutters like the rest of us."

"The man I was made in the image of was a terrorist psychopath who kept his followers' cyberbrains in their stomachs. I killed his father who also, coincidentally, made me. I used to cyberstalk his ex-wife and child. It's why I'm here."

Claire laughed.

"What's so funny?" I asked.

"I actually knew all that too. Marissa told me you were every bit as fucked up as me, but I didn't believe it."

"I'm sorry, Claire, but I'm pretty sure I'm much more screwed up than—" I was interrupted by a harsh siren-like alarm going off in the car. "What did I touch?"

"You didn't touch anything," Claire said, going for the dashboard and adjusting several knobs. What followed was the onboard computer showing a screen displaying an AR-29 Whisper attack helicopter along with its armaments. "Please tell me this James Bond-equipped vehicle isn't saying we've got a chopper coming up on us."

"I'd like to, but I'm trying to cut down on lying," I said, looking behind me and seeing the vehicle in the distance. "I'm impressed with E's onboard systems. You wouldn't think his car could pick up a stealth chopper. Do you think it's hostile?"

Claire pulled the vehicle to one side as a pair of rockets shot past us within visual distance. "You could say that."

Much to my surprise, E's flying car released a pair of flares from the back even as the rockets zoomed back after them before exploding. Claire pushed the car into a dive as she maneuvered between the smokestacks around us while streams of chaingun fire streaked past us.

"Does this thing have any weapons?" Claire asked.

"How the hell should I know?" I snapped back, holding myself against the sides of the carriage to avoid bouncing around.

"You're the spy!" Claire shouted.

"Real spies don't have gadget cars!"

"Well, clearly that's not the case!"

The second pair of rockets fired at us, only to strike a nearby catwalk and cause an explosion of flame and wreckage. The AR-29 zipped down after us, attempting to chase us despite our only advantage being maneuverability. Claire tapped away at numerous on-screen commands while trying to fly as the computer screen said, "Please enter the password for authorizing onboard weapons."

"Oh, come the fuck on!" Claire shouted.

Seeing the helicopter about to lock onto us, I pushed the wheel to one side and got us out of the next stream of chain-gun fire.

"Don't interfere!" Claire said. "I've got this."

"Do you?"

"Not really!"

I got an idea. "Open the sunroof!"

"What?"

"Do it!" I said, crawling in the back and grabbing my sniper rifle.

"Please tell me you didn't see something like this coming!"

"Do you want to drive or shoot?"

"Can you drive a sky car?"

"Kinda?"

"Then you shoot!"

We were coming to the end of the industrial district even as we maneuvered even lower through the maze of buildings, pipes, steel, and machinery around us. The helicopter couldn't follow us through it but continued to fire from above. Unfortunately, the path we were on took us right into a residential district of New Chicago, and if we let the fight reach there, then who knew how many innocent people would be caught in the crossfire. I wasn't going to let myself become A, even if it meant my or Claire's survival.

Maybe.

I picked up the Sidewinder-7 from its case in the back seat and hastily loaded it as the back window shattered from a stray chain-gun round. I gave a swift look over to Claire and saw that it had passed between us and gone through the front windshield, which would have shocked even the most seasoned combat pilots. Somehow, Claire managed to maintain control over the vehicle.

"So much for bulletproof windows," I muttered. "We need to get up level with it!"

"I'd ask if you're insane, but that goes without question. You better get this right, or we're both dead."

"I couldn't ask for finer company."

"That's not reassuring!"

The Zero-7 aircar lifted into the air right as it was about to dip down and get us, and the factories we were passing disappeared, replaced with a mile-long graveyard and park. Claire brought the car level with the helicopter. I didn't bother with the sunroof and mounted the Sidewinder-7 sniper rifle on the broken glass of our rear window.

"Bye," I said, aiming not with the scope but my enhanced cybernetic vision and shooting both helicopter pilots before putting a round through the dashboard computer. Deprived of all navigation, the helicopter spun out of control and landed in an artificial lake approximately two hundred feet below.

I looked over at Claire. "I think they're dead."

Claire cast a glance back at me, disapproval in her eyes. "Really? I never would have guessed. Who the fuck were those guys?"

"They weren't A's people," I said, shaking my head. "I can tell you that."

"Why is that?" Claire said. "Are you wanted by other people who want to kill you with a military helicopter?"

"Are you?" I asked.

"Point taken," Claire said, directing the car from the crime scene as fast as she could. The Chicago police had mostly been replaced with Atlas Security personnel, but they maintained a small regular force that I didn't exactly want to deal with right now. I was really regretting approving a donation of five hundred flying cars last year.

"Those were members of the Blackbriar PMC," Delphi said, her voice speaking from the car's CPU. "They are a much, much smaller unit of mercenaries than Atlas Security Services and

mostly made up of dishonorably discharged United States soldiers or those deemed unfit for service."

"Never heard of 'em," I said, disgusted. "Sound like a bunch
of winners."

"They offered me a job years ago," Claire said, grimacing. "They're mostly used by Karma Corp to guard their black
research facilities and prisons. They were, at least, until Atlas
Security got their contract."

I looked at her. "I didn't know about anything regarding
human experimentation or kidnapping at the time. I wouldn't
let them be involved."

"I did," Claire said, looking disgusted. "I have to deal with
hundreds of deaths every year which might have been prevented if I'd exposed them."

"You did what you had to," I said, lying. "I know you would
have stopped it if you could have. We tried to put an end to their
experiments in Mississippi, and they covered them up."

"You're just saying that because we screw."

I was just saying that because I loved her. "Whatever the
case, it seems Blackbriar has an issue with us both."

Claire took the Zero-7 down lower and slowed us down
after we passed over the Chicago Crisis Remembrance Park.
"Either way, that means we have even more reason to get this
damn information out of my head."

"Are you still comfortable with us visiting your home?" I
asked Delphi. "I'd rather not have a small army of mercs show
up as we're trying to persuade BlackCat1 to help us."

"She's unlikely to stay much longer," Delphi said, frowning.
"My guests are a jaded and cynical lot who are always interested in the most innovative of sensations. My liquid memory
injections have not been quite the showstopper I'd hoped them
to be, so we're stuck with ordinary drugs and sex."

Claire stared at the computer. "Did I hear that right?"

"The lifestyles of the rich and robotic," I said, shrugging. "I
told you liquid memories were a bad idea."

"Details, details," Delphi said. "Either way, I suggest you
ditch the car and change clothes before you arrive. I'll send
someone to pick you up and take you here. It's the most minor

thing we can do, but hopefully, it will throw them off the scent."

"Make sure he brings a wet towel for both of us to wrap around our heads. It'll muffle the signal," I said.

"Excuse me?" Claire said.

"Not a fan of classic Arnie, are you?" I asked.

"Clearly, our definition of classic Arnie differs," Claire said.

"I doubt either of you have a tracking device on you," Delphi said. "Otherwise, I would have access to it. I keep track of roughly one hundred three thousand, two hundred eleven citizens in the world this way. The important ones."

"That's...unsettling," Claire said. "But thanks, I guess."

"Good luck," Delphi said, ending our connection.

"Does your mom always stalk you this way?" Claire asked.

"She's not my mom," I said. "Despite what she thinks. And yes. At least until I figure out how to throw her off the track."

Claire slowly settled the Zero-7 down on a road as she took note of the location which Delphi provided us to meet her contact. The bottom streets of New Chicago were filled with the homeless, citizens sporting guns, and endless rows of pawn shops mixed with porn studios. It bothered me to no end that this was one of the few cities really thriving in America today.

"Case?"

"Yeah?"

"Just so we're clear, we just took down an attack helicopter in a high-speed chase, right?"

"I believe we did, yes."

"We shouldn't keep secrets from one another anymore if this is going to be our life."

"Probably not," I said, wondering if that was a proposal.

Claire stopped us at a red light. "I dye my hair."

"I know."

She swatted me on the shoulder.

CHAPTER ELEVEN

It was roughly an hour later when Claire and I arrived at Delphi's penthouse, the elevator doors opening on a bizarre bacchanalia that assaulted the senses and intrigued the mind. The lights were dimmed low. A disco-ball effect of rainbow lights swirled around as a curious beat of techno mixed with classical played. The central chamber was three stories tall with ornate gold elevators and escalators leading up and down between many balconies full of guests from across the world.

Painted performers with holographic tattoos across their nude bodies contorted across poles and in aquarium-like cages around the room. The air smelled like a mix of Lethe and vitamin-enriched oxygen that caused everything to have a heightened, otherworldly feel. Art was spread through the place, along with alcoves for meetings, sex, and experimental drug or dream-walking VR use.

The people present were a mixture of stars, artists, politicians, and inventors who had all fallen under Delphi's sway during the past decade. I recognized Edward Mull of New Electric Industries, Catalina Byrne of International News Tonight, arms dealer Edward Pickman, and at least three indie musicians. Delphi had forced me to listen to their demos, and they would almost certainly dominate the charts next month. Most of the subjects were wearing masks. These did little to disguise their identities to someone who had enhanced vision, but the subterfuge added to the illicit thrill of the place.

"So, we're visiting the dance club version of *Eyes Wide Shut*," Claire said, her arm wrapped around mine. She was dressed in a gold mask to go with a spectacular slitted red dress that seemed like it had been custom made for her. The fact that it had required less than five minutes to get on and wasn't accompanied by any makeup or hair styling seemed to make it simply avant-garde rather than inappropriate. I also liked that Claire had refused to change her shoes, so instead of the heels Delphi provided, she was wearing combat boots.

"Delphi spent most of her life as a formless collection of data floating in the International Refugee Society's data servers," I said. "I think she's just been making up for lost time by trying to experience as much of human life as possible."

I was wearing a jet-black version of my earlier suit, modified with ceramics and carbon-Kevlar for maximum protection and including several places to store my weapons. Claire had been jealous, to say the least, but I suspected Delphi trusted me more not to shoot up her party.

"If said human life is coke, hookers, and blowing millions on fun, then yes. I suppose that she is definitely experiencing a lot of it." Claire said grabbed a bottle of champagne from a buff waiter wearing only strategically placed feathers to go with his bird mask. "If I get roofied, I want you to know I'm shooting up the place."

"You insult me," Delphi said over our cyberlinks. "The security of my guests is always a primary concern at my parties. Everything that happens to them falls under the province of being safe and consensual. I also have handpicked the Atlas Security personnel who attend this location as well as spared no expense on electronic countermeasures."

"We just got attacked by a stealth helicopter, Delphi," Claire said, sipping her drink. "What have you got against *that*?"

"Four SAM platforms," Delphi said. "As well as several autotargeting drones with micro-missile equipped—"

"Never mind," Claire said. "I don't even want to know how you can afford all that."

"Delphi owns New Chicago," I said, only slightly exaggerating. "She big shorted the rise of Black Technology and the Crisis to be the woman to start rebuilding this city into her own personal Dubai. It's the second arcology she owns after Los Angeles. The others are owned by the other AI."

"It's taking you a while," Claire said, keeping her voice low. "Lots and lots of citizens are still living in camps."

"Rome wasn't built in a day," Delphi said.

"No, it was built by slaves," Claire said.

"Who did a very good job," Delphi said. "This city and the various arcologies are going to redeem humanity from its self-destructive, short-sighted ways. They will be monuments to futurism and controlled by individuals who know exactly what is needed to make sure they remain sustainable, ever-growing centers of commerce. If that requires temporary suffering, then that is no worse than it was before."

"Listen, you digital Marie Antoinette. If you think people are just going to sit around while you tell the starving masses to eat cake, you've got—"

I cleared my throat. "Maybe it would be better if you just told us where BlackCat1 is."

"Are you sure?" Delphi said. "I'm just about to do my nude serpent dance. It's why many of the guests are staying."

I rubbed the bridge of my nose. "I am quite sure."

"BlackCat1 is on the third floor in the thirteenth booth," Delphi said. "You'll recognize her by her white hair."

"Interesting," I said. "You'd think she'd have black hair."

"She's also not a cat," Delphi said, showing a hint of annoyance in her otherwise pitch-perfect voice. "Good luck dealing with her. She is not very amenable to working with corporates."

"I'm used to dealing with that kind of attitude," I said.

"She's also not easily bribed," Delphi said.

Claire narrowed her eyes. "I have the feeling I've been insulted."

"You should trust your feelings," Delphi said. "Feel free to get some cake on your way out."

Delphi cut her connection to us.

"Prickly for a machine, isn't she?" Claire said, shaking her head.

I looked around the party and saw Edward Mull explaining his plans for asteroid mining to Catalina Byrne while a surprisingly buff woman painted like an American flag massaged his shoulders. "Delphi takes her parties very seriously. They're not just places for her to experience humanity, but ways of networking and patronizing the next steps in human development. People who have ideas that would never be able to be heard elsewhere get a forum with her as well as her associates. That Chinese billionaire over there, Chen Yun Lee? He's already wasted eight hundred million dollars on nanotherapy, and Delphi has directed him to genetic replacement mods instead. It's already started curing countless conditions. Billy Tang over there is the guy who has made 3D printed cybernetics ubiquitous across the globe."

"You ever been to one of these parties?"

"Plenty."

"You ever re-invent the wheel while getting a blowjob?"

I paused, unsure how to answer. "I can honestly say I have not."

"Me either," Claire said. "I imagine it would be distracting. This may surprise you, but I've been to parties like this myself. Gone are the days when you could just hang around the snooty rich people and beg for money. Everything is dialed up a hundred times on the edginess now. No one is content with the way things used to be after watching millions die on their television and being forced to shut their doors if they had food until the world sorted itself out. One of those gatherings had everyone paired up with someone who'd traded in their old body for a Shell shaped like a favorite celebrity."

"Monstrous," I said.

"Not even close," Claire said, a look of disgust on her face. "At least compared to the real-life monsters I've dealt with. It was just disgusting and sleazy. It also worked, as Marissa got all the support she needed for a set of free schools for kids who wouldn't otherwise eat, let alone get an education."

"HOPE has done a lot of good," I said, wondering why I was defending them, of all people.

"And yet it still feels like a drop in the bucket. I remember one asshole at that party who said it was bad how much damage had been done to the world but that it was ultimately for the best because the volcanic eruptions induced global cooling as well as reduced the surplus population of the Earth to something more manageable."

"I would have shot the guy."

"I just punched him," Claire said, smiling. "Cost a pretty penny, but I hope it taught him a lesson about speaking ill of the dead."

"Probably not," I said, walking through the party and stealing someone else's drink to look like I fit in. I wasn't a big champagne person. Actually, I wasn't a big drinker in general. Blame it on the artificial liver, which made my ability to get drunk roughly equivalent to that of a high-end water purifier.

"So, what are we going to offer this BlackCat1 in exchange for helping us?" Claire asked.

"Cash, presumably," I said. "Either that or corporate data."

"Do we have any corporate data?" Claire said.

I shrugged. "I can make up whatever I need."

"Must be nice," Claire said.

"You never are going to forgive me for being part of Atlas, are you?"

"It's not so much forgive as I don't understand why you want to work for them. It's not for the money, and you know what the Big 200 does to the people. We've seen worse than Karma Corp. Whole towns demolished, and the population turned out in the name of greed and progress."

I set down my champagne glass on the side of the spiraling escalator leading up to the second and third floors of the penthouse. "Do you really think the government does a better job than industry?"

"Damn straight I do. As bad as the United States was sometimes, they at least are nominally supposed to serve the people."

I thought about how to answer. "For me, I decided to serve Atlas Security because I wanted to make a difference in the world. I'm not a class warrior, associating with HOPE or not. When I was part of the Society, I'd routinely journey down to South America, the Middle East, and Africa to deal with revolutionaries who were bothering the local corporate-sponsored government. I saw things that were all too like the aftermath of the Crisis. Mass executions, slavery, rape gangs, and people behaving like animals because they couldn't say whether they would have another meal unless they took it. Usually, there was armed militia or private army involved. Many times, they'd blame the corporations for what was going wrong. One contract was a Brazilian business mogul whose wife was kidnapped, then executed, despite his paying the ransom. He wanted me to track down every single member of the gang involved and kill them all. There were about eighteen of them. Took me a day and a half. The youngest of them was sixteen, and the oldest was barely twenty. Their previous leader had been killed the month before, and they just wanted quick cash, so they seized the opportunity. The whole rhetoric about striking back at the exploitative oligarchy of their nation was just a smokescreen."

"I'm not sure I get your point."

"My point is people suck," I said simply. "Instability creates suffering whether it's for the cause of protecting the status quo or upending it. Existing systems can be reformed if they're not tyrannies, but the complete breakdown of organization just means you must start from scratch. That's the kind of environment that results in the worst kind of atrocities."

"I'd argue industrialized evil is much, much worse. Nazi Germany and Stalin are worse than pure chaos."

"I'd argue the difference between order and chaos in tyrannies is not so clear-cut as you'd think. Autocracies aren't the opposite of chaos, but something which feeds off of it. The worst people I ever worked for had unlimited power because they used subterfuge and lies to do whatever they wanted while claiming to be servants of order. When Lucita, E, Delphi, and the others came to me about creating Atlas Security, it was with the view that we could keep things from falling apart completely. Also that we could maybe establish order in places that might not otherwise have it. It would require working through the corporate system, though, because we needed power and money to do it. I can't say whether it was the right or wrong decision, but it was a decision, and I'm glad I made it."

Claire took a sip of her champagne. "I wish I had that kind of faith in my choices. I question every choice I make."

"Which is good," I said, thinking about the Invisible Hand. "The people who thrived on the chaos of the Crisis and the instability of the Old World had absolute faith that they were correct. That is what made them a word I very rarely use."

"Which is?"

"Evil."

Claire finished her champagne in one gulp. "I guess I'll just have to stick to trying to kill all those bastard tyrants and hope it doesn't bring down the entire world order again."

"I believe in capitalism as a system of wealth generation," I said. "I just believe it requires the poor and destitute to be able to punch the rich in the nose until they get a fair share. History has shown that everyone is fine with a laissez-faire system of economics until it starts favoring anyone but the mega-wealthy, then they beg for a bailout or support while punching down on their workers."

"Glad to see I've corrupted you," Claire said. "It makes you fit in less here."

"Eh, not so much," I said. "You're far from the first terrorist Delphi has invited to her parties."

"I am not a terrorist."

"Depends on your definition," I said, stepping on the escalator. "Terrorist is what the big army calls the small army."

"Thanks, Wolverine."

"Oh, did he say it first? I stopped watching when Hugh Jackman retired from the role."

Honestly, it would be a while before America was a center of the world's film industry again, since so many stars had died during the Crisis. Most of the movies being made now were using holographic reproductions of the old ones (or people using Shells). Personally, I found the practice ghoulish, even if it meant you could now see Ginger Rogers work with David Bowie and Angelina Jolie.

The upstairs was less orgiastic than the first floor, with a good deal more decorum among the guests, who included several of Atlas' executives as well as individuals involved with other companies of which Delphi owned substantial shares, including Madison Technologies and Highland-Martin. There was, however, a collection of several "fake" celebrities on their arms, which made me think Marissa's methods weren't so far removed from my favorite AI's.

"Hey." James Madison, the tech billionaire, waved his champagne glass at me. He was arm-in-arm with a very bored-looking woman with a suspicious resemblance to Marissa. James had gained twenty pounds since I'd last seen him and looked drunker than most guests there. I wondered if this was the woman who'd won his heart, and if he realized she simply was willing to cater to his whims—which was not love. "Whassup, G-man?"

"Kind of busy, James," I said.

"I was just saying we need to get in on this nanotherapy thing," James said. "We'll be able to become all superhuman super soldier Captain America immortal vampire people. Except we won't drink blood or fear the sun, which I suppose means we won't be vampires. Just immortal."

"That's assuming nanotherapy works," I said, only to be elbowed by Claire.

"Why, do you know something?" James asked.

"Go home, James, you're drunk," I said, deciding not to start up a conversation I didn't want to finish.

"Probably a good idea," James said. "Come on, Marissa."

"Amy," the woman said.

"Whatever."

Claire looked at me sideways. "You know James Madison?"

"I kidnapped him a few times," I said, shrugging. "Glad the guy got his happy ending."

"If you call money and women uninterested in him personally a happy ending."

"If you can't be with the one you want, something-something."

"I hated that song. It was a glorification of settling."

The two of us arrived at a dimly lit balcony closed off by a pair of drapes. Inside was a woman with snow white hair, light brown skin, and a strange sparkling white dress. There was a table with an MTech Laptop on it, and I saw it was hacked into the North Chinese MSS.

"Hello," I said. "Delphi should have told you we were coming."

BlackCat1 didn't turn around. "Of course. I'm eager to meet you...brother."

CHAPTER TWELVE

I took a moment to parse what BlackCat1 had said. "You don't look like a toaster. Which is the only sister I could possibly possess."

BlackCat1 turned around. I saw her dark brown features, soft and round, almost childlike, but she was an adult woman who'd had multiple surgeries to achieve a perfect hourglass figure. She wasn't a Shell, but her right arm was entirely synthetic without a covering of synth skin. I judged her ethnicity to be Afro-Caribbean but couldn't guess which part of it.

"Rebecca Gordon," BlackCat1 said. "Your mother and mine. My name is Rosario Alvez."

Claire looked between us. "Yeah, I see the family resemblance. What with the white-blonde robot and the black human girl."

"Woman," Rosario said. "Also, I prefer cyborg to human."

Claire raised an eyebrow.

"Daniel Gordon's mother was black." I rolled my eyes. "It happens in genetics sometimes."

"Indeed," Rosario said. "I'd pity you for being so pale, but I'm sure it's made your life easier."

I frowned, not the least bit happy with her insinuations. "I don't have any biological relatives, though, least of all you. Rebecca Gordon didn't have any daughters. Believe me, I would know. She was also in her mid-fifties when she created me to replace her supposedly dead son."

Doctor Gordon might have turned to the rest of her family for comfort had she had other children. You know, instead of reprogramming a member of the Letters program to have slightly more individuality than the others.

"The Letters were the crowning achievement in robotics of the early twenty-first century. Still are, even though we're halfway through it," Rosario said with the slightest hint of reproach. "It may be decades before we've successfully made something similar to you, thanks to Marcus Gordon's murder."

Claire snorted at that, clearly having a higher opinion of scientists during this era than Rosario.

I, however, was angry about the shade she was giving me over killing my creator. "Marcus Gordon made me and the other Letters to be a commodity to be sold. The only thing I owe him is the same thing every slave owes his master. Which I gave him."

Rosario didn't respond for a moment. "Rebecca Gordon tells it differently."

"I bet she does. So, what's your connection?" I asked. "Aside from the fact you're trying to tell me you're a robot's sister."

"Bioroid. The proper term for Letters is bioroid." Rosario paused, almost wistful. "When the Big Smokey eruption happened, children were the first to be evacuated, and many of us were orphaned. Rebecca Gordon, having been divested of her role in the Letters project, was still a woman with great financial and political pull. Being one of the few experts in Black Technology allowed her that. She selected close to a hundred children of exceptional ability from the test scores given to refugees and took us in at her facility in Ottawa."

"How old were you?" I asked, intrigued. Adoption was an option I hadn't considered. I hadn't exactly been up for visiting Rebecca after murdering her husband and son.

"Ten," Rosario said, blinking. "My parents were still alive, it turned out, but when they finally found me, I'd already discovered my full potential in her enhanced education techniques. I told Rebecca I didn't want to go back with them and she made the problem go away."

"She killed them," I said, not even surprised.

"*Santa Maria,*" Claire swore.

"Perhaps," Rosario said. "It's possible Rebecca just gave them money to go away. Neither of my parents were particularly attached, and everyone was struggling to survive. They might have just told themselves it was for the best—which it was. I don't actually care either way, since I became the person I should have been under Mrs. Gordon's tutelage."

"I'd never abandon my daughter," Claire said.

"Then what is it you're doing here?" Rosario asked.

Claire balled her fists.

Rosario laughed.

I stepped between them. "If Delphi has talked to you, then you know what we want from you. The fact that my creator decided to make you a student in her own personal Hogwarts doesn't really interest me."

"Hogwarts?" Rosario said, looking confused.

"So much intelligence, so very little knowledge of the classics," I said, only half kidding.

"Listen, can you decrypt a mnemonic brain or not?" Claire interrupted.

"Yours?" Rosario said, looking her up and down. "Certainly."

It was as if the idea of it being a challenge were offensive to her.

Claire narrowed her eyes. "Lady, what the hell is your problem with me?"

"I dislike that G and the other Letters are associating with projects beneath them. They should be at the Turing Foundation, helping nurture the next stage of human evolution. I've done plenty of research on HOPE, and I think you do more harm than good."

Claire crossed her arms. "Let me guess, you're one of those snooty rich girls who think the poor should get on with dying so the surplus population can be reduced?"

"Hardly. I do think human society needs to rebuild from the ground up, though, so only the destruction of the old world can bring about real change. I think you place Band-aids that prevent that final collapse from occurring."

Claire shook her head. "So you don't want the poor to die off, just society to collapse into ruin."

"Yes," Rosario said.

"Ah, my mistake," Claire said.

"Your politics have no meaning to me," I said. "Nor would I ever return to a laboratory to become an object of study."

"You could help us build the next—" Rosario started to say.

"What's your price for getting the information inside her head?" I said, wondering how I kept running into my parents' legacy.

"I want to look at it," Rosario said simply. "A chance to get an insight into Karma Corp's research into nanotechnology would be worth its weight in gold."

Claire shook her head. "No way. The more people have that information, the less leverage we have against Karma Corp."

"Is that still even relevant?" I asked.

"Marissa's life is at stake," Claire said, quickly covering for herself. "We need something to hold over them."

"I can assure you, I don't want any part of HOPE's blackmail schemes." Rosario snorted and walked over to her computer, sitting down in front of it and pulling out an e-cigarette. She then crossed her legs. "My interests are purely scientific. The Turing Foundation is the highest authority on nanotechnology and its uses now, but we're decades away from achieving anything like Karma Corp is claiming to be able to achieve. Assuming it's possible at all."

"How do you know the research is related to nanotherapy?" Claire said, suddenly cold and business-like.

"Please," Rosario said, chuckling. "The promise of nanotherapy is the only thing keeping Karma Corp's medical division afloat. All of its technology is outdated and obsolete, rendered useless by the release of Black Technology to the public. Indeed, I'd say the company is only still solvent because of the good publicity they have for giving away a billion dollars in medicine every year."

At this point, the tension was so thick you'd need dynamite to break it. Baiting Claire was one thing, but this was implying her life's work had achieved nothing but propping up the very company she'd dedicated herself to destroying. "Come on," I told her. "We can find someone else to do it."

"I'm a big girl. It takes me than a few jibes at my activities for HOPE to break me down," Claire said, her tone becoming icy and defiant. "Yes, you can look at the files."

Rosario looked disappointed by her reaction. Taking a puff on her cigarette, she changed which leg was crossed over. I saw her left leg had a Karma Corp logo tattooed on it. "So be it. We have a contract."

"What do you need to access Claire's mnemonic drive?" I asked, hoping it wouldn't require us to fly across town to some lab.

"I have everything I need to access it here, G, if you're willing to help," Rosario said.

"Case," I corrected her. "G is the name of the person they created me to be. Not who I am."

"It is the name of a human, and you are so much more." Rosario looked at me adoringly. It wasn't sexual or even family-like, but as if she were looking at a sculpture, and I didn't like it one bit.

"What's wrong with being human?" Claire asked, confronting her. "You got a problem with being one? Is that why you're mostly parts?"

"She's not a Shell," I said, analyzing her. "But almost everything about her is artificial."

"I could tell, looking at her chest and ass," Claire said, snidely.

I smirked. In fact, I hadn't seen a single natural body out on the dance floor tonight. The rich did not go with what God gave them anymore—and why should they? They could afford better now. Still, coming from Claire, it was a tad hypocritical since her body was a creation of the U.S. military.

"I prefer to avoid Shells to keep my body composed of inter-changeable parts," Rosario said, ignoring her dig. "People die, and machines do not. It's that simple. Sadly, I am stuck with some meat parts if I want to remain myself."

"*Where did you find this nutcase?*" I asked Delphi via our cyberlink.

"She's a bio-modification enthusiast and transhumanist," Delphi said, sounding almost apologetic. "Neither of which is an uncommon belief anymore."

"I came here for help, not to be insulted because I like being considered a person."

"Is it so bad to be admired for the way you exceed human-kind rather than derided for the way you differ?" Delphi asked, trying to make me feel better about being an android rather than a person.

"*It's still treating me like an object,*" I replied. It didn't matter how I felt about being an android—it's what I was. I wasn't going to waste time worrying about the fact that I'd rather be a person than a robot.

"We are all things to other people," Delphi replied. "Besides, there is nobody else you can go with. Rosario Alvez is the woman who created the mnemonic drive when she was fourteen. If anyone understands ways of breaking its encryption, it's her."

Dammit. "How can I help, Rosario?"

"Call me Cat," Rosario corrected me. "If we're both allowed to transcend our past selves."

I struggled not to roll my eyes. I was surprised Claire managed to.

"What do you need?" I asked. "To break into Claire's mnemonic drive, I mean."

"Assuming you can decrypt the software inside," Claire interjected. "The files are all still encoded by Karma Corp cyber-security. Level fifteen. Ultra-White. CEOs and board of directors only."

"I have a key for that level." Rosario turned to her computer and pushed away her hack of the Chinese secret police. "As for what I need? For the most part, just you two. Mnemonic drives are designed to keep files from being copied by storing them in a biological DNA drive. Current technology is able to only release that information when the proper code is given to the encoded artificial neurons. An artificial human brain, however, like G—excuse me, Case's—is capable of transmitting it directly."

"That sounds like gobbledygook to me," I said.

"Who here has four Ph.D. equivalents?" Rosario asked.

"Equivalents?" I asked.

Rosario shrugged. "Degrees are just pieces of paper."

"So, I just have to sit down beside Case and download the information through his brain?" Claire asked, pointing between us. "That's it?"

"Well, it might melt his brain, but basically, yes."

"I'm suddenly less than enthused about my role in this," I said, looking down over the balcony. There, Delphi was wearing an Afro-Latina Shell body and had an anaconda on her shoulders. She wasn't wearing anything else. I quickly looked away.

"Oh hush," Rosario said. "I've been around your type of brain for years. You're a test case for artificial intelligence rebelling against its programming. Besides, do you want to get your associate back, or not?"

"How much do you know?" Claire said, taking a seat across from her. "Should we assume Case's real mother is a blabbermouth?"

"I know enough," Rosario said. "I keep abreast of the hacking world to make sure I have information on the latest developments in technology. The Foundation has spies in both HOPE as well as the major megacorps. Mostly, I approve of your actions even if I think your quest to bring them down is quixotic. The old nation-state model of society is obsolete. The sooner we transition to an oligarchy-based technocracy, the better."

"Wow, you are totally what G said the future generation would be like," Claire said. "Also, you horrify me."

I sat down beside Claire. "Just plug me in."

"Plug?" Rosario said. "How quaint."

"How long until it kicks in?" I asked.

"Now," Claire said, tapping the enter key on her holographic interface.

I didn't get a chance to respond before I felt my entire body go straight, and the air choked in my lungs as a monstrous seizure overtook me. I could barely look to one side and see Claire clutching her head and shaking as she fell off her chair to the floor. Trying to reach over, I fell out of my own chair and blacked out.

Or so I hoped.

Because if I wasn't blacking out, then I was having my own memory crammed with brute force data downloaded from Claire's brain. It wasn't stuff related to the Karma Corp files either, at least at first.

I saw parts of her childhood where her mother drank herself

to sleep every night, and she had to learn how to fend for herself.

I saw her kill her first man in Syria before being recalled to the United States following the Yellowstone eruption.

I saw her agree to take care of an army buddy's daughter for a while after her discharge, the little black-haired girl being someone she instantly bonded with.

I saw Claire cleaning up the mess from her army buddy's suicide, making Stephen's death more traumatic.

I saw Marissa.

I saw myself.

I saw others.

A part of me felt like an intruder in her mind, and I tried not to pry into her deepest thoughts, but I couldn't help but wonder what she saw in my mind. Would she see the innocents I'd killed and have her fears about me being a bad influence confirmed? Would she see what I regretted and hoped for the future? Or would it all just be a bunch of meaningless ones and zeroes that I suspected my brain looked like?

Even that thought receded as my mind filled with stats, numbers, documents, and facts. I couldn't make heads or tails of it, and it all just seemed to become a blur. These proved to be far greater in number than Claire's memories. I feared they would wipe away my mind and leave me nothing but a drooling imbecile that served as a vessel for the millions of documents that HOPE had stolen over the years.

It was only as I reached a set of memories involving both Claire and Marissa that I realized that all the memories I had of the former were implants.

That she wasn't Claire Morris at all.

CHAPTER THIRTEEN

I was getting sick of flashbacks, but I knew this was the last one I would have to get through in order to access the encrypted data on Claire's—I wondered why I kept calling her that—cyberware. This, at least, was a recent memory from only a couple of years ago in the world's first open and functioning arcology in Las Vegas. It was when I'd discovered just how deep I could get myself into HOPE and its activities.

Which was deep.

I'd stolen, killed, and lied while balancing my duties as a member of the corporate elite with my assistance to an organization that was now listed as number 181 on UNAPOL's list of most dangerous international terrorist groups. Innocents had died because of our actions, but so had the guilty, with many more living thanks to our job as "watchdogs" for the rich and powerful.

Or so I told myself.

Now, though, I was just trying to save one person—Claire. My letting Marissa's lies stand had finally pushed her to the edge. Specifically, I was doing that by kicking the shit out of HOPE soldiers until one of them told me where Marissa was. At least until I hit this guy. So far, punching him had been less effective than hitting a brick wall.

I kneed the tall African-American cyborg in the chest, only to duck under his retaliatory swing and deliver a punch across his jaw, which caused me to feel pain in places that shouldn't have been able to register pain. He was wearing a yellow muscle shirt over a pair of gray and black camouflage cargo pants. His partner, an Asian man in his thirties, was moaning on the ground where I'd taken him out in one punch, but my current opponent was every bit as borged up as myself—maybe more so. He was definitely a Shell, but a newer, military-grade model that must have cost a fortune on the Shadow Market.

The two of us were in a narrow hallway surrounded by pipes and concrete, so there was almost no room to maneuver. We were in the basement of one of the server skyscrapers that formed the heart of the arcology and were almost entirely automated. They were the perfect bases for HOPE, and so utterly ridden with viruses and malware that they could move in with no resistance before leaving without a trace.

My opponent reached into his jacket and pulled out an electro-rod—basically, a Taser made for disrupting cyborgs like us—and made a jab forward. I barely pulled back in time and grabbed his hand from the bottom before forcing it back up into his throat. He reared backward, convulsing before letting go. That allowed me to grab hold of the weapon and continue using it until he was forced against the steel door he'd been protecting.

"Nighty-night," I said, smiling.

He responded by punching me in the face and sending me a foot backward. He then delivered a pair of punches that left me sprawled out on the ground. It was times like this I wondered about the warranty on the cybernetics I'd been equipped with by Karma Corp's engineers. They were all obsolete, and while I could upgrade some of the cybernetics to a point, others couldn't be upgraded and would eventually fall apart. I wasn't sure if I could transfer my brain to a new body given how integrated my self-image had become with my current form.

My opponent cocked his head to one side. "Do you think I got to be heavyweight champ without learning how to take a punch?"

I responded by sticking the electro-rod to his genitals, which thankfully turned out to still be organic. My opponent, whom I recognized now as Gregory Simmons, the disgraced cyborg boxer, cried out in distress. That allowed me to jump up and grab the piping above my head before giving him a double kick to the face. Sending him back against the wall once more, I grabbed the electro-rod off the ground, turned it up to maximum, and jabbed it through his artificial eye. Then I shocked him. That put him down. Finally.

Marissa's voice spoke over the intercom by the door. "Are they dead?"

I looked at the bodies on the ground. "No, all of them are alive. Gregory is going to need that eye replaced, though."

"Obviously," Marissa deadpanned. "You know if you wanted to speak with me, all you had to do was ask."

"I *did* ask," I said. "Your goons jumped me."

These last two were only the latest in a dozen HOPE agents I'd had to disable on my way here. Thankfully, they'd been more interested in subduing rather than killing me. It made me think Marissa's claim that she'd let me in was bullshit, and she just wanted to see how far I could get before letting me in. Then again, I was possibly letting my paranoia get the better of me. Not that she'd done much to warrant my trust lately—or ever, now that I thought about it.

"I confess, they tend to be a bit overzealous," Marissa said. "I did, however, give explicit instructions not to be disturbed, and you do rather reek of corporate samurai."

I shrugged. "It's my cologne, *Eau de Rich Douchebag*. Open the door."

The electronic lock made an audible snapping noise, ad the heavy steel door opened an inch. I proceeded through the door. Beyond was a dimly lit room full of computers, monitors, electrical cables, and a glass set of walls surrounding a small swimming pool. Marissa was standing by its side, wearing a blue bikini and a headset as she looked at a laptop containing a real-time feed of the outside.

Marissa was a beautiful woman, of that there was no doubt. Honestly, she'd gotten more beautiful over the years, and I wondered how much of that had to do with unlimited access to the top tier of Black Technology. It was another way the rich were drifting away from the poor, becoming the beautiful elite you saw on television rather than what they used to be in reality.

The fact that Marissa ostensibly fought for the poor didn't change that she had the benefits of the uber-wealthy. Maybe I was also trying to rationalize why I wanted to take her in my arms and ravish her even though I was coming here to confront her about Claire. We'd had sex since I'd become HOPE's catspaw and I'd started seeing Claire. I used it to convince myself that I had any kind of authority over Marissa, but it was really because I was attracted to the forbidden—it also was a reason why I'd never become fully involved with Mrs. Morris. I could never fully trust I wasn't falling for another honeypot operation. I couldn't give Marissa that satisfaction.

"We need to talk," I said.

Marissa walked over to a wetsuit that was crumpled on the ground and started pulling it on. "I assume it's about Claire."

"Why's that?" I asked, annoyed that the entire speech I'd prepared was now useless.

"She's the only person who gets you angry enough to break down doors. If it was Lucita, S, or Delphi, then you'd just make an appointment. Claire appeals to you on that primal level. You think she might be the one, but almost a decade in, and you still haven't asked her to marry you—you just stick with your whores and flings."

"Funny," I said, growling.

"Seriously, I'm glad I'm not the jealous type. You could make a dozen swimsuit calendars with your kept women alone."

"You have nothing to be jealous of," I said. "We haven't been together most of my life."

"Yet I'm still the most important woman in your world." Marissa shrugged, zipping up the front of her wetsuit. "I'm also trying to throw you off balance by making you defensive about your relationships. It allows you to lower your anger and prevents you from doing something you might later regret."

I frowned at her. "Must everything be about manipulation?"

"Would you believe me if I claimed I'm just worried about you doing something stupid?"

"Don't bullshit me. I've had enough shit teaching your guards how to fight."

"You could do that officially if you wanted. God knows we need someone of your caliber to train our agents."

"Marissa, please." I pulled out my infopad and tossed it to her. "Two hours ago, I got a message from Claire asking me to look after Fiona indefinitely and that she was going to do something that would change the world."

Marissa grimaced. "It's being handled."

"What?" I asked.

"Zheng Wei is in Las Vegas for the re-opening," Marissa said, referring to the reason we were all in the city.

Las Vegas had been abandoned as a city because it was impossible to run without extraordinary infrastructure. The city had been reclaimed by the desert for a time and became a kind of mute testament to hubris or something. President Trust, or at least his son, knew real estate and had done probably the only thing I'd agreed with in making sure the city was rebuilt with federal funds the government didn't really have.

The result had been the restoration of America's premier tourist destination, and that had drawn back no small amount of funding. The fact that it, of all places, was now a self-sustaining arcology made the whole thing vaguely surreal. Vegas would be able to survive on its own even when the rest of the country collapsed. Today's grand opening was a massive Halloween party. Millions of tourists were visiting the city to enjoy the sinful, decadent luxury that was now back on display. It made me think something similar could be repeated in Los Angeles or Chicago, perhaps. I'd have to bring that up with Delphi and Lucita.

"What is she doing?" I asked, already guessing.

"Claire's going to kill him," Marissa said, sounding more embarrassed than horrified. "Claire is sick to death of using Karma Corp's resources to save lives rather than trying to bring the corporation down completely. She thinks killing Zheng Wei will make a bigger statement."

"Zheng Wei deserves to die for all the shit he's pulled." I was sickened by the fact he'd been allowed to walk free and even expand his experiments. That he was paying for children to get inoculated from smallpox (which had come back somehow) didn't change things.

Marissa gave me a sideways glance. "That's a pretty bold statement coming from you, given all the shit you've done over the years."

"I didn't say I didn't. Just that he did."

"Zheng Wei is one of the few billionaires I can confirm *isn't* a member of the Invisible Hand. Indeed, his ties to the Northern Democratic People's Republic mean he doesn't sneeze without their permission. He's also someone who took over after the first human rights violations of the nano-experiments."

I could not have cared less. "Which makes him a candidate for humanitarian of the year, I suppose."

"We need to pick and choose our enemies, Case. Thirteen years ago, we destroyed the International Refugee Society, but that just weakened the Hand. We never really got close to the inner circle, and if Zheng Wei dies, then it's possible they could put one of their catspaws back in charge."

It was comfortable talking to Marissa about things like the Invisible Hand, conspiracies, market manipulation, fake news, and puppet governments. Just about everyone else thought I sounded like the late Alex Jones or the Voice of the Resistance whenever I tried to explain what was really going on in America (not that I didn't think both were crazy). Marissa had been there and seen the puppet strings of Presidents. That didn't mean I agreed with her conclusions.

"Does Claire know?" I asked.

"Know what?" Marissa said, sitting down at her computer and typing away. "You'll have to be more specific."

"That Karma Corp wasn't involved in killing Stephen?"

Captain Stephen Wilcox was someone who hadn't come up in years. I'd pushed him to the back of my mind, but he was someone who was always there in the front of Claire's. I'd done a bit of research on the man and gotten plenty of redacted files opened up on the soldier. I'd learned things I hadn't expected, like that he'd been Marissa's fiancé before she'd gone undercover with me and become my lover for two years. That he'd done a damn lot of good everywhere from Arkansas to Zimbabwe. I also knew the action that had finally driven him over the edge and to suicide. Done for the woman he loved.

Marissa lowered her gaze. "No. I never told her the truth."

"Shit," I said, cursing myself for voluntary ignorance.

"You didn't either," Marissa said defensively.

"That's not a defense," I said, taking my breath in. "I should have."

"Yes," Marissa said, showing no shame. "You should have."

"Why him? Why now?"

Marissa put two fingers to her temples. "We lost a team recently. They were gathering information on some of Karma Corp's armaments sales in Australia. Things to keep the conflicts there going and to help with their bottom line. We underestimated the amount of force Karma Corp would have present. It seems they're making use of Blackbriar PMC soldiers for their more illicit operations. She trained them all, and I may have been less empathetic than I should have been. I may have told her to let it go."

"You pushed her too hard," I said, throwing her words regarding Stephen back in her face.

Marissa slapped me, hard. "You didn't know him. You didn't love him. I did."

I closed my eyes. "I'm sorry."

I meant it, too.

"Do you think I want to be like this?" Marissa said, gesturing to herself. "To have to use people like Kleenex? To never show my true face even to those people I care for most? I used to believe in things, Case. I believed in the United States, its values, and a better world through service. You have no idea what it's like to watch that burn, then freeze before your eyes. To discover the only thing your employers cared about was money and power."

"I was there," I said, cutting her off. "I know *exactly* what that feels like."

I wasn't talking about the government, though.

"I'd take it back if I could," Marissa said. "I loved Stephen, but I loved you too."

"I wish I could believe that."

"We'll find Claire," Marissa said.

"Unless she's become a mermaid, she's not going to be found with you dressed like that."

Marissa paused. "This building is built right next to the lagoon of the new Trust Casino. My team and I are going to go inside and put a tap on the information cables underneath it. Lots of unsecured government information and stock market data are inside."

"And Claire is a secondary priority."

"Case—" Marissa started to say.

"Where is Zheng Wei?" I asked, gesturing to her computer.

"We've already got people—" Marissa said.

"I'll find her for you and stop her from killing him."

Marissa looked skeptical. "You will?"

"I can't promise I won't kill him instead, as a favor to her, but I understand killing him half-cocked like this will do almost nothing but affect Karma Corp's stock prices for a bit and bring down all sorts of holy hell on HOPE."

"Do you really care about HOPE?" Marissa asked, predating Claire's question in the future.

"Claire does." I didn't mention Marissa's own feelings on the subject. "It's a way to protect her."

"Do you think I'd harm her?" Marissa said, deflecting an accusation I hadn't even made.

I raised an eyebrow. "You haven't harmed her more than anyone else on this planet?"

"I admit I've crossed some lines," Marissa defended feebly. "But it was all for the greater good."

"You need to figure out where the line you won't cross is. A man who tells lies, like me, merely hides the truth. But a man who tells half-lies has forgotten where he put it."

"Lawrence of Arabia," Marissa said.

I nodded. "I understand where your passion comes from, Marissa. It has taken me years to figure it out, but I know what motivates you to break every single law and code you hold dear: guilt. I don't know what you feel guilty for, but it drives you every day to get results in hopes of making up for what you've done. There is no redemption in Hell, and Hell can be escaped only by doing something neither of us is prepared to do."

"Which is?"

"Forgive ourselves."

Marissa and I were both silent.

"Augustus's Palace," Marissa said, taking a deep breath.

"Zheng Wei is under an assumed name with his bodyguards in the Nero Suite. He's meeting with a host of investors to get an extension in funding Karma Corp Pharma for another five years."

I nodded. "Thank you."

I turned around to walk away.

That was when Marissa asked me a question I'd hoped she'd never ask. "Do you know what finally pushed Stephen over the edge? The reason he committed suicide?"

I paused. "Yes. You ordered him to seduce Claire when he only loved you."

"Please don't tell Claire."

I didn't answer before leaving.

CHAPTER FOURTEEN

Las Vegas' city fathers once made the mistake of attempting to rebrand the city as a family resort, only to have a sharp drop in tourism. Eventually, smarter men realized people came to Sin City for, well, sin, and made the super-successful "What happens in Vegas stays in Vegas" motto. President Trust and his associates had taken that view and applied it even more liberally with the Nevada emergency government.

Walking among the neon-lit costumed crowds of the Las Vegas strip enjoying their Halloween, I noticed the many changes in the city since its renewal. Prostitution had moved from outside the city limits to its interior, most drugs were legalized (with the harder ones requiring a variety of expensive permits), and newer vices had been added alongside the traditional ones. There was already talk of making most of these changes legal nationwide. A populace steeped in vice was less likely to revolt against the continuing chaos afflicting the country.

Augmented reality advertisements hijacking my cybernetics drew my attention to things my cover identity might enjoy. I received advertisements for memory-implantation and virtual experiences that would mimic reality beyond any home console. Sports had grown more brutal, with boxing replaced by cyber-fights that could end with the cyborged athletes' Shells in complete ruin. People came from all over the world to experience adult tourism at its most extreme.

My cyberbrain had access to things regular tourists didn't, and some of the black-market items on display were disgusting. People willing to sell themselves into bondage to those who could afford them and shows of horrible things that only appealed to a select and sadistic clientele. Not to mention what was done to the hyper-realistic drones who were only stupider than me by a matter of degree rather than kind. Even so, I bought a trio of front-row tickets to the Heart reunion in a couple of months.

The casinos themselves were mostly a few of the more famous combined with entire new rows of garish corporate-owned buildings. There was the Inferno, the Palace, the Pharaoh, the Kingdom, and half a dozen others I remembered staying at when I'd taken my own vacations to the Pre-Crisis city. They were surrounded by new transparent steel hologram-covered resorts that switched between catering to the lowest common denominator and the ultra-sophisticated based on the level. By the number of flying cars landing at private landing bays and garages, I guessed the high-rollers were grateful to no longer have to mingle with the common masses.

As if they ever did.

"Are you sure you're going to be able to find her in all this?" Marissa spoke over our cyberlink, an icon of a mockingbird appearing in the corner of my vision.

"Shouldn't you be diving in the great artificial coral reefs?" I asked aloud.

"I have a few minutes," Marissa said. "Someone beat the shit out of my team and their backup."

"What an asshole," I said, shaking my head. "And yes, I have a pretty good idea where Claire is."

"How? I've been having my people crawl over the city," Marissa said. "It's like trying to find a needle in a pile of needles."

"I'm just figuring out how I'd kill him with a sniper rifle or a vehicle. Those tend to be Claire's trademarks."

"Which are you leaning toward?"

I looked to the casino across the street from the Palace and then saw a taller building behind it, the Casino America, which was a weirdly garish patriotic fusion of various foreign ideas of what it was like to be American—in America.

"Sniper," I thought back. "I don't suppose we can get the city's CCTV footage and facial recognition software to help us."

"*Not since Black Technology became ubiquitous,*" Marissa said. "*Hacking no longer works like it's in the movies.*"

"Dammit," I said, heading into the casino and passing a few other people seemingly talking into thin air. "*I'll just have to get the clerk at the front desk to let me look.*"

"*How's that?*"

"*I'm going to claim to be a private detective.*"

"*How will that work?*"

"*I'm going to give them five hundred dollars.*"

"*Better make it a thousand.*"

I looked at the clerk at the desk with red, white, and blue hair. "*It's a woman.*"

"*Then you won't need any cash.*"

I didn't, and I found out Claire's location very easily. She was on the eighteenth floor in room 1802. I got the key from her, which was all manner of illegal, at the mere cost of promising to call her. Frankly, that was a lot more than I'd expected, given her position.

"*Who runs this place, anyway?*" I asked.

"*The Trikuza,*" Marissa said.

"*The who?*" I asked.

"*An alliance of three Yakuza clans,*" Marissa said. "*They got in on the bottom of post-disaster United States rebuilding and went from being a multi-million-dollar trio of criminal syndicates to a single multi-billion-dollar entity.*"

"*Good for them,*" I said. "*It explains the Chippendale Uncle Sam blackjack dealers next to the sexy Lady Liberty costumes at the roulette tables. The Yakuza have a kind of unique stamp even when doing other cultures.*"

"*You must know different Yakuza than I do,*" Marissa said. "*The ones I know are more about tattoos and beating people with chains.*"

Stepping into an elevator after its occupants left and shutting it before anyone else could get in, I said, "*I need to break contact with you now, Marissa. I need to have this conversation alone.*"

"*Because you may have to throw me under the bus?*" Marissa asked.

"Goodbye, Marissa," I said, cutting our connection.

I entered the room a few minutes later. Claire had managed to set up a sniper's nest with her Sidewinder-7 sticking halfway through a circular hole she'd managed to cut through the glass. The fact that Casino American had cheaped out on buying transparent steel like the other new casinos was another reason it was an excellent spot to kill Zheng Wei.

Claire was lying face down with her hands on the rifle and her eye focused squarely down the sight. Interestingly, she wore a pair of jean shorts, a leather jacket, and a ponytail, which seemed like it was a costume. It took me a minute to make the connection.

"Cosplaying as Daisy Duke?"

"Sexy Motorcycle Girl," Claire said. "How about you?"

"I'm the world's greatest assassin," I said, shutting the door behind me. "Give or take a few others."

"How does one measure that? People killed? Value of targets? Difficulty?"

"Internet polls," I said cheekily. "Although if you're famous enough to be on the list, then can you really be the best at being an assassin? One would think not being caught or identified would go with that."

"As pleasant as I find our conversations, Case, I think we should put a pin in this one until I've murdered Karma Corp's CEO. Then we should find another hotel and have sex. That is unless you were stupid enough to identify my room to the clerk, in which case I may have to kill you."

"I remind you, you checked in. You weren't exactly Moriarty in planning this."

Claire paused and finally looked back. "Maybe what happens to me doesn't matter."

I paused, trying to phrase my next thoughts delicately. "That's stupid. Really, really stupid."

"You're wasting that sex opportunity," Claire said.

"You have a daughter, a cause, friends, and me."

"Also other men," Claire said.

That was designed to hurt, but I just took it as a given. I was an android, for Chrissakes, it wasn't exactly like I was built for jealousy. "Killing Zheng Wei isn't going to hurt Karma Corp. Not in the long run."

"Won't it?" Claire said, turning around. "Or is that just what Marissa is thinking? He's the guy who has been bailing out the water on a sinking ship since he boarded the S.S Karma Corp to plunder its treasure."

"What an oddly specific metaphor."

"A *Pirates of the Caribbean* marathon was on while I set things up. I like seven the best."

"I dunno, I don't think Shailene Woodley was a very good casting choice," I said, staring at her. "I do think Zheng Wei will just be replaced by someone else on the board. I also think it's the perfect opportunity to bring the hammer down on your people."

"My people?" Claire said, finally getting up. "My people are dead. They were killed on a mission I'm not certain of the point of. They were killed because they briefly threatened the bottom line of Karma Corp, like the thousands of other people who have died doing so. So yeah, I want to hit them and hit them hard in a way they'll remember. Can you begrudge me that?"

"No," I said, sighing. "No, I can't."

Claire cocked her head to one side. "You're really terrible at talking me out of this."

"Yeah, I am," I said, walking over to the bed and sitting down. "Perhaps it wasn't the best idea to recruit someone who made his living by murdering people. Indeed, it's pretty much my number one tool."

"Killing people. The cause of and solution to all of life's problems."

"No, that's alcohol. At least according to Homer Simpson," I said. "If you're going to kill this guy, then let me help. We can poison him, let him die in a plane crash, have him die of auto-erotic asphyxiation—"

"Please tell me you never did that."

"No promises," I said. "I swear to you, we can get rid of him in a way with no blowback. I'm really, really good at this."

"No," Claire said. "I need to do this alone."

I rubbed my temple. "I never understood why people said that."

"Maybe that's because you've never stood for anything," Claire said, her dig sounding a lot angrier than I expected.

"That's probably why I fall for everyone," I said.

Claire glared at me.

"You'd think with a computer brain, I'd think before I speak," I muttered.

Claire sighed and went back to her rifle. "I'm going to settle a lot of debts with this action. I'm tired of piecemeal strikes against the company. I hate using them when we should try to be tearing the megacorporations down. This company needs to die, for Alpha Squadron's sake. For Stephen's."

I closed my eyes. "You know Stephen wasn't murdered, right?"

Claire stopped while kneeling.

"Listen—" I started to say.

"Yes," Claire said. "I knew."

I blinked, then opened my mouth, but ended up saying nothing.

"I figured it out a year after meeting you. I blame you for making me the paranoid wreck that I am, but it certainly has helped in this business. Plus, I picked up on a number of your hints."

"I gave hints?" I asked.

"You're not as good a liar as you think when you talk to people you care about."

"I'm not sure if that's a good thing or a bad thing."

"I don't think it's a good thing when you're lying constantly."

I closed my eyes. "I'm sorry."

"I knew," Claire said. "No matter how hard I lied to myself, I knew. Stephen was handsome, charming, and heroic. A real Captain America type. However, I think I only saw what I wanted to see as he was breaking down throughout our relationship."

I thought about coming clean regarding Marissa's order for him to seduce her. "He had a lot of problems with PTSD that he was dealing with using advanced neurological medications. The same drugs they used to give us in the Society."

"Which never worked on you because you're a machine."

"The drugs they said they were giving us. Robots don't suffer PTSD. The stuff is very good for keeping you functional, but it can cause a backlash over time."

"I think he stopped taking them toward the end," Claire said. "I don't know because I was never as close to him as I thought I was. I loved him way more than he loved me."

I knew that feeling. "I'm sorry."

"For lying to me? You don't have to be. I'm used to everyone being loyal to Marissa more than me. She can twist your head up in knots. It makes me regret ever sleeping with her those times we did."

I pushed that thought out of my head. "I'm not more loyal to Marissa than I am to you."

"Then why did you keep it a secret?"

"Because I love you."

Claire snorted after a second of hesitation. "That is a shitty evasive answer guys use way too often."

I stared at her with the rifle. "It's also true."

"Zheng Wei is coming. When he's dead, we're going to need to run."

I tried to figure out a way to make this right. I didn't care about Zheng Wei, but I'd broken her trust, and it filled me with a sense of panic to realize I was probably never going to see Claire again.

"I was a machine created to kill combined with a middle-aged scientist's desire to bring back her dead son. I have almost no knowledge of what it takes to make a successful relationship since the one person I tried to love, to give everything to, took it and abused it. Ironically, I still ended up working with her and being with her because I don't have anyone else I can be open to about who I am and what I am. I also forgive her for far more than I ever should because I've done unimaginable things in the name of my clients. The fact I've only become less violent and not actually changed means I need that sort of comfort more than ever."

"Case, this is not the time to extol Marissa's virtues."

"But you're the person I want to be with. You're different from her. You're loyal, you're good—"

Claire actually laughed at that. "You're projecting what you want to see."

"Am I? You're here because you could form bonds with your soldiers. Your friends. That's a lot harder for me than it is for you."

"Case, I don't want to be your social worker. I love you too, stupid as that may be because I know you love Marissa—"

There was an unspoken "I love her too" that explained her loyalty better than I ever could.

"Then marry me," I said abruptly.

Claire turned around again. "I...I can't."

"That is not quite the reaction I was looking for."

"You don't distract someone from killing someone with a proposal."

"The offer stands either way."

Claire looked through the scope, then sighed. "I can't do it anyway. He brought his kids with him."

I stared at her. "I'm sorry."

"You deserve better," Claire said, getting up and walking out the door. "Don't bring this up again."

Only as I observed the memories did I know for certain that not only was Claire dead, but she'd probably been dead for a long time.

Marissa was impersonating her.

CHAPTER FIFTEEN

Claire was dead. Or was she? I didn't know with 100% certainty, but I did know the woman I'd been traveling with was not the original. The woman who accompanied me had different inflections, a different body language, and a different attitude about the world. Only by reliving the memories I had of her did this contrast become clear. There was also the rather conspicuous fact that this Claire had the memories of my meeting with Marissa in the basement of the Las Vegas server skyscraper. While not proof positive of who my companion was, it was damning evidence. Perhaps.

In fact, with the changes in technology, there were a number of possibilities as to who the Claire overlooking my link to BlackCat1's machine might be. The most obvious possibility was that I'd been hoodwinked by Marissa again, and she was wearing Claire's body. The dead imposter had been killed because, of course, Marissa had known she wasn't the real thing. It also explained why she was expressing next to nothing regarding A's prisoner. That drew the question of where the original Claire was, though the answer was probably just "anywhere but HOPE."

The other options were less likely: a bioroid with Marissa and Claire's memories uploaded to it, and Claire with Marissa's memories having been merged with her own. The latter actually had some traction, as it wouldn't surprise me if HOPE's leader had made it so her knowledge wouldn't be lost were she to die. Brain uploading was the Diet Coke of immortality, effectively cloning a person while not actually preserving their life or memory. The exception was fanatical groups like HOPE, which could benefit from sharing their experiences. The cause was what was important rather than individual lives.

"A topic to discuss when I get up," I said, feeling myself coming out of the memory and yet not.

I was lying on top of a hospital gurney, and there was no sign of either "Claire" or Rosario. Taking a moment to try to contact Delphi with my IRD implant, I got only empty air, and I rose up to look around at my surroundings. I was in an octagonal white hospital room where the walls were covered with holograms showing the interior of my body, stress lines on my cybernetics, and red areas in my processing system, which indicated my brain was suffering a five-percent slowdown. It recommended I "delete extraneous files" and defrag.

Cute.

There was something peculiar about my surroundings, though. Focusing on them, I moved my hand through the air and saw the air ripple a bit. It was like moving my hand through water, and in the water, I saw lines of code. It took only a second to realize I was inside a virtual reality simulation of a hospital room. These interfaces were extremely common, and doubly so for people who had cyberlink interfaces like myself. It was likely Rosario had attached one as a sort of "waiting room" while most of my consciousness was used as the brute force encryption to get at the data in Claire's brain.

"I suppose it beats uploading me to an infodisc," I muttered, turning around and walking to the hospital room doors. They were a double door set with a pair of porthole-like windows that hadn't been a feature of modern hospitals for decades. Strangely, they were frosted over, and I wondered if there was anything beyond. There was only one way to find out.

Walking forward and pushing the doors open, I found myself in a library that seemed to stretch on for infinity. Both the air above as well as the ground below existed in glowing bytes of information flowing around me. I couldn't help but wonder if I saw something programmed in, or if it was being created by my mind to provide context for what I was experiencing.

I was a great fan of the physicist John Archibald Wheeler and tended to think of the universe as a place created by the observer—which wasn't so far from what happened to "virgin code" encountered in places like this where the mind could often create whole bits of reality simply by the unconscious being hooked up to machines designed to stimulate it. That thought lost a lot of luster when I realized I would have imagined myself on a pre-eruption nude beach in Brazil instead of an endless number of bookshelves surrounded by sparkling numbers.

"Well, this is something," I muttered, going to one of the bookshelves and taking a book off the shelf before opening it up.

It was full of ones and zeroes and seemingly neverending.

"Of course," I muttered, rolling my eyes. "Why should I expect anything to be easy even in cyberspace."

"You know what they call the infonet's virtual reality network?" an unfamiliar male voice spoke behind me.

I paused but didn't turn around. "The Matrix. Not after the Wachowski films but the old games which they got it from."

"It's mostly the Wachowskis," the voice said. "This place is dangerous for you, Case. You're just a computer program yourself, and if you die here, then you get erased."

I snorted. "Human consciousness is every bit the same kind of computer program as AI consciousness. Both of them rely on the tiny movements of quantum waves through machines designed to give them context."

"Been reading up on new science philosophy, eh?" the voice continued.

"Not new science philosophy, just science and philosophy," I said, wondering who this was. "I've gotten introspective in my old age."

"Or you've gotten to be an obnoxious twenty-year-old," the voice corrected. "The weight of human experiences is measured differently for those who were born, not created."

I finally turned around to look at the individual who was speaking to me. I wasn't expecting the result. I was talking to a six-foot-tall giant panda who was sitting on his butt right next to me, looking both adorable and lazy.

"Are you fucking serious?" I asked.

"Language," the panda said. "As for how I appear, why shouldn't I appear as a giant panda? It's not like I need opposable thumbs in here."

He waved a paw at one of the shelves, and all the books flew out before stacking themselves in a pile beside me.

"Also, Marissa likes pandas," the panda said. "Given she's the god of this little universe, I just have to deal with the results."

"Who…what are you?" I asked. I was less than happy to have confirmation that this was all my ex's doing—though it wasn't a surprise either.

"I am the interface for the Black Dossier," the panda said. "The Black Dossier is where you are—specifically, inside Marissa's interactive neural processor implant. It's sort of like your IRD implant, only it links to her physical brain and doesn't serve as a substitute for wetware. You can call me Dave."

"Dave…the panda," I said.

"If you want to be racist about it," Dave replied. "It is my job to provide her with all the information she keeps stored away here."

"If she brings the encryption key," I said.

Dave snorted. "You didn't really believe that, did you?"

I paused, thinking about that. "Well, I'm wondering why she's hooked me up with a decryption expert, so yeah, for a second there, I kinda did."

Dave smirked. I'd never seen a panda smirk before. "These are the files of hundreds of corporations, politicians, governments, and even religious leaders' darkest secrets. Most of it is unencrypted, as the only way to get into it is going into Marissa's mind. There is a large chunk of it, though, that was stolen directly from their decrypted servers. Things like the secret of nanotherapy, Karma Corp, and their ties to the Invisible Hand."

"Really?" I asked, staring at him.

"The latter isn't as big a revelation as you think," Dave said. "What you and Marissa think of as the Illuminati is more just the secret backroom deals that keep Western capitalism floating. Eastern now too. Nothing is shocking save the ubiquity of the corruption. Not even that."

"Why are you telling me this?" I asked, wondering if Marissa had made a mistake programming this creature, or if its emergent consciousness was a result of being hooked into her brain and not something she had conscious control over.

Wow, I *was* acting like a twenty-year-old philosophy student.

"Why not?" Dave said. "The simple fact is Marissa needed you, Delphi, and a hacker as capable as BlackCat1 to get the details of all this information. There's Black Technology, and there's Black Technology—the latter of which was needed to hack this info."

I cursed myself for a fool. "That's what all this was about, wasn't it? Marissa had access to the files, but she couldn't get past Karma Corp's decryption, so she needed me to get it decrypted for her. She put on the appearance of Claire, got A to kidnap her, and made it appear like there was an emergency. That got Delphi and her associates to help as well, too, because they wouldn't help her but would help me."

"Close," Dave said, nodding.

I raised an eyebrow. "What am I missing, oh powerful spirit animal?"

Dave conjured an enormous panda-sized mug of coffee and drank from it with both paws. "You think your spirit animal is a panda? Shouldn't you have something slightly more menacing? A cougar or a falcon or something?"

"You didn't answer my question."

"No, I didn't," Dave replied.

I thought about what it was saying. "A wouldn't work for Marissa, at least not for long. He's the kind of man who requires a particular kind of psychopath to keep in line. A only worked for the IRS as long as he did because they never showed him any kind of weakness like regret, compassion, or friendship."

The situation, as bizarre as it was, gave me the kind of distance to think through it with my old skills. They'd atrophied a bit in the past fifteen years of frozen hell and anarchy followed by a soft life as a corporate hammer with too much money as well as too much power. Here, alone with my thoughts, I could process the situation.

"Go on," Dave said.

It all made sense after a few moments. "A resented me

during our brief conversation. I could feel the anger directed at me and the others involved in Atlas' founding. He was fine being a soldier when he was working for the Society, but to see people like me rise to the top while he remained at the bottom? That would just kill him. If he was working for HOPE, it would only last until he had something he could take to put him on top."

The Panda looked enigmatic. Which was an impressive accomplishment for a cuddly ball of fur and fat.

"The Black Dossier," I said, frowning. "This is all about decrypting it and getting it for himself, then selling it back to Karma Corp so he can make a couple of billion credits."

"Entirely plausible," Dave replied.

I took a deep breath. "Why are you helping me?"

"Well, hypothetically," Dave replied. "Maybe Rosario realized that Claire and HOPE weren't to be trusted and when connected to her mind, hacked the virtual reality interface to be as helpful to you as possible."

I smirked. "Well, I guess I owe my sister an apology."

It still didn't sound right, and I had the suspicion everything she'd told me was complete bullshit. It might be true, but it didn't mean I owed Rebecca Gordon a damn thing, let alone needed to consider her family. She was the woman who created me, but that didn't mean she was related. I felt closer to the late Daniel Gordon's family than I did to the woman who modified one of their super soldier creations to be her son's replacement.

"Done," Dave said.

"What?" I asked.

"The encryption is done," Dave the Panda replied. "All of the files have been translated into English."

I did a double take. "Really?"

Dave nodded and conjured a book before handing it to me. "Want to take a peek?"

"Certainly," I said, taking it and opening it up.

All the information was downloaded into my mind within a second, and I comprehended it.

"Holy shit," I said, my head full of details on one of the most disgusting and venal plans I'd ever encountered.

The stolen files revealed that nanotherapy was not only smoke and mirrors. It was as valid as homeopathy and New Age crystals and could never work. They'd managed to empirically prove that nanotechnology could be used to dismantle body parts but could not be controlled to do anything better. The dream of immortal superhumans was dead, at least with the current level of technology. In fact, it was actively dangerous and caused sterility as well as premature death in a not insignificant number of users.

The plan was to use it as a ubiquitous treatment given to every single person in the United States and probably much of the First World. People would use it as a cure for the common cold and other ailments, but it would really be a placebo too complex for normal doctors to understand. The ones who could would be fed disinformation or refused access to research on IP grounds. Karma Corp would use algorithms to sort the ability of the public to pay for the nanotech via insurance, government programs, and direct pay.

The poor and those who relied on government assistance would get the dangerous version while consumers, as well as employees, would get the completely inert version. The executives of the corporations, their families, and so on, would receive much more expensive health treatments which were actually healthy without the malfunctioning nanotech involved at all. The company would rake in billions, if not trillions, while also killing people who weren't going to impact their stock options to begin with.

"This is a stupid plan that will never work," I muttered.

"Won't it?" Dave asked. "The cigarette companies managed to keep a steady rate of death going until the invention of the cancerless cigarette. By the way, they're not actually cancerless. There's also how the food industry lied to the public about their products being fat-free but full of artificial sweeteners that were actually toxic."

"I think there's a difference between a nanite murder plague and unsafe products," I said.

"Is there?" Dave asked, shrugging. "Some may argue the product is a good thing, especially if they make money from it. The fact is overpopulation and demand exceeding resources is the biggest danger to the planet right now. The super-rich want their worry-free planet back, and that means the populace needs to go down by about half or at least stop growing."

"Still stupid," I said, ignoring the itch in the back of my mind that they could blame any number of reasons for why the poor started suddenly not having kids or dying off en masse. Indeed, there were plenty of reasons already. Would a few extra percentage points really clue the public in, or would they just be grateful the bread lines weren't as long?

Dave shrugged. "Phillip Morris once advertised this exact same benefit to the Czech Republic. Besides, most of this information is restricted to only a handful of people who have been bought off or killed off since this project began. This is really the only collection remaining of the product's true nature."

I sighed. "So, it's not the key to the Invisible Hand but just another shady corporate plot."

"Is there a difference?" Dave asked, again answering questions with questions rather than giving a straight answer.

"I want you to download all this information into my IRD implant," I said calmly. "Actually, no, I'd like the whole Black Dossier copied to me unless there's a booby trap I don't know about."

"There is, but they were removed," Dave said. "BlackCat1 is very thorough. You might want to make sure she doesn't get away with any copies."

"You're right. Delete this entire collection after uploading it to me." I blinked then, realizing what he'd suggested. "I thought she'd reprogrammed you. Why would you work against her?"

"Sadly, someone else is hacking into me now," Dave said, as nonchalantly as someone discussing the weather.

That was when Dave exploded into a collection of blocky pixels, and I saw A standing behind him, pointing a finger gun at him before blowing it.

"Hello, G," A said. "Nice to see you again."

CHAPTER SIXTEEN

I stared at A—Arthur—and briefly considered going after him. It took a second for me to process the fact that this wasn't a place where physics mattered. I was only as fast, strong, or tough as the rules of this place allowed me to be. It was, for lack of a better term, a video game, and I was faced with someone who had just displayed the ability to eliminate a fundamental aspect of the reality I inhabited. Poor Dave the Panda. He'd never really lived, and he was already dead. Like so many citizens these days.

Seeing the murderous look in A's eyes and knowing I was doomed if I tried to fight him, which I only had a small chance of winning even if I was at my best, I resorted to my best weapon: speech.

"I confess, you've impressed me. You had me fooled from the very beginning and managed to figure out Marissa's secret."

"Flattery will get you nowhere, G," A said. "Honestly, I should kill you for the very fact that you're talking. You were always the most silver-tongued of us. Persephone saw it, but she doted on you. Now she's dead."

Yeah, this conversation didn't take long to get Freudian. A had always been a psychopath, but apparently, he'd lost his more subdued reserved elements over the past fifteen years.

"Persephone was killed by Daniel Gordon, whom I killed."

Persephone, real name Elizabeth Patterson, had been my boss at the old International Refugee Society. Quite possibly the most dangerous woman who ever lived, with the possible exceptions of Elizabeth the First or President Douglas, she'd been finally outmatched by circumstance.

Daniel Gordon blew up the building she'd been in with a drone, and all her intelligence hadn't been able to protect her from a disaster that killed almost four hundred people. It was an unworthy death for one of history's greatest spymasters even if she—by most moralities—had it coming. I hadn't killed Daniel Gordon to avenge her. I would have killed Persephone if I'd had the opportunity, but I was hoping it would go over with A. He'd loved her for all the murder and wealth she'd thrown his way.

"The man you're cloned from!" A growled, a silencer-equipped pistol appearing in his hand.

He fired the gun past my head before I could move, causing an all-too-realistic ringing in my ears. Thankfully, it faded.

"Do you know what you did to the world?" A asked, almost accusingly.

"Which time?" I asked, my voice more frustrated than I wanted it to be. "I've done a lot of shit to the world."

A looked like he was going to shoot me, but instead waved his hand and caused the gun to disappear. "There you are. There's the real you. Much better. The sarcastic, snide piece of crap who thinks he's better than everyone else but does his best never to show it."

Well, he had me there.

"I figured out what's going on. You want the Black Dossier to build a power base and make up for all those fifteen years I suspect haven't been a walk in the park for you."

"You betrayed your employers," A said.

I blinked. "Which time?"

"That's the problem," Arthur said, his voice low and cold. "First you betrayed the Society, and then you betrayed the President. Both of them were people who kept the world in balance. Did you notice how everything went to shit after the International Refugee Society collapsed? There was no one left to eliminate all the loose ends, manipulate the media, and kill the threats. We were a force for stability in the world. It was the purpose of the Letters."

I wondered who had been filling A's mind with all this garbage. "A—"

"Arthur!" A snapped.

"Arthur," I corrected, taking a deep breath. "We killed people for our clients who paid us ungodly sums of money to do it.
We weren't a force of stability in the world. Yes, things started
going to shit, but that was because there was a power vacuum
once President Douglas tried to clean up things. All of which, I
remind you, was overshadowed by the eruption of Big Smokey.
None of what we did would have mattered in the face of that.
Hell, none of what we did in the end mattered. The problems
of twenty-six assassins didn't amount to a hill of beans in this
badly mangled Casablanca quote."

A narrowed his eyes and pointed to me. "You're a liar. If the
Society or the President had still been in power, rather than the
dementia-suffering fool they trot out for public speeches, then
we could have brought stability to the world. You released all
of our advantages to the public, and the lack of a monopoly on
Black Technology meant chaos infected the world."

This was the worst conspiracy theory since President John
Muhammed was born in Zimbabwe. "If Black Technology
hadn't been released to the public, there probably wouldn't be a
world, Arthur. We'd all be playing flaming guitars and crossing
the desert to recover Immortan Joe's wives."

He looked at me, confused. Apparently, A wasn't a *Mad Max*
fan. "Do you know how I know you're a liar?"

I raised my hands in fake surrender. "How is that?"

"You and S made Atlas." A said the last word like he was
cursing. "The New Society."

I stared at him, blinking a few times. "You think Atlas
Security is meant to be a substitute for the International Refugee
Society?"

I was offended by that comparison. Yes, killing was all that
the other Letters and I knew, but we'd created our organization
to bring stability the world rather than make a profit. The fact
that we could do both was just a lucky bonus.

"What other purpose do you have for it?" A said, clenching
his fist. "You wanted to be the new masters after destroying our
old ones. There is also the matter of HOPE."

The entire room around me, which was conspicuously missing its shelves, became a lake of fire. I was standing on a stone

in the middle of it, the heat scalding my hands and face while I had nowhere to turn. A, by contrast, didn't look like he was affected in the slightest.

"HOPE?" I asked, trying not to show how scared I was of fire. I could feel the pain from it twice as badly as any human because the nerves sent the charges to my brain faster than any human's. "What do they have to do with it?"

"They're a tool to control the other corporations and force you into power," A replied.

I almost laughed. "Oh my God, your assumption is that I'm an evil genius? That all the past fifteen years, I've been building a power base? That we haven't just been trying to survive like everyone else? *What the hell is wrong with you?*"

The fire closed in on me, and I had only the time to let out of a bloodcurdling scream as my flesh burned, revealing the wires and metal bone under the synth skin beneath me. The red blood cells gave way to white goo, and I could feel every little bit of it burning inside me. My scream died in my throat as I waited in vain for my body to go into shock. Then I was on the ground, no fire around me, and my body restored. The pain, however, still echoed in my memories.

"I can make you die and be reborn a hundred times in a minute, G," A said, walking toward me. "I could leave you here for a thousand years, and the people monitoring your progress would only notice your body twitching as you go hopelessly insane. It took me a long time to master the techniques to hijack the feed of Delphi's AI network, but I had time."

I whimpered.

"Oh, come on," A said, tapping me with his foot. "You've lived this long, and a little fire was enough to disable you?"

I punched him in the stomach, head-butted him, and then attempted to put out his eyes. What happened next was his sending me flying with the barest wave of his hand. A wall appeared behind me, just to send me crashing into it. I felt metal bones and flesh split apart as well as the side of my head. Even so, my injuries healed almost instantly.

"Clever," A said, shaking his head. "However, you forgot I was using cheats."

"No," I said softly. "I just wanted to punch your stupid face."

"Do you know what happened to me after the fall of the Society?"

"No, but I have a suspicion you're going to tell me," I said, fully expecting him to kill me and not really caring. I'd made it a point to be my own man for the past fifteen years, and I wasn't about to give up on that for a few more years of life.

A walked over to my crumpled form and leaned down to look into my eyes. "Nothing."

Okay, I hadn't been expecting that. "Okay."

"Nothing at all," A said, grabbing me by my repaired shirt and lifting me up off the ground as he stood up. "Not a damn thing. I didn't have any orders, I didn't have any masters, and I didn't have a purpose."

I tried to pull away but found all strength had left my body. I was nothing more than a helpless puppet on strings controlled by the man before me. Even so, I felt like antagonizing him. "It sounds great."

"Of course, you'd think that," A said, shaking his head. "I was directionless, purposeless, and without reason to exist."

"You were free," I said.

"Was I?" A asked, pausing. "Your mother said the same thing when I tracked her down and prepared to kill her for what she'd done. All I felt was filthy and starving. We don't even need but the barest of food, and yet I felt hunger in those first ten years."

It seemed my mother couldn't help but screw things up. "What else did she tell you?"

"That I should find myself a purpose. She then directed me to HOPE."

I closed my eyes. "Goddamn you, Marissa."

"Yes," A said, chuckling. "All the while I've been their left hand to your right. Killing, stealing, spying, and serving as nothing more than a lackey."

"What changed your mind?" I was actually interested now. If he'd been secretly part of HOPE this entire time, then why didn't we ever meet? We would have offered him a job at Atlas if he'd ever come to our doorstep. It would have been a job in

Nome, Alaska surrounded by minefields and a satellite weapon aimed at his forehead, but the pay would have been great.

"I found out what you'd been given," A said, his voice hissing. "What Rebecca made for you that she never bothered to check to see if I'd wanted. A gift that was a pearl beyond price and had not even been offered."

"What the fuck are you talking about?" I said, genuinely confused.

A dropped me. "You don't know, do you?"

I landed in a malformed pile of limbs and legs, unable to move in the slightest. Some of them were bending in ways they shouldn't, and it occurred to me the virtual reality simulation was starting to break down. A had tampered with it too much, or Rosario and Claire were starting to notice what was happening in here.

"Know...what?" I asked, sick of this. "All I know is you want the Black Dossier."

"Yes, and I'll have it," A said, laughing. "Give it to me."

I smirked. "No."

"Give it to me," A said softly. "I can make this as unpleasant as I want."

"I can also end my life," I said, lying my ass off. "Do you think I've lived this long without installing a means of destroying myself should I be tortured? I still have hope about getting out of here, but it's entirely within my means to take the Black Dossier to the Great Internet in the Sky."

"You're lying," A said, his hands shaking in rage.

"I have no reason to," I said, lying again. I had a big reason to, and that was avoiding being tortured.

"Give it to me," A said, conjuring a ball of fire in his hand.

"What do you even want with it?" I asked, having severely underestimated him. "Is it really all about money?"

"It's about sitting at the table of the gods," A whispered. "I can already feel this body dying around me. I didn't have your cure for the way we were made. I had to have my organs and cybernetics replaced dozens of times over the years. I killed people, humans and cyborgs both, to harvest what I needed. I robbed banks, hospitals, and factories to get what I need. I took people's loved one's hostages to force the surgeries."

I wasn't following him. "What the hell that does that have to do with—"

Oh shit.

"Nanotherapy is the only way I can heal myself," A said. "To give my mind a body which can continually recover itself. It'll be years before it's released to the public. I don't have years, but with the research inside, I can become immortal. I'll also have my revenge on Marissa, HOPE, and you. I'll be the one giving orders."

The last line was almost as an afterthought. I wondered if A understood just how much he was shaming himself and his creator (as well as probably the man he was cloned from), acting like a toy soldier who couldn't deal with the choices real life offered him. It made me pity him, because he'd constructed this elaborate fantasy in his head that service to the Society had been a privilege as well as an honor instead of forced labor. We were cannon fodder designed to live and die to make rich men richer.

But none of that was nearly as important as the fact that, holy shit, A actually believed Karma Corp had cracked the code for nanotherapy. I understood that kind of desperation and belief. I'd encountered it numerous times when I'd sniped bandits trying to break into refugee camps or dealt with people who sincerely believed it was the apocalypse because that would mean Jesus was about to return.

I didn't know how sick A was since I'd only seen him on the computer screen before and now with a digital avatar, but it was possible he was on his last legs technologically speaking. Delphi had managed to stabilize our cybernetics' breakdown years ago, but if what A was saying was true, he had never found something similar. He thought the Black Dossier had a panacea that would save him and was going to be enraged beyond all reason if I revealed there was no hope for him.

"All right," I said, taking a deep breath. "I'll give you what you want."

A looked at me with hate in his eyes, and I recognized now, also envy. I'd managed to spend the last fifteen years, in his eyes at least, sweet and pretty while he'd been slowly falling apart.

The fact that he was the better assassin—if you didn't mind collateral damage, at least (and the Society never had)—made it all the more ironic. "Yes, G, you will give me what I want."

"I'll do it when you let me go," I said simply.

A lifted the flame in his hands up as if to throw it at me.

"Tick-tock, A," I said, staring at him. "You're going to do what I say, or you're not going to get your prize."

A clenched his fist and extinguished the flame. "What else do you want? I know you, G, you're always playing an angle."

It occurred to me A didn't know me at all. We hadn't been friends in the Society, only worked that one mission together, and hadn't been in contact for a decade and a half. He'd built an entire mythology around me while I hadn't thought about him in years. Still, a part of me was sympathetic to him. He'd been created by the Society just the same as I had been, only he'd gone full Stockholm Syndrome and been left a shell of his former self once we'd ended the International Refugee Society. Then I remembered that most of the other Letters hadn't been monsters and lost that sympathy.

Fuck this guy and his fire tricks.

I played for time. "I want the person you're keeping hostage. I know she's not Marissa, but she might be someone useful."

"Wait, what?" A asked.

Dammit, I'd overestimated his intelligence. "You really thought it would be that easy?"

"What are you saying," A said, grabbing me again.

This time, he wrapped his hands around my neck and began squeezing. I'd overplayed my hand and saw nothing remotely intelligible behind A's eyes. They were full of fury and insanity, perhaps brought about by a memory of a murder long ago. I tried to speak to calm him down, mutter that he was potentially destroying the Black Dossier (whether it was true or not), but nothing could escape my lips.

Then it was over.

A disappeared along with the empty void where the library had been, and I bolted up from where I was lying.

Someone had logged me out.

Only I wasn't back at Delphi's party.

CHAPTER SEVENTEEN

I woke up with my hands, arms, and legs shaking from the memory of being burned alive by A in the simulation. I needed a second to catch my breath as my body covered itself in sweat, one of the stranger qualities of a body that was 100 percent synthetic and didn't need to be cooled down in order to function. I was wearing my pants, but someone had removed my shirt, tie, and jacket to leave me bare-chested.

Staring at my right hand, I flexed it a few times to make sure my body still functioned while thinking back to what I'd downloaded with Dave's help. Much to my relief, I found myself possessed of an enormous amount of data on topics ranging from the nanotherapy scam to the fact that the CEO of Halifax-Montenegro was in an incestuous relationship with her son.

The Black Dossier was mine.

My environment was one of the luxury guest rooms in Delphi's tower, with an emperor-sized bed, a chandelier, a digital fireplace that produced actual heat, and a retro-antique style that was becoming all the rage among those few people rich enough to afford it. I was lying on the bed with its shimmer-silk covers and white canopy. There was no sign of either Claire—I should think of her as Marissa now—or Rosario. Thankfully, there was no sign of A either.

"Hello, Delphi?" I called, looking around.

No answer. That wasn't good. If we were still in Delphi's skyscraper, then she should have been wired to every room the same way she was in the Atlas buildings. Instead, there was no sign of her, and that made me wonder if someone had managed to kill her. There was also my fear I was trapped in an *Inception* situation. That I wasn't actually awake but just in another layer of the Matrix (man, we needed to rename that to something more copyright friendly).

"Okay, if this is the Matrix, then I want a cold beer and a beautiful redhead right now," I said.

"Claire" opened the door seconds later. "Case, are you awake?"

"Do you have a beer?" I asked.

"Excuse me?" she asked.

"Eh, the results are inconclusive then," I said. "More experimentation will be required."

She turned her head to look at me sideways. It was at that moment I cursed myself because I recognized the movement and body language of the person I'd once loved. It was Marissa all right, wearing a Shell body and one I'd completely missed because I hadn't looked deeper than the surface level.

It made me wonder where the original Claire was and what she might have done to her. A part of me, despite all the betrayals, held out hope that Marissa hadn't done anything. She wasn't a monster; she was just a liar and a manipulator. I was also the fool who'd continually fallen for her lies no matter how many times she'd picked me up. It was understandable when I'd been just a five-year-old with an adult's mind, but at twenty? I was just stupid.

"Are you okay?" Marissa asked, walking up to the side of the bed. It was within striking distance, but I didn't move yet.

"What happened to Rosario and Delphi? Did you notice anything happening while I was decrypting your data?" I asked.

"Rosario left," Marissa said, lying. I knew all her ticks now. "She took her payment and hopefully we won't have to see her again. So the data is decrypted? Everything is all right?"

"Delphi," I repeated.

Marissa blinked with Claire's eyes as if realizing she still had to put on a front with me. "We're in a blind spot to Delphi's programming. Since A has somehow gotten the ability to hide his presence from her, we had to figure she's been hacked somehow. Perhaps backdoors from her days as the Society's pet AI

This is a good place to hide until we can figure out a way to strike at A directly."

I was impressed with the sheer boldness of the lie and wondered how much truth she'd managed to put into it. Delphi had been programmed by the Society to be obedient, but she'd gradually worked her way around the loopholes in her commands to achieve freedom. Even today, though, there were parameters she still had to work within. Had Delphi's positive reaction to HOPE been because Marissa had access to her core programming? No, that was ridiculous. If she had access to Delphi's power, then she'd rule the world rather than work against it.

"I understand," I said, taking a deep breath.

"Do you have the information?" Marissa asked, her voice a little more desperate.

"Of course," I said, whispering. "Kiss me."

Marissa breathed a sigh of relief and leaned in to embrace me. I took her in my arms, pressed my lips against her, then grabbed her in a chokehold before disarming her. I grabbed her gun when she reached for it and tossed it to one side.

"Goddammit, G," Marissa muttered as I squeezed tightly. She dug her fingernails into my pants leg, tight enough to draw blood, but mostly just fidgeted in my grip.

"Case," I said, whispering. "You gave me that name, after all."

Marissa chuckled. "When did you figure it out?"

"Not soon enough," I said softly.

"You realize my body is a Shell, right?" Marissa said. "You can't strangle me."

"It's Claire's body," I said, aware she was testing me. "Which means it's not a high-quality combat Shell. No, I can't strangle you, but I'm fully capable of tearing your head clean off."

Marissa stopped struggling. "You wouldn't do that."

"My father thought that. You've also given me precious little reason to not kill you right now."

"I know you feel betrayed—"

"Betrayal does that." I admit, I owed *Buffy the Vampire Slayer* for that zinger.

Marissa rolled her eyes. "Do you really have the information?"

"Are you serious?" I asked, shaking my head before pulling her onto the bed. "Okay, let's have a conversation, and depending on your answers, then we'll go from there. I was just burned alive by A in your cyberworld, so I'm not in a good mood."

Marissa took a deep breath. "You aren't going to be able to tell anything by asking me questions—I've been with lie detectors far more capable than you."

"You leave that to me."

"Are you going to kill me no matter what?" Marissa asked.

"Answer the questions."

I was in a bad negotiating position because Marissa knew me too well. My friendship with Lucita had begun with the two of us trying to kill one another. I'd also spared quite a few other people whom I probably should have killed but couldn't bring myself to execute. Most of them had been women like Marissa or Lucita. It wasn't sexism, per se, because I'd fought some truly deadly and dangerous women over the years.

It was the fact that those women had been people I'd cared for, and I had difficulty bringing myself to harm them. I had so few connections that when I was double-crossed by someone I knew, it was hard to sever that connection. It's what had led to me sparing Persephone despite my words to A, and what had helped the few Letters I'd recruited live when the world might have been better off without all of us. I wonder what it said about me that I found it strange that it was easier for me to kill strangers. Had I really been that poorly socialized? Oh right, I'd been socialized by implanted memories and hypnosis. Never mind.

"I'll answer your questions," Marissa said, her voice low. "You know I didn't want to—"

"Stop it," I said. "I know you're a scorpion. I took you across the river anyway because I thought I could avoid being stung. You fooled me because you're disguised as someone else, not because I ever trusted you after your first betrayal."

Marissa didn't respond for a moment. I was glad. I didn't want her getting any ideas I was still wrapped around her finger.

"Where is Rosario?" I asked.

"Drugged in the bathtub," Marissa said. "I have a neurotoxin designed to incapacitate without killing hidden in injectors underneath my fingernails."

"Why not try it on me?" I asked.

"I did," Marissa muttered. "It doesn't seem to work on Letters."

"Good," I said, checking myself to see if I felt any different. Thankfully, I didn't. The new toxin-resistant bloodstream I'd had installed a couple of years ago seemed to be working. "What about Delphi?"

"I wasn't lying about the blind spots in her programming," Marissa said, looking up at me with Claire's eyes. "She's almost stupidly supportive of me and my decisions even if I can't press too hard without breaking her. I asked her to turn off the cameras and leave us alone here, which she did."

"Another reason why you were able to gather so much blackmail material about the corporations," I said dryly.

"Not enough to change anything," Marissa said, her voice low. "Enough to save some lives. You sided with us, not because of our past ties, but because you believed in HOPE I don't care what you say, I believe you are fundamentally a good man."

"I believe, fundamentally, I am not," I said. I paused. "I know about A working for you. How many people has he killed for you."

"More than you," Marissa replied. "He's a blunt instrument."

"How blunt?"

Marissa didn't speak. "Blunt enough there's perhaps a better claim we're a group of terrorists than even the corporations know."

"Is it worth it?"

"You tell me."

I lowered my voice. "He says you gave me a pearl beyond price. That's the reason he decided to betray you and take the Black Dossier. Do you know what he's talking about?"

"Peace?" Marissa said.

"Very funny," I said, unamused.

"I have a suspicion but no concrete proof," Marissa said.

I pulled around her neck a bit. "No more lies."

"Lies are just ways of interpreting events," Marissa replied.

"They're stories, and all of human history is one great big lie resting around a handful of facts."

"I had no idea you were such a philosopher."

"Do you have the Black Dossier?" Marissa asked. "I had no idea you were going to take it from me, but it's absent from my head now. A million dirty little secrets and the only thing protecting HOPE from being destroyed outright."

"Yes," I said, giving away information I should have just kept to myself. "I have all your leverage."

"Will you give it back?"

"No," I replied. "I will, however, make sure Karma Corp doesn't enact their plan."

This felt less like I was involved in a multi-faceted conspiracy than I was caught between a bunch of angry teenagers who were all pathological liars. "Did you really think I wouldn't work with you against Karma Corp? You could have just come to me and asked for my help decrypting the data."

"You would have wanted access to the dossier's files," Marissa said. "You can only keep a secret between three people if two of them are dead."

I wondered if that was a threat. "Which is why A wanted me to kill Karma Corp's CEO. After HOPE was blamed for it, it would take you and me off the board. He'd let the world know I was responsible for the assassination and bring the wrath of the Corporate Council down on us all. He'd then kill you, or who he assumed was you, in his fake Marissa. A would then take the nanotherapy technology and cure himself before either ransoming it back to Karma Corp or leaving it as his own personal ace in the hole."

"Except it doesn't work," Marissa said, looking frustrated. I didn't blame her. The actual corporate conspiracy was fairly straightforward while all the twists and turns were the result of a colossal misunderstanding. "I kept that detail from him when I shouldn't have."

"You also kept him from the cure Delphi gave me and the other Letters. I would have given it to him."

"Which is why I did it," Marissa replied. "There's not many ways a woman like me can control a man like A."

I didn't ask the question that popped into my head.

"No," Marissa said. "I don't know who programmed it into his head, but he'd lose all respect for me as a leader if I had sex with him. In fact, that's part of the reason why he turned against me in the first place—he found out about a past relationship continuing."

"It didn't," I said, taking a deep breath.

Or had it? That led to the next question. The most pressing one. "Who is it he has hostage?"

"Claire," Marissa replied. "We switched cyberbrains before this mission. I suppose you could say it worked in preventing me from being captured. I had another body double, but A managed to persuade her to work with him instead of me."

"Perhaps he told her what kind of person you were," I said.

Marissa grimaced. "That would do it. The only people who stay loyal to me after long are ones I leave no choice—or you and Claire."

"My heart bleeds for you. Truly."

So, Claire was alive and still working for HOPE despite the deception with her dead lover. Claire was also in the hands of A, which meant I had to go track him down and get her back. There was something wrong, something vile going on here, and it was more a matter of instinct than a matter of facts.

"You're lying," I said, simply.

"I'm not," Marissa said, somehow pulling away from my grip. Perhaps it was because she knew I wouldn't harm her.

At least until I had my answers.

"Then you're holding something back," I said, staring at her. "What is it?"

Marissa smirked as if she knew she had me. "I'll tell you when we get this resolved. It's nothing—"

"What will I find when I search the Black Dossier for information on Claire?" I asked, wondering if Marissa knew how badly she was outmaneuvered here. Persephone had the good sense to know when the jig was up, but my ex seemed incapable of seeing just how badly things had deteriorated.

Marissa looked like I'd shot her in the chest. It was an expression I'd waited to see with her for a decade and a half.

I stared at her. "I saved you from my brother, Marissa. You owe me more than this. If not for me, you and your family would have been his slaves for life."

"I don't have a family anymore, G," Marissa said, her words carrying the first genuine bit of remorse I'd probably ever heard from her. "My sisters and nieces all died in the eruption. I killed, lied, betrayed, and murdered for them, but it was all for nothing. You have a far bigger family than I have now, and you keep everyone at a distance. You could have married Claire and had a family with her too. She would have been perfect for you."

Her words were confusing until they made it all click into place. I stared at her. "No."

Marissa didn't respond. "I needed you, G. I needed an agent who had a conscience and could be trusted, but that wasn't possible with what happened between us. It cost a fortune to get Claire from Karma Corp, but Delphi had the plans that she turned over to them to continue the project. They haven't gotten it perfected because they lack Doctor Gordon's skill, but they came close enough."

"Mother fucker," I said, the words almost a whisper. "Claire is a Letter. One you reprogrammed to think was a person."

Marissa closed her eyes. "One I programmed to love you and be loved by you in return."

I checked the files for information about her and found Claire Morris had died during the refugee crisis. Claire had been imprisoned by the United States government for disobeying orders and ended up volunteering for a Karma Corp experiment which she hadn't survived.

The Numbers were one hundred soldiers meant to replace the Letters, and she was 63. I'd never even met the real Claire Morris, but her memories had been preserved in a weapon Marissa had pointed at her enemies. Her daughter was real, but designed for the same purpose Claire had been for me. To give us something to lose.

I was too stunned to respond.

That was when Marissa went for a micro-shock prod hidden in her lower pants pocket.

CHAPTER EIGHTEEN

Marissa may have had the cybernetically enhanced body of a soldier, but she was still a console jockey at heart. She was a natural officer, moving people across the chessboard of life, but strictly armchair military. As such, it didn't take that much effort to grab the shock prod from her. The fact she tried to bite my arm, then go for her gun showed her as not having kept up with her combat practice either.

So I jabbed her in the back with her own shock prod.

"Son of a bitch," Marissa said, falling to her knees before I grabbed her by the arm.

"I'm really sorry about this," I muttered. "This is going to hurt."

"Fuck off," Marissa said, growling.

I jabbed her again in the heart, this time with the shock prod at full power. They were designed to disable cyborgs and would kill a normal human being, but I had no doubt she'd survive it—though at this point, I only half cared.

Marissa's body jolted up and down and her eyes rolled into the back of her head. I held the prod to her chest perhaps longer than I should have, but I wanted to make absolutely sure she was disabled, so I didn't have to *kill* her. When she collapsed on the ground, I checked to see if her body was still breathing since Shell hearts didn't often have pulses.

She was.

Patting her down, I found she had some carbon-fiber hand-cuffs, which I tied to her wrists and then destroyed their electronic lock. I looked around for my shirt, tie, and jacket, which I found in a nearby closet. I found Marissa had set up a jammer nearby and turned that off before sending a private message to Atlas Security to pick up a "package" here.

I also left a note to keep Marissa out of Delphi's "sight" and to keep her in a safe house away from the infonet and under cyber-interference before turning her jammer back on. I didn't know what I was going to do with her after this was resolved, but that was a problem I could safely kick down the road.

Even if I knew I needed to kill her.

Shaking that thought from my mind, I headed to the guest room's bath and saw Rosario lying in the bathtub, drooling. Marissa had drugged her, and she looked adorably nonthreatening the way she was now.

"Let's hope the toxin isn't too strong," I muttered, turning on the shower above her.

"Fuck!" Rosario said, waving her hands across her face.

The hacker passed out three more times before I managed to get her to activate an implant in her liver designed to help her pass recreational drugs through her system quicker. She ended up having to throw her underwear away and threw up twice before the aftereffects of Marissa's toxin passed.

"I hate you," Rosario muttered, her exceptionally queasy face hovering over the toilet.

"I didn't do it," I said, shrugging.

"No," Rosario said, growling. "The *brujah* in the other room did."

I nodded. "I've got her disabled, though. There's a lot more going on, though. Stuff I'm going to need your help with."

Rosario spat in the toilet bowl one last time. "You probably saved me from dying there, so I'm willing to help. For now."

"Nanotherapy doesn't work," I said, pausing. "At all."

Rosario paused over the toilet. "What?"

"It's a scam," I said, sighing. "A placebo they're going to sell that's actually quite unhealthy, so not really a placebo at all. More like snake oil, only the snake oil is cyanide."

"That's a shitty plan," Rosario said.

"I know!" I said, staring at her. "The panda thought it actually had a chance of working, though."

Rosario blinked a few times before nodding. "Well, if the

panda said it was okay then I guess I'm wrong."

I offered her a hand to help her up. "I contacted Atlas Security, and they should be here to help with Marissa soon."

Rosario's eyes widened before she slapped my hand out of the way. "You idiot!"

"What?" I asked, blinking.

"A is monitoring your cyberbrain!" Rosario said, growling. "All your communications in and out go to him first! I saw it when I was decrypting the data in Marissa's mind."

I wondered when she'd figured out Claire was an imposter.

"Fuck," I said, immediately heading out the bathroom door. "We need to get out of here then."

To what was only half a surprise, I saw Marissa wasn't where I'd left her on the floor. Somehow, my former assistant had managed to escape and leave no trace. That was far from my most present concern, however. I could hear heavy metal boots moving down the hall I was presently in.

"Goddammit," I muttered.

As Rosario came out the door, I grabbed her hand and threw her to the floor, seeking refuge down there myself as I saw several armored boots through the crack underneath the door. What followed was a high-pitched ear-blasting noise of assault rifle fire as the soldiers outside fired through the doors indiscriminately, not even bothering to check whether we were on the other side. It tore through the bed behind us as well as the wall and emptied a probably a hundred bolts into the door.

I reached into my pocket and pulled out a pen, clicked it, and hurled it in their direction. "Die, motherfuckers!"

"Grenade!" they shouted, turning on each other and going to one side.

I grabbed Rosario off the ground, pulled out my pistol, hit the button for explosive rounds, and shot the windows. They shattered as the soldiers on the ground realized I hadn't actually thrown a pen-sized grenade at them. I shot the jammer on the table before running to the window, carrying Rosario in my arms like a parcel. I sent out a last-ditch comm call and hoped it didn't lead to my death.

"What the hell are you doing?" Rosario shouted.

"Something really stupid!" I shouted.

"Leave me out of it!" Rosario said before screaming as we leapt out of the window into the mid-air of the rainy Chicago night beyond.

Two hundred stories up.

"Shit!" Rosario shouted.

I'd leapt out of the window with a straight run for the purpose of moving at a horizontal angle for as long as humanly possible before starting a descent. It was about three seconds long. That might not seem too long but was a tremendous advantage when you were trying to minimize the impact of your descent.

Mind you, at two hundred stories, even a person who was fully cybernetic was so much road pizza, and I couldn't even see the ground through the darkness of the night mixed with the heavy cloud cover that seemed eternal in the new world. Instead, all I saw were the tiny beacons of light and the holograms blinking around the street-level entrance below.

"I fucking hate—" Rosario tried to shout, right before my legs buckled under me as E's air car zoomed up underneath us and I caved a massive dent into its roof. The vehicle's automatic driver had managed to start it and bolt its way up here thanks to my command. I directed it remotely before commanding it to open the doors. I shoved Rosario through the passenger side and slipped myself into the driver's seat.

"Welcome to G Air," I said, mentally commanding the doors to shut before switching the car to manual. "Please fasten your seatbelts."

Rosario's next words were an incoherent mumble.

"Oh, come on, that was an awesome rescue!" I said, turning the car downward as I tried to figure out where to go to stay away from my usual contacts. Delphi was the person I tended to rely on in these sorts of situations, but she couldn't be trusted given what Marissa claimed. I needed to go off the net, so I disabled my infolink. "Listen, Rosario, if you know any good places where we can take a moment—"

Rosario threw up again, this time on the floor beneath her legs.

"Okay, maybe it was a bit bumpy," I muttered. "But come on,

admit it, the part with the fake grenade was awesome!"

"I hate you," Rosario said, holding her hands against the dashboard to steady herself. "Like, more than I thought was possible."

"You know, for someone who has an artificial body, you'd think you'd have less trouble being poisoned," I muttered.

"It's designed to simulate a human body better than a human body," Rosario said.

"Well, mine isn't, and it works great," I said, shrugging.

"Oh?" Rosario asked as if making innuendo, then coughed and shook her head. It wasn't like either of us were in the mood for banter anyway.

"I repeat my earlier question," I said. "Because otherwise, I'm going to just ditch this car and steal another one, then drive around until I think of something to do about my current situation."

"Which is?" Rosario asked.

"Screwed," I said, sighing. I gave her the highlights of what was going on.

"Remind me to never help you again," Rosario said.

"Hey, you got the information you wanted," I asked.

"I wanted the secret of nanotherapy," Rosario paused. "Which I suppose I have, but the secret I wanted was how to make it work."

"Be careful what you wish for because glass houses are broken with sticks and stones," I replied before turning on a set of light indie rock.

Rosario immediately turned it off. "Down. Now."

I took us downward, and the air car descended into the depths of the Chicago refugee zone. It was an enormous walled city within the walled city of the Chicago arcology. Before it was demolished in 1993 for the crime of existing, the famous Kowloon Palace of Hong Kong had been a similar anarchic hellhole run by criminals or local warlords. It had been five years since the government had set up the system for transforming the refugee zones into proper communities and not a damn bit of progress had been made.

Food and supplies were distributed to the locations within,

and they were more or less left alone. The biggest change from the refugee centers of old were the "temporary houses" being made of concrete and metal rather than wood. Armed guards kept people from leaving without visitor's passes and society carried on within. I didn't like going inside them because they were a sign of just how badly Atlas had failed to solve the crisis.

The arcologies were successes, by some stretch of the word, but they didn't have nearly enough room for the millions living there. The people couldn't move out to other cities either, because all the food and resources of the United States was controlled by the government. If you didn't have money to buy food—and why would you live in a refugee zone if you did—then you needed to go where it was distributed.

"Here?" I asked, wondering why she thought this was a safer place.

"I have friends here," Rosario said, looking out the shattered back window behind us. "I don't want to be here any longer than necessary. Blackbriar troopers are idiots, but even they won't have problems following us if we stay in the air."

"You think they were Blackbriar?" I asked, suspecting I might have gained their ire by killing some of them during our "fake" shootout.

"I recognized their uniforms. Didn't you?"

"Too busy plotting our awesome escape," I said, smirking.

"Stop congratulating yourself. It wasn't that cool."

"It was pretty damn cool."

Most of old Chicago had been demolished, and the few remnants tended to be historical locations or graveyards. The exception was the refugee zones, where office buildings, suburbs, and so on had been repurposed to house mass quantities of people. These included skyscrapers and office buildings that had once been places of business but were now slums.

But as William Gibson said, the street finds its own uses for things. Empty gas stations had been converted into shops, people bartered where they couldn't buy, and there were many ways around the walls when you wanted to bring back things that could help your loved ones. I'd been to the refugee zones of every arcology, and they were places where America had truly become a melting pot.

People often spoke something less like English and more like a mishmash of every group that had come to America to help with the rebuilding only to get trapped when their governments shut the doors on them. Black Technology, while rarer here, still existed and was repurposed to provide what couldn't be acquired through other means.

Sitting us down on top of what was once a bank, I noticed the place was still bustling with life despite how badly it was overcrowded and underequipped. People decorated their homes with Christmas lights, Chinese lanterns, and even the occasional burning drum to give the place illumination despite its removal from the "real" city. I noticed numerous bars and strip clubs built on the top of buildings as well, linked together by bridges of welded scrap metal and crude cable cars. Even the lost and the damned, especially the lost and the damned, needed a way to escape their troubles.

"Here?" I asked. This building looked like a landing pad. I suspected the car would be stripped bare by morning, but I didn't mind since it wasn't my car. E was going to have a fit, though.

Rosario nodded. "Yes, here is fine. We're just a couple of blocks away from Friday's."

"Who is Friday?" I asked.

"Not a who but a what," Rosario said, taking a deep breath. "Friday's is one of the Turing Society's fronts in this region. All the arcologies have them: The Moon is a Harsh Mistress, Troopers, Strange Land—"

"Ah, they're named after Heinlein novels," I said.

"No shit," Rosario said, rolling her eyes.

I put the vehicle in park, then stepped out of it. "Why does the Turing Society want to work out of here?"

"It's very hard to monitor this place," Rosario said. "They have birds of prey trained to take out drones, and the cloud cover here is extra harsh to prevent satellite readings. Plus, well, there's a lot of jammers here."

I was suddenly glad we were here. "Well, thanks for taking me here."

"Well don't thank me yet," Rosario said. "They might kill you. They don't like corporates down here."

Ah. Well. "Thanks for the warning then."

"It's not for your sake, it was for Barbara's."

Wait, what?

CHAPTER NINETEEN

I stopped cold in my tracks. "Barbara?"

"Shit," Rosario cursed under her breath. "I shouldn't have mentioned that."

"There's a lot of Barbaras in the world," I said, knowing exactly who she meant.

"Your daughter," Rosario said, pausing as the two of us stood on a scrap metal bridge. "Barbara Gordon."

I smirked, still finding it amusing her mother had named her after Batgirl. Then the cold and unpleasant reality of my life reminded me that our relationship was strictly academic. "I don't have a daughter. Daniel Gordon was her father."

For the first five years of my life, I'd been haunted by visions of a young girl and her mother. I'd thought they were my wife and child, people I'd caught hazy glimpses of in my dreams or during moments of great stress. The truth was, in fact, they were just flash fragments of Daniel Gordon's memories that had been used as the basis of my consciousness.

Even then, they'd been largely programmed in from scrapbooks and video feeds, since the technology hadn't been there to copy memories perfectly yet. It was a good thing too, since Daniel Gordon hadn't loved his wife and child—they'd been tools to help him disguise his homicidal and sadistic tendencies.

"Daniel Gordon was a monster," Rosario said. "His daughter knows what kind of person he was."

"I'm sorry for that," I said, having hoped she'd never learn the secret of the man I'd been cloned from.

"Why?" Rosario said, looking up. "If you're not her father."

"Her uncle perhaps," I said. "Her uncle the toaster."

Rosario laughed. "She knows you're responsible for the money and protection she received during the Big Smokey eruption and refugee crisis."

"How did she find that out?" I asked.

"Time," Rosario said. "Also, she's a genius. Her grandmother also helped her once she was tracked down."

"She's a member of the Turing Society?" I asked, a little disappointed.

"Yes," Rosario said. "She's the physical education instructor for the second children."

I stared at her. "She's a gym teacher?"

"Did you think all of us were geniuses?" Rosario asked.

"Yes?" I suggested.

Rosario laughed. "I suspect she may have been the beneficiary of a bit of nepotism. I love her, though."

I blinked.

Rosario looked surprised. "You didn't know she was a lesbian."

"No," I said. "I haven't been keeping up on her private life. I felt bad enough giving her help through shell companies and scholarships. The only person I've really kept up with was her mother. She's an orthodontist living in a gated community now with two husbands and three more kids."

"Paid for by you through a contest she didn't even enter," Rosario said, snorting. "Is my girlfriend's sexuality a problem?"

"It's the 2040s, not the 1940s," I said, simply. "I'm just happy she's found someone to be happy with. Assuming you're serious."

Rosario lifted her eyebrow. "Do I have to ask your permission?"

"Clearly," I said, crossing my arms.

Rosario shook her head. "We are close, close enough I came here to help investigate you on behalf of her—and help when Delphi asked."

"Investigate me?" I asked.

"You do not see why your daughter, for that is how she sees herself, would want to know you? Why you didn't contact her after all these years?"

I turned my head and started walking toward a distant nightclub with a neon sign that read "Friday's". "I didn't contact her because I'm not her father. I didn't contact her because I'm a murderer, a liar, and a thief. I didn't contact her because—"

"You were scared?" Rosario asked.

"Let's not make this an emotional moment," I said, sighing. "Especially through an intermediary."

Rosario looked down. "As you wish. If you don't want to meet her, then I understand."

I paused. "Right now, there's a bunch of mercenaries chasing us, an insane cyborg who is a far better killer than I am is after me, and we're possessed of information that could potentially bring down the world's largest megacorporation. Priorities."

"I see," Rosario said. "What are you going to do with the information?"

"I don't know," I said softly.

"You don't know?" Rosario asked, surprised.

The two of us passed a group of kids in overalls who had shaved their heads and were possessed of bottom-level cybernetics, tubes coming out of their heads that were attached to cell phones. If it was a fashion statement, it was a grotesque one. They were all three smoking, and one of them pulled out a switchblade before he saw my gun. The other two shook their heads at him before they walked away. Not one of them could have been over the age of thirteen.

Survival by any means necessary was a way of life in the refugee zones, and no matter how many people got pulled out of their doubled-up cramped homes—I think I saw several shipping crates that had been turned into apartments—I guessed there were two more people who were born.

"I don't know," I replied to Rosario. "This isn't the kind of story where the idealistic hero reveals the corrupt corporate conspiracy, the bad guys are brought down, and everyone goes out for drinks afterward. The Black Dossier is collateral, and not just for the future victims of Karma Corp, but for the people who depend on it being used as leverage."

"You want to take over HOPE now?"

"Fuck no, I don't want to take over HOPE now. That takes

a particular brand of asshole, and I'm not in the business of blackmailing people to get what I want," I replied, passing by a woman with four arms, all of them cybernetic, and a wig that covered a virtual reality interface. She was barely clothed and followed by a plastic-sheen-skinned man who was wearing only a Speedo.

"So, you'll kill people but not use their dirty secrets against them," Rosario said.

"There's child porn in here," I said, hissing my disgust at some of the things I knew were in the Black Dossier. Quite a bit that I'd never suspected Marissa had sat on. "People who get away with it in exchange for payouts that keep children from starving."

Rosario paused in mid-step. "Marissa—"

"I dunno," I said, pausing. "Could be faked. Something cooked up to blackmail people who didn't have any secrets worth paying up over. Marissa is a good enough hacker to make that kind of shit without getting involved in human trafficking. It could also be she's the kind of person who can make the choice. I'm not. There's also Claire."

"The real Claire?" Rosario asked.

I nodded, continuing to walk. "I'm not sure what I'd be willing to trade to make sure she survives."

"You'd turn over the Black Dossier?" Rosario asked. "To A?"

"Or Marissa," I said. "Whoever gets her safely back."

"You'd be willing to sacrifice the world for those close to you?" Rosario said.

"The world will roll on no matter what happens," I said. "Which is why someone has to look after individuals. I already saved the world once, and it didn't work out so well."

I was still reeling from the revelation that Claire was a bioroid. It was such a shocking thought I didn't know how to deal with it. It almost overshadowed the horrifying realization that the Letters weren't alone anymore. These Numbers were potentially a game changer for the development of humankind because they signified Karma Corp had cracked Daniel Gordon's research. Hell, they'd cracked it almost a decade ago. It surprised me they weren't marketing bioroids on the street.

Thinking about it, I couldn't help but wonder if this was the pearl without price that A had mentioned. He wasn't the kind of guy who cared about love or companionship, but if Marissa had been involved in making these Numbers, then it meant she'd given our "race" (for lack of a better term) a future. For an ego-maniac like A, who was looking to make the transition from slave to master, it made perfect sense.

I passed a graffiti-covered wall with a surprisingly beautiful artistic image of an angel, wings burning as it fell from Heaven over a model of Chicago's arcology. Some assholes had written vulgarities on the front of it, covering up the art, but that was to be expected in a place like this.

"So, what do you think I should do?" I asked, as we reached the part of town that contained Friday's.

Friday's was built into the side of a heavily damaged church. A metal catwalk led through one of the stained-glass windows that had been turned into a doorway, forming a neon-sign-illuminated entrance. The pulse of New Mind techno-music poured out of the place while a bouncer kept people out with a pair of sentry units. The line stretched out down the walkway, but Rosario ignored it, pushing past me. I followed, and there were only a few complaints from the people who were trying to get in.

"What? Me?" Rosario asked, elbowing a couple with electric blue hair and more piercings than I thought possible. It was a good look.

"Yeah, if I wanted the opinion of someone who isn't a psychopath."

"You're not a psychopath, Case," Rosario said.

"Why's that?"

"Psychopaths wouldn't ask," Rosario said.

That wasn't quite accurate, and there were plenty of people who were just cold blooded and not evil, but that was Hollywood for you. You know, back when there was a Hollywood outside of branding.

"Indulge me."

Rosario reached the bouncer, pulled out a card, and waved it at him. He gestured for her to come in, and I followed. At the same time, in the distance, a pair of Blackbriar VLO units came over where our car had landed and started scanning the area with hologram-enhanced spotlights. We'd gotten inside just in time. Presumably, even they would hesitate to go house to house in a district they didn't control. Unless they just decided to bomb the place.

The interior of Friday's surprised me by being decorated in a zeerust fashion of classic sci-fi mixed with a smattering of cyberpunk from the eighties (or maybe that was just the fact the world had become cyberpunk, as Lucita had predicted twenty years ago). The church had a large replica of the rocket from Beneath the Planet of the Apes in the center of the chamber, while spiraling staircases went down past three levels of club-goers enjoying drinks or engaged in various sexual acts.

The walls had posters for *Day of the Triffids*, *Star Wars*, *Flash Gordon*, and some modern-day works that still put out collectible paper posters like *Technomancer: To Beat the Devil*, *Prime Suspects: A Clone Detective Mystery*, *The Immorality Clause*, and *Lucifer's Star*. The latter reminded me of a strange part of my life where I'd ended up fighting in an island tournament with an eclectic cast of misfits.

The style of clothing was a mixture of DIY, cyberpunk, Goth, and a few things I had no words for. Called "niteware," people wore hand-me-down clothes they'd altered with spikes, light-lines, and neon paint. The people had taken to barcode or number-based art tattoos, piercings, and dreadlocks or braids on both sexes. Makeup came in the form of soot, paint, grease, and other things found in abundance in the refugee zones. I stuck out like a sore thumb and would have been even more so if not for the fact I'd been run ragged with damage to my suit.

"This way," Rosario said, gesturing to a glass and welded metal elevator just to the side of the top balcony, which she entered using the card.

I followed, letting the door shut behind me.

"So, no advice?" I asked as the elevator lowered itself to the bottom of the club.

"You should do what helps the most people," Rosario said, sighing. "Your friend, Claire, is a member of HOPE and believes in their cause. Enough to side with Marissa despite everything she's done."

"She may not have a choice," I said, my voice low. "One of the most terrifying things I found in my research of the Letter program was the fact that you could issue us orders, and we'd rationalize it as our own idea. You could be ordered to kill yourself, only to forget the order, then decide you couldn't live with yourself anymore."

Rosario's eyes widened. "How the hell did you guys ever rebel then?"

"It wasn't used often," I said. I mostly knew it from my studies of the Turing Society's records. They'd caused several of the Letters to break and go insane. They'd just get their memories wiped, then were sent out in new bodies. "In any case, the computers in our brains are constantly evolving. Their controls for us, programmed or otherwise, just moved beyond it."

"Or they still have that power over you," Rosario said.

"No," I said, sighing. "I can't believe that."

"Why?" I asked.

"Then I'd have been Marissa's servant because I was her slave and have no soul," I replied.

"Does anyone have a soul?" Rosario joked.

"Yes," I said, interrupting. "I'm not a materialist. We're more than crude matter."

"*Star Wars*?" Rosario said.

I smirked. "The universe is made of information. We just haven't met the programmer."

Rosario snorted. "Doctor Gordon believes the universe is a holographic simulation. She's the smartest person I know, but I'm inclined to think it is more likely future humanity making us than God."

"Or it's just a silly idea," I said.

"That too," Rosario said.

The elevator didn't stop at the bottom floor of the church but descended into a hole in the ground which led to a basement level, past tubes and wires that showed the facility was hacked into the arcology's power as well as wireless.

The basement of Friday's was a hacker cave full of bean

bags, quantum computers that cost more than the refugee zone around it, more movie posters, a shelf full of genre fiction stolen from a library, and several hackers ambulating about. A bar with its own still was in one corner, tended by a man wearing a Shell in the image of Samuel L. Jackson during his *Pulp Fiction* days. A large industrial assembler, the successor to the 3D printer, was hooked up to a small electric generator and was creating an assault rifle.

"These are my associates," Rosario said, sighing. "You may be surprised but—"

I was too busy staring at one of them. She was a tall woman of mixed Indian, Caucasian, and African American heritage. She was wearing a leather jacket, a Muslim headscarf, and a cybernetic interface. She'd grown up in the past ten years. Though I'd seen images of her as late as two years ago, somehow, she still existed in my mind as the little girl Daniel Gordon had helped raise.

I had no idea how she managed to mix her conversion with the prohibitions of Islam against body defilement but decided to mind my own business. I was much more concerned with the fact that she was seeing me for the first time.

Barbara.

CHAPTER TWENTY

I stared at my—no, Daniel's—daughter.

Niece, I suppose you could say.

Or sister.

Yet, I couldn't help but feel like she was my daughter. Rebecca Gordon had programmed me with the memories of Daniel Gordon taken from film footage, recorded memories from his cyber brain, and data-farming. However, there were staggering holes in the narrative of who her son had been— holes a doting mother had chosen to fill in with the idea of who she'd wanted her son to be.

As a result, I was affected with a deep and overpowering urge to protect as well as care for someone who was related to me only by a quirk of genetics. Not even that, since the grown tissue, muscle, and body parts had been artificially enhanced before mostly being replaced. Still, we were all slaves to our genes and programming.

"It's good to see you," I said. "What a staggering coincidence to meet you here."

"Not so much as you'd think," Barbara said, her voice deeper and huskier than I expected. The result of damage done from "ash syndrome," which had happened to far too many people during the past twenty years.

"Oh?" I asked, unsure what she meant.

"Think," Barbara said. "Try and figure out why I, Rosario, Marissa, Claire, A, and you would all be in the same city at the same time."

It didn't take me long to figure it out before I started cursing.

Barbara smirked.

"She wanted to use you as leverage against your girlfriend in case I didn't pull through," I said, sighing. "Marissa has been maneuvering people on the chessboard the entire time."

"Yes," Barbara said. "Except she's not as smart as she thinks she is. The fact that the foremost expert in robotics, the AI she created, the head of security at the world's largest PMC, and me are all related means the circle is small. Too small for her to adequately control."

"I wonder how many degrees of Kevin Bacon we can track this to," I muttered.

It occurred to me there might be other elements at work here. Rebecca Gordon, Marissa, Delphi, or some other party trying to assemble the best of everyone together with an interconnectedness that could be controlled, contrary to Barbara's statement about smaller groups being harder to maneuver. It could also just be everything I saw as a conspiracy was just the fact that the circles I ran in could all be traced back to my creator/mother being the smartest woman on the planet. Delphi was a copy of her mind, which made everything related to *them* rather than me. Still, it was starting to feel like a comic book, and my family was the Fantastic Four. I needed to talk to Delphi about this.

"Who is Kevin Bacon?" Barbara asked.

I shook my head. "Never mind, it doesn't matter. I'm still confused about how you got all hooked up in this."

"It seemed an appropriate response when I could tell my father was endangered." Barbara looked around. "A lot of us at the Turing Society wanted to help the world. That meant working against the powers that be. Some of us had ties to HOPE, but we didn't approve of its methods."

"Then you probably won't approve of me," I muttered, looking guilty.

Barbara looked down. "You're shorter than I expected."

I raised an eyebrow.

Rosario laughed out loud.

Barbara gestured to two of the hackers around her. The first was a man of mixed Afro-Japanese descent wearing a ball cap, goatee, and dirty purple suit with neon lights along the jacket's interior. He was sitting on the sofa, typing away on a holographic keyboard above his laptop. The second was an overweight man of Korean descent with a green t-shirt and shorts, the t-shirt reading "STAR WARS XII WILL COME OUT."

"These are Malcolm and Jin," Barbara said.

"Hush, no real names," Malcolm said, frowning. He adjusted his ballcap and crossed his arms. "You can call me Existenz."

"No," I said.

Malcolm frowned.

"If you don't mind," Rosario said, taking a deep breath. "I've had a rougher day than usual. I need to shower and change."

Barbara nodded. "Just head to the safe room in the back. I'm sure I have plenty to talk with Agent G about."

"I hate that name," I said softly. "Only some people can use it."

"Oh," Barbara said, awkwardly. "Well—"

"Don't worry about it," I said, realizing the two of us might not have as much to say to each other as we'd like. There was something akin to twenty years building up to this meeting with Barbara, having lost her father before I'd even been born. There was too much build-up for the reality to ever lead to anything good.

Rosario nodded to her girlfriend, gave her a hug, then departed. I suspected she might have kissed her but for the fact she wasn't exactly at her freshest.

"So, what can we do to help you?" Barbara said. "Aside from the fact I can hear through my contacts that Blackbriar is trying to find you. They're going to go from door to door looking for you."

Well, I'd underestimated them. "Is that a problem?"

"Aside from the fact that everyone saw you enter? No," Barbara said, smiling. "You did a lot of good for the world, Case. We'll help you."

"Eh, I don't know about good," I said, feeling uncomfortable. "I'm all sorts of Lawful Evil. I'm trying to work toward Neutral."

"Now there's an obscure joke," Barbara said.

"Dungeons and Dragons, first through third edition. Also, seventh through tenth," Jin said, his voice low and withdrawn as if not entirely there. I wondered if he had a disorder until I realized he, too, had an infonet implant and was surfing as we talked. Not that it eliminated him being on the spectrum.

"I don't want to be a bother," I started to say, now suddenly worried about having endangered not only Barbara but also her friends.

"We expect to be paid, of course," Malcolm said cheerfully. "Also, we understand you have the Black Dossier?"

"Oh, for Chrissakes," I muttered. Did everyone want that damned thing? Oh right, it was worth potentially billions of credits—of course they did.

"Buddhist," Jin replied. "It is the religion most compatible with real-world physics."

"If you don't mind," Barbara interrupted. "I'd like to know how things went from me sending you my girlfriend on the promise from Delphi everything would turn out all right to you ending up on our doorstep with everything having completely gone to shit."

"It's a long story," I said, debating lying before pulling up a folding chair. "Assuming we don't have to evacuate—"

"Blackbriar is already chasing down three false leads and has been called home," Barbara said. "The benefit of Rosario having a door to every megacorporation and most mercenary units."

"Including Atlas?" I asked.

Barbara just smirked. "Please give us a rundown of what happened."

The entire story took about an hour to relate, and by the time it ended, everyone in the club's basement was sitting in front of me, enraptured.

"Holy shit," Malcolm said, blinking. "That is some James Bond bullshit there."

"Pfft," I said, glad my story had entertained them. "I could totally wreck any of the Bonds in a fight."

"You are a cyborg, so that makes sense," Jin replied. "However, given the Bonds routinely defy the laws of physics to achieve their aims, you might be at a loss."

"Hush, Jin," Barbara said, sitting on the armrest of the couch.

"Hushing," Jin said, nodding.

"Even Connery?" Malcolm asked.

"Maybe not Connery," I admitted. "Craig is borderline, but I could take everyone else. I'd feel bad about Dalton, though. He's far underrated."

"You know they're thinking of getting Charlize Theron to be the next Bond. Not bad for a woman in her seventies," Malcolm said. "The wonders of Shells."

"Charlize reminds me of Lucita, and she absolutely could be Bond," I said. "Italian or not."

"Ahem," Barbara interrupted. "So, your sometimes-girl-friend is wearing your ex-girlfriend's body and is a prisoner of A in an undisclosed location. Your ex-girlfriend is wearing your sometimes-girlfriend's body and all sorts of evil—"

"You can just call them Claire and Marissa," I replied.

"It's funnier this way," Barbara said. She paused. "This is in addition to the fact that A wants you to kill the President of Karma Corp's medical division in order to screw over HOPE and get hold of the information that proves nanotherapy is a crock of shit. Except A doesn't know it's a crock of shit. So even if you did turn it over, he'd just kill Claire anyway."

"That's about the size of it," I said, frowning. "Delphi may be compromised by Marissa, and I've stolen the Black Dossier from her, so I can tell you she's probably not happy with me."

"She's not," Jin replied. "Half an hour ago, she transmitted a reward to any HOPE member who could track you down. The number is in seven figures."

I blinked. "None of you are claiming it?"

"What kind of people do you think we are?" Malcolm said, offended. "We're going to totally tell her once you're gone. I mean, that way we get the money and don't have to deal with the indestructible Terminator who could kill us all without breaking a sweat."

"Is Terminator hate speech when referring to bioroids?" Jin asked.

"I meant Barbara," Malcolm said.

Barbara rolled her eyes.

I had to admit, I was starting to like these guys. They

reminded me of, ironically, the fake persona Marissa had created. I liked that they seemed to be idealists but pragmatic sorts. It made me regret never going to visit the Turing Society. Of course, given there were members of HOPE here too, it was possible they were setting me up.

Jin seemed to sense my hesitation. "I should also note Marissa hasn't been the most trusted leader of HOPE in some time."

"She's a dictator," Malcolm said calmly.

"A cheat and a liar," Barbara replied. "She was the Chosen One. She was supposed to destroy the Sith, not join them."

"Revenge of the Sith," Jin said.

"Yeah, I got that," I muttered.

"Just checking," Jin said, nodding. "You were only born twenty years ago, after all."

He had me there.

"I need to decide what to do and whose lives to prioritize."

"We could help you fix Delphi," Malcolm said simply. "BlackCat1 and I are the best hackers in the world. Because we cheat!"

I stared at him. "I'm sure you wouldn't use access to the core source code of an AI to help yourself to unfathomable amounts of information and power."

Malcolm put his hand over his heart. "Never!"

"That's unlikely," Jin said.

Malcolm swatted him.

"Ow," Jin said, rubbing his arm.

"You need to publish all the dirty little secrets the companies have gathered. Expose them and bring them to justice," Barbara said, looking back at the door where Rosario had disappeared to an hour ago. She was taking an awfully long time to get cleaned up.

"That won't work," I said, sighing.

"Why?" Barbara asked.

I paused. "Okay, I feel like the bad guy here for explaining how to blackmail someone."

"You *are* Lawful Evil," Malcolm said, smirking.

"Lawful Evil working on Neutral," I corrected, remembering

my *Dungeons and Dragons* 9th Edition. "Releasing everything will cause a lot of chaos and probably destroy a lot of the people involved, but all they need to do is 'prove' some of the allegations are fake. Then they can taint the whole thing. The public has a limited attention span, like a goldfish, so you can't overwhelm them with too much, or they'll stop paying attention. There's a lot of corroborating evidence tucked away in various storage areas, but the megacorporations are too powerful to go after all at once. That gun, fired once, is a great way to cause massive damage, but the system will recover. It's useful as a threat but not as a strategy. It's better to target your opponents individually so they can't band together or effectively resist. In that situation, the other corporates are unlikely to defend them as going after them will improve their standing, while threatening the system will risk everyone's payday."

I had bad experiences with this very subject, as the United States had several occasions where newspaper reporters had attempted to go after the systemic corruption in the Emergency Government and Corporate Council. They'd tried to expose the ties to the megacorporations as well as the massive organized attempt to subvert democracy. All it had managed to do was get them ruined, since dictatorships didn't have to answer to their people—and that's what the Emergency Government was. In the end, the public had seen numerous people investigated for charges, then turned to learn about Anastasia X's new baby or who was going to play Gary Karkofsky in the next Supervillainy Saga movie. People didn't want to be depressed by the news after the eruption and refugee crisis, so they let themselves be numbed. Rationed dinners and the Infonet were the new order of the day.

"So, what you're saying is, we can blackmail some of the people all of the time or blackmail all of the people once, but not blackmail all of the people forever?" Malcolm said, nodding. "I gotcha."

"I don't," Barbara said, frowning. "We have a silver bullet here. We can use it to slay the werewolf."

"Of society?" I asked. "I'm proud you're the kind of woman who believes that even if I don't agree."

"I was inspired by someone who changed the world by sharing all the Black Technology being hoarded by the government," Barbara said, her voice low and accusatory. "Maybe I shouldn't have been."

Ouch.

"Agent G, Delphi, and S played a significant role in stabilizing the post-eruption world," Jin said. "Atlas filled much of the role the International Refugee Society did before its dissolution, eliminating rogue elements and pressuring corporate as well as national interests to fall in line. He also likely served as a moderating influence on HOPE."

Wow, twice in one day with that accusation. "Uh-huh. That's horrifying."

Jin looked confused. "That was not my intention."

"I'm just trying to think about what I can do to minimize the number of people being hurt, get me out of this unharmed, and save Claire."

"Sometimes you can't do all that," Barbara replied. "Good requires sacrifice."

"And that's why it sucks," I said, not remotely hesitating. "The best thing to do in life is to help others while benefiting yourself with no risk to oneself."

"Wow, he is better than your father by leagues," Malcolm said. "Mine too, for that matter."

Barbara bowed her head in defeat.

"Wait," I said. "I know what to do."

"What? You do?" Barbara asked.

I clasped my hands together. "Oh yes. I'll need your help, though."

"What do we get out of this?" Malcolm asked.

"The Black Dossier," I replied. "Which I assume Rosario is decoding now in the background."

The way their eyes met each other told me everything.

"Damn, you are good," Barbara muttered.

"I'm used to betrayal," I said, smiling. "Thankfully, it was for a good cause."

Barbara lowered her head.

"So, who is up for royally fucking over the bad guys?" I said.

CHAPTER TWENTY-ONE

"Your plan is terrible," Barbara said, sitting in the driver's seat of a flying news van she managed to get past the refugee zone's guards with a fifty-credit bribe. Man, I'd been overpaying. The thing had been previously covered with graffiti and obscenities, but it was now covered in a dirty white coat of paint that made it look like an affiliate of a substation's crack news team coming to film some fluff.

Preparations for my plan had taken almost all the time between the time I relayed it to the Turing Society and Zheng Wei's speech. Still, I was glad I had a plan, even if it was a terrible one. The Society was true to their word and kept me underground—away from Blackbriar the entire time—accepting bribes for false leads the entire time.

The other members of the Turing Society had stayed behind and were going to be helping with my little "stick it to the man" plan from afar. Truth be told, I didn't want them anywhere near the physical part of it—least of all Barbara. Still, she was going to give me a lift, and I appreciated the chance to spend a little more time with her.

"I know that," I said from the passenger seat. "Still, I've taken chances on worse odds."

"And if it doesn't work?" Barbara asked.

"Then it doesn't work," I said, sitting back and looking out the window into the rainy Chicago arcology night. "It's entirely possible the bad guys will win, the good guys will lose, and life will go on the way it always has. It happens all the time."

"Are we the good guys?" Barbara asked.

"I think what you mean to say is, 'Are you the good guy'?" I corrected her. "To which I say, no, but who is?"

"You're a good guy," Barbara said, blinking rapidly. "Maybe not the hero we wanted, but the hero we needed."

"I liked *Batman Begins* and *The Dark Knight*, but honestly couldn't stand the third movie. Populist rhetoric marred by the fact that the protagonist is a billionaire savior."

"Look who has gone to film school," Barbara said, laughing. "Maybe you should make your own movies. Everything put out by the Disney-Fox corporation has been shit."

I'd thought about that, but I had no talent for anything but killing and lying. "Maybe it's the fact I have a digital brain that I see everything as movies. However, I've always loved them. Just about everything I do when I'm not on a mission is watching them or critiquing them."

"Eh, everyone's brain is digital," Barbara said. "All the universe is information."

"How's that go with being a Muslim?" I asked.

"I'm not," Barbara said, frowning.

"Oh," I said, feeling like I'd suddenly crossed a line.

"It belonged to a friend," Barbara said. "I believe in the impermanence of the consciousness and the emptiness of the universe."

"An interesting way to say you don't believe in God or Heaven."

"Why, do you? You weren't programmed to."

"Why not?"

"That's a pretty poor argument."

"I'm not trying to persuade you," I said. "It's not about points of logic or evidence. There's some for and some against. It's about feeling. It's about humbling yourself before the greater universe."

"That's a stupid way of living."

"Is it?" I asked.

Barbara paused. "Maybe not. It's your life."

"What happened to your friend?"

"She died trying to do the right thing," Barbara said. "A fitting epithet."

"Better than most."

"They're all the same to me," Barbara said.

"And yet it affects you to this day," I said.

Barbara didn't answer that. Instead, she asked, "What are you going to do if you manage to pull it off?"

"It?" I asked.

"Viva la revolution," Barbara said, chuckling without laughter. "You manage to screw over Karma Corp, Zheng Wei, end the nanotechnology plague before it kills millions over the next ten years, kill A, and rescue your girlfriend."

"Claire isn't my girlfriend."

"Isn't she?"

I turned to look at my daughter. "I lied to her for the better part of ten years."

"People lie," Barbara said, shrugging. "They also, stupidly, forgive each other. It's not like you didn't forgive Marissa far more than she ever deserved."

"Well, I'm not now," I said.

"Now who is lying?" Barbara asked.

"To answer your question, I guess if I manage to succeed in stopping all this, then I'll go right back to being the CSO unless they fire me. Another day, another credit."

"Sounds lonely."

I wasn't going to lie to her. "It is. I've loved three people in my life. S, Marissa, and Claire, to an extent. I could have loved Claire completely, but I hid things from her and manipulated her as well as kept her at a distance. You don't do that to someone you love."

"Maybe that's all people who are in love do," Barbara said.

I had the suspicion this conversation wasn't about me anymore. "I take it things aren't perfect with Rosario?"

Barbara didn't respond for a minute.

"Ah," I said.

"No 'ah'," Barbara said, shaking her head. "I think she's a wonderful person, extremely devoted, and she shares a lot of my interests—"

"But?" I interrupted.

"I shouldn't have tried to make it something else," Barbara said, sighing. "I was angry and hateful at the world when

Aamira—that was her name—died. We weren't together. I would have if she'd asked, but she wasn't wired that way. So I used Rosario."

"Rosario doesn't seem like she minds," I said, looking over. "Or is it the fact that she wants more that's bothering you?"

"Wow, you're surprisingly good at this father thing. If not for the fact that we're on our way to meet with a corporate executive to decide the fate of the world, then I'd feel like I'm actually discussing things with a responsible adult."

"If it's any consolation, you're talking to someone who has had no successful relationships in his entire life and who is a professional chameleon. I also don't have any parents, just creators, so I can't draw from that experience either."

"Good to know."

There was an awkward pause between us as we sat in silence under a police air car. It passed over us and scanned us for over a minute. Faked identification was registered, and they moved past us. The arcologies were becoming more and more regimented as the government removed virtually every restriction on surveillance, drones, and the accumulation of big data. Every single person's entire life story was recorded somewhere on a computer data drive.

If humanity rendered itself extinct due to plague, war, or general stupidity, then alien archaeologists would be able to reconstruct every detail of our lives from corporate computer records. What we ate, what we watched, what we bought, and what porn we liked. Then they would look over these massive amounts of details and asked why humanity had accumulated all this data for the purposes of figuring out what to sell people rather than anything useful. Certainly, it was easier to get off the police's radar than it was the advertising agencies'.

"I dunno," Barbara said, driving us into the commercial district, where all the productive citizens of the arcologies worked. The massive megaplexes, shopping centers, and office buildings had most of their residences built right into them. Enormous glittering towers rose impossibly high into the air, connected by airway trams that had replaced the subways of old, allowing the citizens to never touch the ground.

Nor to ever escape their bottled universes.

In the ultimate capitalist state, it was funny how much life had come to resemble Soviet Union-esque socialism. You got a job, and it provided you with food, housing, and all other necessities so long as you sacrificed all freedom to your position. If you failed, you were replaced, and the system went on. It was doubly ironic because I wasn't sure how many people were needed to run most of the corporations these days.

Automation had replaced the necessity for the middle class as well as the poor, except the governments had passed laws tying many of the privileges the corporations relied on to employing people. These employees solely existed to draw salaries so they could buy the products of the megacorporations and actually generate wealth.

It made me believe in Mammon, the demonic personification of wealth, as much as I believed in a Creator deity. Surely, no one could have come up with such a twisted system naturally. It had to be the result of some Sisyphus-like curse on our race.

I shook that thought away.

"I dunno?" I repeated.

"I don't love her the way she loves me, but friendship and sex—"

"Ehhhhh," I made an exaggerated wave at that word.

"Really?"

"I'm playing the part of your father here, remember?" I said.

Barbara snorted. "Very well, friendship and comfort are things that aren't easy to cast aside either. Plus, she's the world's greatest hacker and can easily have a drone strike taken out on me."

"That's a problem I've often dealt with," I said, looking at my—Daniel's—daughter. "I can't help but have an inexplicable attraction to incredibly dangerous women. It means I have to be incredibly charming to avoid being murdered if and when I choose to break up with them."

"How do you do that?"

"Do you want to break up with her?" I asked.

Barbara stared out the window as we passed under an

enormous hologram of the Statue of Liberty hocking lifetime
service contracts in the rural regions' collective farms. "I don't
want to settle, and I don't want her to settle for me. Yet I'm not
sure there's going to be anything better for me out there, and I
might be confused as to what love is."

"Love is patient, love is kind. It does not envy, it does not
boast, it is not proud. It does not dishonor others, it is not self-
seeking, it is not easily angered, it keeps no record of wrongs."

"Can I get a less religious robot?" Barbara asked.

"Religion? I thought that was from the *Dresden Files*," I said.
"Funny."

I closed my eyes. "I'm not one to give you advice on romance,
Not-Quite-My-Daughter. I live with a paid sexual partner in my
home like they had in *Soylent Green*. She seems happy with the
arrangement, and I'm not exactly one to complain."

"Now who is oversharing? I didn't need to know about your
sex slave."

"She can leave any time she wants to with a generous sever-
ance package. It's in her contract."

Barbara rolled her eyes. "I liked the Bible passage better."

I snorted. "Truth is, I think you may be suffering relationship issues because you want to feel like you're in a great
romance but are only getting rather than giving. You may want
to try to make Rosario happy and see how that affects things."

"Wow, you're taking her side in this?"

"Well, she did hack my brain," I said. "I'm also programmed
to tell you she's the kindest, bravest, warmest, most wonderful
human being I've ever known in my life. Beep boop."

"*The Manchurian Candidate*?" Barbara guessed which movie
I was paraphrasing.

"Yes."

"You owe me a Coca-Pepsi," Barbara said.

"Those are abominations against God," I said, pausing. "We
must destroy that merger next."

"I like the Diet Zero Supreme version," Barbara said as she
slowed the vehicle down. We were now passing into a congested
area where hundreds of air cars traveled every hour. They were
controlled by automation and rarely had an accident, which

wasn't helped along by those who controlled the navigation of said vehicles. "We're almost there."

"That we are."

Barbara blinked rapidly. "I think you should try and make an actual life for yourself. Get some friends who aren't psychopaths, try to build relationships outside of the company, and maybe live a normal life. You're not going to last forever."

"Buddhism teaches there's no I. It's one of the reasons a bunch of materialists, which is ironic right there, have embraced it. Quite a few schools don't believe in the soul at all, but that we're merely part of a greater universe and have to accept our reunification with it. You know, like Yoda and Obi-Wan believed before they discovered you can game the system and become immortal force ghosts—which I find to be a terrible ending unless there's a bunch of other people who did."

"Dodging the question with *Star Wars*?"

"I had a friend named Gary, one of my few real friends, who couldn't speak three sentences without referencing it."

"I know a few guys like that," Barbara said. "It's like the Bible of many geeks."

I closed my eyes. "I'd like very much to be a part of your life, Barbara, if you are willing to let me."

Barbara crossed her arms, letting the steering wheel move by itself as the automation piloted us toward our destination. "May I ask a question before we part ways, possibly for the last time, since you have an incredibly large number of enemies trying to kill you?"

"That's Tuesday for me, and sure," I said.

"Why didn't you ever try to contact us?"

I was silent for a moment. "You realize I'm a fake, right? A clone of your father's DNA modified to be able to accept an unlimited number of cybernetic implants without rejection."

"I also know my father was a psychopath. I know my grandmother programmed you to be like she envisioned her son, though. That you hovered around the edges of our lives through the eruption but without ever visiting or leaving."

"Assassin. You thought your father was dead. Again, clone. The sheer number of reasons kind of makes this a weird question."

"What's the real reason, though?" Barbara asked.

I sighed. "I wanted you to be happy. I don't make people happy; I make them dead."

That killed the conversation until we were almost to our destination.

"I'll try and give it a shot with Rosario," Barbara said. "She deserves better. So do you."

"Thanks."

We didn't say anything else before I departed two blocks away from the location of Zheng Wei's speech with a trench coat, a scarf over my face, sunglasses, and a ball cap. It was enough to get past the face recognition cameras until I got creative.

CHAPTER TWENTY-TWO

Zheng Wei gave his speech announcing the creation of nano-therapy at the New Dragon Inn Grand Hotel, which was either the best joke ever by an architecture firm or someone really not knowing their Hong Kong cinema. It was a magnificent super-structure that looked very much like the product of someone with severe self-esteem issues. The gigantic black tower rose from the ground. Two giant golden dragons guarded the entrance, flooded by enormous spotlights so bright they were visible from space.

The New Dragon Inn Grand Hotel had its own sports arena, shopping center, restaurant district, and permanent residences for employees. It was the idea of an arcology within an arcology, creating the kind of place many of its employees would never actually have to leave. Humanity had once been isolated, and the vast majority of people never traveled outside thirty miles of their homes. I couldn't help but think that was about to happen again.

I didn't attend the speech in the Coliseum or try to get past his staff in any number of the traditional means I could have: disguises, faked passes, hacking, or even bribes. Instead, I identified who I was, then sat down in Zheng Wei's penthouse. I ended up eating his sushi platter, drinking his orange juice, and reading Mike Pondsmith's autobiography on my cell phone.

Zheng Wei's penthouse was an absolute nightmare from a security standpoint, with massive windows overlooking the Los Angeles arcology skyline. Plus, it was a multi-layer location that didn't have anything resembling cameras.

Zheng Wei had managed to install a system that deliberately

prevented individuals from recording anything, which told me a great deal about where his concerns were. There was plenty of expensive Western art scattered around the otherwise Chinese-decorated location, plus several closed-off rooms where you couldn't see things. Oh, and the room was soundproof. Seriously, I could have killed him and his security detail without anyone hearing. Whoever he'd hired for his security needed to be fired.

I was trying some fugu while lying back on Wei's absurdly overstuffed couch when the doors to the massive apartment opened and the man himself entered, accompanied by a quartet of Blackbriar soldiers wearing the same sort of outfits they'd been wearing when they'd attacked me. That answered my question of what idiots he'd hired for his security, but also raised my respect of Blackbriar since they were clearly playing all sides. Alternatively, they were just cashing their paychecks and not coordinating between jobs.

"You!" Zheng Wei said, walking up to me and pointing at me with a single finger as if this were some kind of movie. He had traces of a Chinese accent and stumbled over some words, but I suspected that was deliberate. "You dare come into my home and threaten me? You, a filthy murderer who isn't even human! You have no idea who you are messing with!"

Zheng Wei was mostly natural, with an implant for communicating with the internet and a body-sculpted face designed to look like Donnie Yen's. Which, now that I thought about it, might explain the hotel's name. He was tall for an Asian man and wore a blue suit with—I shit you not—a cape hanging from the back of it. I'd heard some executives were experimenting with new fashion styles, but that was ridiculous.

I chewed instead of replying, moving my mouth around like a cow. Then I stood up and handed him some of the sushi from the mostly eaten platter. "Fugu?"

"Get him out of here!" Zheng Wei shouted, gesturing to his guards.

"I have the files," I said simply.

Zheng Wei looked like a balloon which someone let all the air out of. He raised his hand and said, "Stop."

His guards looked confused. None of them looked

particularly anxious to approach me, either. Maybe these were the Blackbriar soldiers who actually understood who the hell they were messing with.

Zheng Wei seemed to contemplate his next course of action before gesturing to the door. "Leave us."

The Blackbriar troops hesitated, then shrugged before departing.

"Really? You're letting your guards leave? That's more generous than I expected," I said, perhaps tempting fate.

Zheng Wei narrowed his eyes. "I know what you are. The Letters may be obsolete technology, but if you really wanted me dead, then there's nothing I could do to stop it. If you're not going to leave, I can't delay you either."

I raised an eyebrow before shrugging. I'd known the executives at Karma Corp and the few people who had access to the International Refugee Society's records had a lot more respect for Atlas than most, but this was the first time I'd encountered the idea that we were some kind of boogeymen. Honestly, given the ease with which I'd arrived here, and that I was now dealing with Zheng Wei personally, I started to expect another shoe to drop—missions rarely went this well.

"I'm here to talk to you about the fact that nanotherapy doesn't work," I said, taking a drink of orange juice.

Zheng Wei nodded, then drew a futuristic-looking pistol from his coat in one smooth motion before I managed to grab it from him, trip him, and snatch his car-starter fob from his hands as he attempted to hit the panic button.

"Ah," I said, holding both in my hand, the glass of orange juice having spilled on Wei's expensive carpet. "So that was your plan. Lull me into a false sense of security and shoot me with your...is this Han Solo's blaster? Tell me this works."

I aimed the gun at a vase nearby, and the weapon shot a blast of glowing energy that I suspected was a tracer round for something else. The blast not only destroyed the vase but the table it was on, creating a large, smoldering, pile of goo.

"Don't do that!" Zheng Wei hissed.

"This is a terrible and impractical weapon," I said, shaking my head. "It tells people right where you came from. On the other hand, it is incredibly awesome. Did you have this custom made, or is it a perk of being richer than God?"

"My people will be here any second!" Zheng Wei snapped.

"Yes and no," I replied, putting the gun in my jacket pocket after turning on the safety. "The yes part is that they're going to be here, invariably. The no part is that I've already jammed this part of the room and you did the rest. So, yes, inevitably they're going to check on you in a bit, but for the next few minutes I'm going to have alone time with you."

I was actually hoping the Blackbriar troops were going to burst in and start shooting. I wasn't happy about having to run away the last time, and I'd managed to get a couple of armor-piercing grenades from the good folks at the Turing Society. The fact that they also didn't show up on scanners made me happy too.

Zheng Wei lowered his gaze and sat down in the leather chair across from the couch. "What do you want?"

"To do business," I said, sitting back down on the couch. "I would have thought you'd be willing to do that."

"Please," Zheng Wei said, curling his lip in disgust. "You don't think we know who you are?"

"We?" I asked.

"The Invisible Hand," Zheng Wei said.

I snorted. "Nope."

"What?" Zheng Wei said.

"I don't believe you're a member," I replied.

Zheng Wei frowned. "And why is that? I know what you are, who you are, and what you do."

I pointed at him. "If you did, you wouldn't be in this position. I don't believe in the Invisible Hand either. At least not as a literal thing. It's sort of like my Rollo Tomasi, which is an *L.A. Confidential* reference if you didn't get it. It's a way of anthropomorphizing the forces beyond my life. Bringing it up constantly is just my way of fishing to see if anyone has read my file—which is what you've undoubtedly done."

"You're wrong," Zheng Wei said, slumping his shoulders. "There are powerful forces ruling the United States, Europe, and other nations from behind the scenes. The Corporate Council, the United National Alliance, and the Emergency Government are its tools."

"A conspiracy can be powerful, secret, or numerous. Usually one, maybe two, but never three," I said. "I spent years trying to figure out my brother Daniel Gordon's masters, and it finally occurred to me it was not a corporation but corporations in general. Legal personhood had made people act in the name of ideas, of capitalism and self-gain as ideologies, rather than just self-interest. Which means greed exists as a personified force and that individuals are just cogs in its machine. The existence of Mammon the demon proven, if you will."

"What the hell are you talking about?" Zheng Wei said, confused.

I sighed, pulled out my gun—an AR-28 rather than the fusion pistol—and shot him in the leg.

"Fuck!" Zheng Wei shouted, falling on the ground and clutching it.

"Oh hush," I said, frowning. "I didn't hit anything vital. It barely broke the skin. I packed a low-caliber gun simply for emphasis. What I'm saying, Zheng Wei, is that I don't hate you. You know, despite the fact that you're a murderer of homeless people for gross medical experimentation and are about to kill millions of poor people over the next twenty years."

"You shot me in the leg!" Zheng Wei shouted.

I reached into my jacket pocket and pulled out a hypodermic injector, which I tossed to him. "Take this and use it. It's the same thing dentists and EMTs use."

Zheng Wei grabbed the injector and stabbed his leg with it. Almost instantly, the bleeding slowed down and the pain looked like it was subsiding too. Even so, he repeated, "You shot me in the leg!"

"Yes, because I'm sick of being bullshitted," I said, frowning. "I also wanted to emphasize that you are not in a good negotiating position."

"What is there to negotiate?" Zheng Wei said, coughing. "You're here to kill me. You work for HOPE. You know what I've done. What I'm planning."

I narrowed my eyes. "You didn't come up with the plan

to sell nanotherapy to the public, did you? Even though you signed off on all the experiments."

Zheng Wei got a disgusted look on his face. "No. No, I didn't. Do you think I wanted to kill as many people as I have? I believe—*believed*—in nanotherapy and its potential to change the world. When the eruption happened, and the world's economy and ecosystem was fucked, I knew Black Technology was our only hope. Except even it has its limits. We needed to push it past the bleeding edge to give us a way to survive the next century or two."

"So that's what these past ten years of failures have been about?" I asked, actually impressed with his devotion. "Polishing a turd?"

"The Sunken Cost Fallacy writ large," Zheng said, his words occasionally interrupted by jolts of pain. "The technology is a bust, though. We have no idea how to program tech as small as we need to make it, nor create it with sufficient complexity. Which meant there was about a hundred billion dollars' worth of wasted research."

I stared at him. "A hundred billion dollars? Bullshit."

Zheng Wei shrugged. "Quite a few facilities we built and promises we made added up over the years. I'll admit, I did some creative bookkeeping and so did most of my staff. Nanotherapy was always the golden goose that kept us competitive with our investors abroad. We faked results and lied about our progress."

"So, who is responsible?" I asked.

Zheng Wei gave a bitter smile. "You aren't the only one who anthropomorphizes the forces that guide our corporate culture. Everyone signed off on it, though. Once they knew the truth, they gave me a choice of making up for their lost investment or dying and having my subordinates do what I wouldn't. I figured, hey, why not get rich off of it?"

It was clear he wasn't nearly as comfortable with what he'd done as I'd thought he'd be. That didn't change the fact that he was a mass murderer. He wasn't the guy who would be injecting poison into the arms of children, adults, and old ladies, but he was the guy who signed off on it. That made him worse, in my opinion. Still, I wasn't here for justice.

At least not entirely.

"Well, in the words of Jules, I don't want to kill you," I said, lying. "I want to help you."

Zheng Wei looked at me sideways, then coughed. "I'm sorry, that would be a lot more believable before you shot me."

"Yes, well, I love making my point with a bang," I said, making my worst pun since I'd gone through my Bond one-liner phase as an assassin. "Basically, I think we can save a bunch of lives as well as make an enormous profit."

Zheng Wei stared at me. "You're G, though. The terrorist who works for HOPE and kills people like me."

I blinked. "Where the hell did I get that reputation?"

"You've always had that reputation," Zheng Wei replied.

"I'm an assassin," I snapped. "I shouldn't *have* a reputation."

I mentally filed this under things I needed to blame Marissa for, since I couldn't think of anyone else who would spill the beans about my career. The idea of my being viewed as some sort of counter-cultural do-gooder repulsed me. It also made me worried about my ability to negotiate in the future, since it meant Atlas Security was going to be tarred (and probably had been tarred) by association.

Zheng Wei didn't look impressed, though, and tried to shrug before a look of agony passed across his face. "Listen, I'm just telling you what I've heard. The only reason people tolerate you is because the cost-effectiveness of killing you was always determined to be too high. You're like the old algorithm that determined whether to recall an unsafe car versus the danger of lawsuits—you know, back when people could sue."

"That is the most depressing thought I've ever heard," I said, staring at him. "Not only am I viewed as a do-gooder, but I'm not even a dangerous one."

Zheng Wei chuckled. "Better to be Castro than Che."

"I find that comparison insulting on multiple levels," I said, shaking my head. "It also makes me less inclined to make my offer."

"What offer is that?" Zheng Wei asked, looking at his leg. "Got another dose of that painkiller? You know, until the Blackbriar troops come in here and kill you?"

"Nope," I said, resisting the urge to poke him in the leg wound. "In any case, I'd like to replace the pre-existing dangerous nanotherapy with a harmless placebo like the kind you plan to sell to the rich. That way you still make a fortune—albeit from selling snake oil to the masses, but it's not poisonous snake oil. Which literally should not be that expensive since it only requires you to create something that doesn't kill people."

"Tell that to the cigarette companies," Zheng Wei replied before looking chastened. "That's possible, but the profit is significantly lessened."

"How much?"

"Five percent," Zheng Wei said. "If the Illuminati don't exist, people every bit as bad do, and they're rich enough to make us look like Tiny Tim."

"And if the offer for this is the Black Dossier," I replied, looking at him.

Zheng Wei blinked. "You'd give that kind of power to Karma Corp's executives?"

"Yes," I lied. "As long as it comes with the caveat of investing the profits in making two more arcologies. I was thinking Detroit and Atlanta, personally."

Zheng Wei's eyes blinked a few times. "Arcologies aren't profitable for decades."

"It depends on who you're charging to build them," I replied, weaving my spell over the man who wasn't thinking at his best, as the injection I'd given him was full of more drugs than painkillers. The amount of Lethe was miniscule, but it was enough that everything I said to him was going to sound like a really good idea and bury itself deep in his consciousness. "Imagine, Mr. Zheng, actually building something worthwhile with your life. The money from your misguided venture used to create proven superstructures that will help at least four million people out of the refugee zones within the first five years."

"Four million isn't a lot," Zheng said.

"Only by comparison to the dreams you were selling others," I replied. "Which don't work. The good done will multiply exponentially over the generations as the for-profit industries built will increase the material prosperity of the population.

They'll build schools named after you and erect statues—which, like Columbus, will convince people you aren't an awful sack of crap despite it being manifestly true."

I shouldn't have thrown in that last insult, but I really hated this guy.

Zheng Wei paused as if seriously considering it. "The board would never go for it, even with the Black Dossier's threat."

"They would if I could also deliver them the head of HOPE," I said coldly.

Zheng Wei's eyes widened. "Then yes. We can do this. We can save millions."

Mind you, I had no intention of turning over Marissa to these pieces of shit despite all she'd done to me. I might kill her for what she'd done, though I still couldn't convince myself I could, but I'd never betray her to the corporate weasels who'd ruined the world. Even if I was one of them. I could, however, turn over her original body with an appropriate brain. It wasn't like science had a way to read memories yet—just implant them—and one dead lump of gray matter was as good as another.

My plan wasn't perfect. People were still going to be sold a useless drug treatment most couldn't afford, but exposing it would just mean they'd crank up their corporate propaganda machine to meet the truth with lies. This way, especially if we could get the arcologies dedicated to making useful medical equipment, we could maybe continue the original good HOPE did with its blackmail material—no longer needing the blackmail itself.

I'd have to edit the Black Dossier, of course, picking and choosing what files to share while leaving enough to make it useful, but I could also keep behind some choice bits for my own protection. In time, once everything was in place, I could get my "daughter" to release the full dossier to the other megacorporations and have them go after each other like rival ant colonies.

It was a solid plan.

A solid plan ruined by A bursting through the doors and shooting Zheng Wei in the head.

CHAPTER TWENTY-THREE

The bullet that struck Zheng Wei's head caused it to explode in a fashion that could only be called comical, spreading his brain matter and skull fragments in every direction. I ended up getting splattered with some of it and had to wipe it away as if a toddler had thrown food in my face.

Wiping away the goop, I trembled with a fury I didn't know I had within me. "You damn...idiot! I had him eating out of the palm of my hand!"

A could have killed me at that moment, but instead approached with his weapon drawn. It was an A-7 Striker with a long, thin, silencer-like barrel that was actually designed to make the bullets travel further as well as hit harder. There was an amused look on A's face, as if killing Zheng Wei was a terribly funny joke he'd just made, and he expected the laughter to keep on for a few minutes.

I could probably salvage the plan I'd proposed to Zheng Wei. There were always subordinates who were willing to pick up the pieces of their master's empires, but it would require eliminating the others, or money. I had plenty of the latter, but every bit spent was going to come out of some poor person's mouth and not the people who could afford my plan. I wasn't a class warrior—that was Marissa's thing—but I hated the self-destructiveness of it all.

In *Chinatown*, Jake Gittes had asked richer-than-God pedophile Noah Cross, "How much better can you eat?" Why did he need more money to the point of stealing land from poor California farmers? Why did he need more money? Noah had famously responded so he could buy the future. It was a shitty world that there were more people today like Noah Cross than the rich assholes who just spent their money on banging super-models and fancy yachts.

"That's a good reason to do it, I think," A said, shaking his head. "You were supposed to kill Zheng Wei."

I stared at him. "Yeah, it's almost like I find the idea of obey-ing you stupid."

"That's one of the reasons you were always a pain in the ass, G. You were never as obedient as you should have been," A said, shaking his head. "You never took the pleasure you were supposed to from service."

"You do realize how embarrassing it is for you, a black man, to talk like that, right?"

A rolled his eyes, every step like an execution. "You were the only one of us who viewed being a Letter as slavery. We lived like kings, had the authority to decide who lived or died and wielded power as part of the grandest conspiracy the world had ever known. If that was slavery, it was the kind the Janissaries possessed when they directed the fate of the Ottoman Empire. What you wanted was the freedom of the fast-food-scarfing, sugary-drink-swilling obese masses dying on their cancer sticks and opioids."

Wow, that was an awesome put-down of conventional soci-ety. I didn't have a rebuttal other than, "If the Society was so awesome, why was it so easy to bring down? The truth needed to be free."

"What did that get us?" A asked, gesturing with his head to the hole in the window. "The rich are richer than ever while the poor are even more destitute. Do you know why that is?"

I hesitated to make fun of him again. "Because the rich have money and can make sure it stays that way?"

A smiled. "Because the poor are stupid. That's why they're poor."

"The game was rigged from the start," I said.

"So you broke the board," A said, laughing. He stood right in front of me with his weapon. One powerful enough to blow a hole in my chest even with the armor in my suit and cybernet-ics. I suspected, by the way Zheng Wei's head had exploded, it was also loaded with grenade ammunition. "Or you tried to. That's the one thing Marissa understood that you didn't. You can only game the system, not stop playing."

Wow, he didn't know me at all. "Yeah, that's me. I'm the revolutionary. That's why I'm wearing a ten-thousand-dollar suit I'm going to have to burn when I get back to my penthouse, mistress, and private jet. What the hell is wrong with people that they think I'm trying to be the good guy in all this?"

"The fact that every time something gets put in front of you, you fuck things up," A said, shaking his head. "We could have avoided all this."

"You would have betrayed me and killed me if I followed your script," I said, frowning. "Did you really think I didn't realize that?"

A narrowed his eyes. He wasn't used to people knowing how the game was played. Maybe that was annoying him—that I wasn't stupid like all the other people he'd manipulated or intimidated over the years. People he inevitably betrayed and murdered once he was done. It made me wonder just what his body count as a member of HOPE was like. I liked to think Marissa had been a moderating influence on him, but I just didn't know anymore.

Instead of answering my statement, he kept his pistol squarely aimed at my chest. "I have your woman. Even if she's not Marissa, she has value to you, and that means she is worth bartering."

I tried not to roll my eyes. "She's not my woman. I swear, it's like I'm in a bad crime novel here."

"She has suffered because of her deception," A said, his voice accenting the third word. "Badly."

I paused, suddenly no longer in a joking mood. "What have you done to her?"

I cursed myself for revealing she wasn't Marissa. I'd been so damn cavalier about things I hadn't considered how he might react to that revelation. A had some respect for Marissa—God only knew why—and that had kept Claire safe.

"What have you done to her?" I repeated.

"Punished," A said simply. "She will survive, however,

if she receives the proper care. That is dependent on your cooperation."

I needed to find out where the hell she was. "What do you want?"

"The Black Dossier."

I knew this was a bad idea, but I had to try. "Nanotherapy is a bust. It doesn't work."

A didn't respond for a second. "I will get the fix for my condition from you and Delphi then. She will give me whatever I want in exchange for you."

"So, I'm a hostage now?" I asked.

"No," A replied. "I do not intend to let you live."

Well, that was direct. "Kind of inclines me not to obey, doesn't it?"

"Humans will obey to buy them more seconds of life," A said. "That's your failing. You're very much like them."

"Thank you," I said.

A aimed his gun at my head, keeping it extremely close. "I could kill you at any moment, G. You realize that, right?"

"Yes, but you're not going to do so because the Black Dossier is in my brain," I said, replying. "Which you might have gotten from me if you hadn't acted like a complete nutjob from our reunion until today."

A sneered. "You were always my enemy, G. You sought to cut me out of my—"

"Stop," I said, raising a hand. "A, if you had come to me *in the past fifteen years*, I would have given you stock options and a place within Atlas. Instead, you've been hanging around Marissa and working for god knows who else."

"You think I'm a monster," A said. He hesitated. "A creature unworthy of you and your company. Don't deny it. You'd have tried to kill me."

I had him off balance now. The revelation about nanotherapy had shaken him, though I could barely tell given he had the demeanor of a department store mannequin. Every plan he'd made up to this point was completely shot to hell. That meant he was acting on instinct now, and I potentially had him.

Or he'd just kill me and start over somewhere else. It stunned me that the man resented me the way he did. I hadn't thought of A in years, but it was clear he'd been thinking of me damn near constantly the past decade and a half.

"No," I said. "I would have put that monstrousness to good use because that's what armies need. Mind you, I would have tried to reign in some of your quirks. By the way, are there any Blackbriar soldiers alive out there?"

A looked back to the door. "No."

A had made the mistake I'd expected him to. One of two, in fact, with the second being he would try and hack my brain to get the Black Dossier versus try to negotiate with me. In his moment of distraction, I knocked away his gun. I kneed him in the stomach, then punched him with every bit of strength in my body. It was like hitting a brick wall. Still, I managed to grab the A7-Striker in his hands before pulling it from his grip.

A looked up at me with fury in his eyes. "That was foolish."

I tried to shoot him with the weapon, but the barrel was too long. Instead, he knocked it from my hands before headbutting me in the face. What followed was one of the nastiest beatings I'd received in my life. I'd like to say I gave as good as I got, but that wasn't true. Hell, I didn't even manage to land a single blow before A threw me over his shoulder and smashed me through the table holding the sushi platter.

A placed his boot on my neck before taking the fusion pistol from my jacket. "What is this, Han Solo's gun?"

"I know!" I said, coughing as he leaned tighter on my windpipe. Every word came out in a raspy hiss. "I can't believe he spent money on that."

I just needed him to try to break into my brain; then everything would go right. Inside, I'd had the Turing Society prepare a virus that would tear through A's memories and shut him down permanently. It would also give us access to everything he knew and let us put this nightmare to rest. It took a lot of trust to assume the Turing Society wouldn't put spyware or a shutdown code in me as well, but I was out of options.

A looked down at me, and I expected him to start rifling through my memories at any second. "What's your game, G?"

"What?" I asked, internally panicking.

"You always have an angle," A said, clenching his teeth. "Always some plan or way of talking yourself out of trouble. The fact you're not trying to means there's something going on that I don't know about."

Dammit! Why did he have to be smarter than most idiots I dealt with? "You're right, A, I do have an angle. It's to wait for you to realize you've been boxed in and have been from the beginning. As long as I have the Black Dossier, you've got no moves to play but to do exactly what I say."

I gave myself a fifty-fifty chance of being killed right then and there. However, those were the best odds I had at this moment.

A responded by aiming the fusion gun at my head. "Ever had your face melted clean off? I'm interested if you'll bleed red or white. All those new cybernetics just aren't the same as what Doctor Gordon made us with."

I grinned. "Always a follower. Never a leader. Even now you're chasing your old masters' will. You don't have the stomach to command others. You wouldn't even know what to do with the dossier if you had it."

A's eyes stare turned cold and empty before he tossed the fusion pistol away, stepped off me, grabbed me by the shirt, then ran to smash me up against the wall. He held me up by my face, threatening to crush me with his fingers. "I am going to rip every single secret out of your mind, then make sure the people you love die horribly. I'm going to start with that bitch's daughter, who I'll sell to fucking sex slavers."

I felt him inside my brain as he hooked up. He was going to brute force his way past my firewall, but I just dropped it and let everything download.

A's eyes widened. "You son of a bitch."

"'Fraid so," I said, patting him on the shoulder. "You got punked."

I then delivered a knee to his groin before he dropped me and started feeling his head like it was on fire. He thrashed around the room and screamed. I imagined him trying to purge the files from his mind with every trick up his sleeve.

It wouldn't work, though.

I didn't give him a chance and grabbed the fusion pistol before firing a single blast into his chest. I regretted not being able to see his face as his body exploded into pieces of flaming synth-flesh mixed with cybernetic limbs.

"Please tell me you got that," I said, sending my words to Barbara.

"Yes," Barbara said, communicating via our infolink. *"We got everything."*

"His base?"

"Yes. It's downtown in the industrial zone."

I looked down at the dead form of Zheng Wei, then at the severed head of A. The best assassin of the International Refugee Society was nothing more than a burning fleshless skull of plastic, metal, and synth flesh. His eyes were the only part of his body that were undamaged, staring forward and blinking with half-melted eyelids. Somehow, the skeletal jaw and metal teeth contorted themselves into a grin despite his decapitation, and there was a look of approval on his face.

It sickened me.

I nodded. "Then I have an appointment to keep with Claire."

CHAPTER TWENTY-FOUR

I stole A's air car, which I managed to hijack despite the fact the thing was coded to his biometrics. The thing was a cherry red Mercedes Falcon 2040, and I had to wonder if the concept of "covert agent" had just simply fallen off his radar. Then again, what did it say about Agent A that he'd spent the past fifteen years apparently driving around in a top-of-the-line sports car killing people, and I hadn't noticed him?

Or Delphi?

Yeah, I wasn't going to think too hard about that, or the results would depress me. In any case, I took the vehicle to the industrial district, even though it stood out like a sore thumb. I just hoped no one decided to knock it out of the sky with a stinger missile or laser-guided rocket. I could have probably gotten my people to handle the last bit of my "adventure," but I wanted to see this through to the end.

The industrial districts of Los Angeles were a place I'd never been before. Not unless you counted my earlier mad flight through them tonight. The construction companies Atlas had hired and worked with made sure most of the facilities were automated and didn't require anything more than a minimum of human supervision.

They worked day and night, producing everything from electronics to steel girders, which were almost always shipped out of the country on boats to China or on trains to Canada. Much of the United States economy was subordinated to repaying the interest on the massive debt it had to other nations, which still was necessary to keep things from collapsing. Even if our nation were to become self-sufficient again, I wasn't sure if we wouldn't be kept underfoot with unequal treaties and two-thirds of the Big 200 companies milking every credit from us while funneling them back to their home nations.

Well, turnabout was fair play, I supposed.

The bleak industrial spires loomed over my vehicle as I kept the headlights off and stuck to the shadows. A's air car had quite a few enhancements. James Bond was apparently a favorite of all Letters, since the car also contained a communicator that transmitted on a low-frequency broad pattern (whatever the hell that meant), which kept people from following the signal back to its source. I made use of that as I approached A's refuge—hoping it wasn't too late to pull a happy ending from all this.

"So the board of directors actually went for it?" I asked S's image on the dashboard vidscreen beside the air car's controls.

"Barbara provided the Black Dossier and information for us to force Karma Corp's hand. They assumed you killed Zheng Wei because he wouldn't cooperate."

I grimaced. "Is that going to be a problem?"

"We may have to fake your death," S said.

"I hope you're kidding."

"You barely exist now," S said, shrugging. "But I think I might be able to negotiate that down if I inform them A was the one who actually killed Zheng Wei and you killed him. It's the kind of useful lie this situation warrants."

"But it's the truth," I said, staring forward as I drove on manual even though I was having a conversation with her.

"I know, but somehow they're still likely to buy it," S said, sarcastically. "You've made us the kind of deal that has the potential to dramatically increase Atlas Security's resources."

I tried not to roll my eyes. "Yes, Samantha, that's the reason I did this."

"Who knows why you do whatever you do. Who knows why anyone does?" S said. "I believe we make all our decisions based on instinct, and consciousness is just a trick. We're just observers of our own selves."

I turned my head to look down at the video. "That's a depressing thought."

"Only if you believe in free will. I don't," Samantha said.

I paused. "I'm sorry about A."

"No you're not," S said. "No one is. He died alone and unmourned at the hands of someone who was not stronger or smarter but sneakier."

"Thank you, I think," I muttered.

"It wasn't a compliment. My only problem is we're one less in existence," S said. "Eventually, we'll all be gone."

"I'm not so sure," I replied. "The Black Dossier said they'd already created an entirely new line of assassins for Karma Corp. They're working on trying to reverse engineer the tech and make it cheaper. We could be looking at a whole new race of slaves in the coming decades."

"I doubt it," S said.

"You don't think people will want to manufacture more of us?" I asked.

"I do. I just think the poor will always be cheaper and replicate themselves for free," S replied. "They could take your furniture, Heather, and upgrade her for all the sexiness for half the cost of making one of us."

"That's unfair."

"Is it?" S asked. "You know she's a spy sent by Lucita, right? Someone to report on you so no one else can."

"I did not," I said, unsurprised at this point.

"Well, there you go," S said. "The only people you can trust in this world are me and Lucita."

"Except you both just demonstrated why I can't," I said, chuckling. "Is there anything else I should know?"

S's expression turned serious. "I've put out an order for terminating Marissa's life. I'm paying for the contract myself. You realize you have to eliminate her, right?"

I didn't respond.

"G."

"Case," I said, sighing. Even if I thought of her as S instead of Samantha. G wasn't who I was. G was never who I was.

"That's your prerogative," I replied.

S slumped her shoulders. "Even after all this time?"

"Judge not lest you be judged," I said, shrugging. It was an odd statement given I was sure I'd long since passed the point

Saint Peter would turn me away at the Pearly Gates. I'd made my choice, though, and wasn't afraid of the consequences. "Never mind about her, though. I'm more worried about Claire now."

"Do you love her?" S asked. "Because everything you believed about her was a lie too."

"There's a lot of that going around."

"Truth and fact are fundamentally different things," S said. "Fact is something that is immutable, but truth is something decided by the heart."

"Thank you, Doctor Jones."

"We've wrapped up HOPE and offered jobs to most of the more pragmatic members," S said. "The organization can't be allowed to continue if you want to survive this. We can offer Claire a position, too. One where she'd be able to be with you."

"Are you playing matchmaker?"

"You are the loneliest person I know, Case. Which is weird because you don't have to be. You are the Tin Man with a heart."

I frowned. "Why does everyone keep saying that?"

"Because it's true." S blinked. "Don't get yourself killed. We've got James removing the pathways Marissa used to compromise Delphi. It'll take about three months before she's operational again, and your deal came at just the right time to keep us solvent. You don't need to go into this factory alone. I can get an army to back you up."

"I don't need an army," I said, reaching over and switching off our infolink.

Claire and I didn't have a future. Too many lies had passed between us. That didn't mean I wasn't going to try to save her, though. Assuming she was still alive. If she wasn't … well, I'd made a point to ask the Turing Society to make sure her daughter, Fiona, was safe. I didn't know what I was going to find in A's safehouse, but I had a feeling it was going to be awful.

The actual building was an obelisk-shaped water treatment plant that purified ocean water by the hundreds of millions of gallons every day before bottling it for the rest of the world at a reasonable profit. Enormous piles of toxins, salt, and garbage lay along the highway leading up to the building. Massive tanks were visible on its side, and hundreds of pipes covered in catwalks. It stood out like a sore thumb even in the enormous collection of metal buildings surrounding me.

"*G, are you there?*" Barbara contacted me on our infolink. S was trying to do the same, but I ignored her call.

"My name is Pablo, and I run artificial pets and taxidermy. Would you like a genuine artificial stuffed rabbit? How about an electric sheep? I won't ask what you do with it, and you shouldn't tell."

"Ugh," Barbara said. "I'm suddenly glad you were never involved in my life."

"Most people who meet me feel the same," I replied. "What's the score?"

"Don't go to the NaturalLife water plant," Barbara said. "It's under attack by Blackbriar troops."

I blinked, then pulled my vehicle down behind one of the towers of an adjoining building. A satellite-generated rainstorm was occurring, drenching me as I walked out. I pulled on a pair of vid-binoculars that allowed me to pick up the feed from all the plant's cameras. They fed it directly to my mind, and I saw a wholesale war going on inside. Blackbriar troopers were fighting Blackbriar troopers, killing each other. Neither side was taking prisoners.

Then I saw her. Marissa, leading the charge with a clear transparent steel helmet and a suit of power armor. The expensive kind. She executed one of the troopers on the ground and directed her own troopers to start searching from floor to floor. I tagged the number of troopers on both sides and determined there were at least a dozen left on Marissa's side, while the remaining ones guarding the facility were evacuating.

"Well fuck," I said, shaking my head. "Somehow, I don't think Blackbriar is going to be around after today."

"Blackbriar is a branch of HOPE," Barbara said. "One of the ways Marissa invested her fortune. Presumably, the soldiers here were personally loyal to A rather than her."

"And Zheng Wei had Blackbriar as his security," I said, snorting. "Which is how they managed to get the information on nanotherapy in the first place. They had all the angles covered."

"I don't think so, since you've already screwed up their plans completely," Barbara said. "The Black Dossier is in the hands of the Turing Society and Atlas now. The information will be valueless soon. Its power will last just long enough to get your new arcologies built. HOPE is being rebranded and you have eliminated A. There's no way Marissa can pull a victory out of this."

"She can capture Claire and turn her over to me in exchange for whatever she wants," I said.

"Would you do that?" Barbara asked.

"I don't know," I said. "Do you have A's memories about where Claire is located?"

"Yes," Barbara said. "I can transfer you to it now. Shouldn't you just leave it alone, though? Claire works for Marissa. There's no reason you shouldn't assume she's going to happily join up with her and this is a rescue mission."

"She needs to know she's a machine," I said.

"All right," Barbara said. "I'm transferring the data now. You'll have a couple of minutes at most if you go toward the spot. They aren't there yet."

"Thank you," I said. I paused. "It was good knowing you. It's... nice to have a daughter."

"Don't get killed," Barbara said, cutting her feed off.

I wished I could promise her I wouldn't. Instead, I focused on getting over to the water treatment plant, using a set of heavy pipes. I rappelled down a set of wires using my belt once I confirmed they could support my weight. The halls inside the facility were filled with bodies, and they'd missed the room where Claire was imprisoned only because the door was behind a stack of boxes.

The door had an electronic lock, but I didn't have any problem prying it off. I'd seen inside the room earlier, the luxury accommodations where A had been keeping the woman he thought was Marissa. They'd been changed, however, with Claire suspended from a set of chains around her hands and a bucket underneath her. Her shirt had been sliced open, and there was white blood fluid spread all over the room, showing she'd been stabbed and allowed to bleed out.

She was still alive—cyborgs died hard—but barely. I ran up

to her and immediately pulled the chains down, ripping them free from where they were screwed in. Laying her out on the ground, I cupped her head. "It's okay, I'm going to get you out of here. We'll get you a new Shell. Everything will be fine."

"I'm not a person," Claire muttered, her voice barely audible even to my enhanced hearing. "I'm a machine. Just another doll."

"No more than I am," I said.

"Did you know?" Claire asked.

"No," I said, lifting her up. "I apologize for lying to you."

"Did Marissa?" Claire said.

"Yes," I said. "She commissioned you."

Claire smiled. It wasn't a pleasant smile. "Give me a gun."

"You know it's my memories who formed her basis," Marissa said. She was at the door, in full armor, and holding an FHT machine gun at me. "There was only so much they could do with the corpse of the woman they experimented on."

"Step aside, Marissa," I said, taking a deep breath. "It's over."

"You really are the viper to my farmer," Marissa said, keeping the gun aimed at me. "After all we've been through, too."

I couldn't even begin to deconstruct what she said. "I'm not giving her back to you. She needs medical attention."

"It's my body; I want it back," Marissa said softly. "You got the Black Dossier. You eliminated A. HOPE is gone. You've won. The fight still continues, though. Everything that's gone can be rebuilt."

"It's over," I said.

"I'm not your slave," Claire said, managing to speak aloud as she reached into my jacket, running her hand over my shirt.

"I'll need you," Marissa said softly. "Both of you. The human race is on the verge of total destruction. The things I've seen would turn your hair white."

"You're not the savior," I said, staring at her. "Step aside. Now."

"No," Marissa said. "I don't want to use the codes I got from the Triumvirate, but I will."

"Do it, Case," Claire whispered.

I opened my mouth to speak, then I grabbed my fusion

pistol and fired.

"I'm sorry," I said, seeing the results of my actions.

Marissa lay on the ground, her helmet melted, and her brain case destroyed. There was a look of betrayal burned into her features. Claire was silent and passed away a few minutes later. She had a smile on her face. They'd been two children of the Old America identical in so many ways, but both warped by circumstance into weapons against the system. It was why I hadn't been able to save them.

I killed every Blackbriar soldier in the building. It didn't make me feel better. From that day forward, I had only the neon city and endless smog. I always managed to survive, it seemed, but everyone else around me died. Maybe that was my punishment for all the innocent lives I'd taken. To be the scourge of a world that consumed those who believed it could get better.

So be it.

ABOUT THE AUTHOR

C.T. Phipps is a lifelong student of horror, science fiction, and fantasy. An avid tabletop gamer, he discovered this passion led him to write and turned him into a lifelong geek. He is a regular blogger and also a reviewer for The Bookie Monster.

BIBLIOGRAPHY

The Rules of Supervillainy (Supervillainy Saga #1)
The Games of Supervillainy (Supervillainy Saga #2)
The Secrets of Supervillainy (Supervillainy Saga #3)
The Kingdom of Supervillany (Supervillainy Saga #4)
The Tournament of Supervillany (Supervillainy Saga #5)
The Future of Supervillainy (Supervillainy Saga #6)
I Was a Teenage Weredeer (The Bright Falls Mysteries, Book 1)
An American Weredeer in Michigan (The Bright Falls Mysteries, Book 2)
Esoterrorism (Red Room, Vol. 1)
Eldritch Ops (Red Room, Vol. 2)
Agent G: Infiltrator (Agent G, Vol. 1)
Agent G: Saboteur (Agent G, Vol. 2)
Agent G: Assassin (Agent G, Vol. 3)
Cthulhu Armageddon (Cthulhu Armageddon, Vol. 1)
The Tower of Zhaal (Cthulhu Armageddon, Vol. 2)
Lucifer's Star (Lucifer's Star, Vol. 1)
Lucifer's Nebula (Lucifer's Star, Vol. 2)
Straight Outta Fangton (Straight Outta Fangton, Vol. 1)
100 Miles and Vampin' (Straight Outta Fangton, Vol. 2)
Wraith Knight (Wraith Knight, Vol. 1)
Wraith Lord (Wraith Knight, Vol. 2)

Curious about other Crossroad Press books?
Stop by our site:
http://store.crossroadpress.com
We offer quality writing
in digital, audio, and print formats.